FOR LOVE OR MONEY

First published in 2000 by Marino Books
An imprint of Mercier Press
16 Hume Street Dublin 2
Tel: (01) 661 5299; Fax: (01) 661 8583
E-mail: books@marino.ie

Trade enquiries to CMD Distribution
55A Spruce Avenue
Stillorgan Industrial Park
Blackrock County Dublin
Tel: (01) 294 2556; Fax: (01) 294 2564
E.mail: cmd@columba.ie

© Tony Flannery 2000

ISBN 1 86023 124 1

10 9 8 7 6 5 4 3 2 1

A CIP record for this title is available
from the British Library

Cover design by SPACE
Printed in Ireland by ColourBooks,
Baldoyle Industrial Estate, Dublin 13

FOR LOVE OR MONEY

TONY FLANNERY

CHAPTER ONE

It took Enda Staunton a few moments to work out whether the scream that had made him sit bolt upright in his bed was real or just part of a dream. The clock on the bedside table told him that it was just after three in the morning. While he tried to figure out what was happening, a loud bang, which seemed to come from the room beneath him, confirmed that there was indeed something suspicious going on. The room in question was a large community room which was used for the purposes of relaxation, like reading newspapers and watching television. The monastery of St Carthage was a large building with three floors, built at a time when young men were beating down the doors to join this way of life. That was no longer the case but the big building survived, even though now it was inhabited by only eight men, and they were mostly old. Seven of them were priests, and the eighth man, Brother Bartholomew, was the last surviving lay brother, and the oldest person in the community.

Enda wasn't a golfer, but ever since the first break-in about five years ago, he always kept a golf club in his room to be used as a weapon in case of emergency. Armed with this, and wrapped in his dressing gown, he made his way slowly and cautiously down the stairs. He was a tall man, strongly built, but with his hairline receding on both temples. Like most of the men in the monastery, he was from a rural background, and despite a long training programme and years of public speaking, he still spoke with a fairly strong country accent. Even though he was in his late forties and had lived in this monastery for over ten years, he still found it to be an eerie place at this time of the night. He was conscious of all the priests and brothers who had lived and died here since the foundation of the monastery in the middle of the nineteenth century. And a great many of them were buried in the vaults, under the high altar of the church. Living that close to the dead might sound like a nice idea in the course of a pious discussion on religious life and the communion of saints on a fine summer's day, but at this hour of the night, and having been woken from sleep by a loud scream and strange noises downstairs, it did not seem like a good idea at all.

There were many stories of ghosts being seen on the stairs and along the corridors. One man, an alcoholic who had been sent there by his bishop in the hope that he might be cured of his drinking, was supposed to have been driven to such desperation that he jumped to his death from a top-storey window at the beginning of the century. A recent visitor to the house claimed to have woken with a start one night to the sight of a hooded black figure framed in the window, arms outstretched, ready to leap to his death, but none of the community had ever seen anything. Normally Enda, who was by nature hard-headed and practical, would have dismissed all these stories with a derisory laugh. But now, with his ears straining to hear any sound, he wasn't too sure.

He felt it was better not to turn on the light so that he wouldn't draw attention to his presence. A pale light from the street lamps shone through the windows on the stairs and the corridor below, but this only served to accentuate the darkness of the shadows. He gripped the handle of the golf club more tightly. He resolved that whether the intruder had come from this world or the next, he would return with the imprint of a seven iron on his head.

As he approached the community room, a figure burst out of the door, stooped over, running. Enda raised the golf club above his head.

'Who are you?' he shouted at the figure advancing towards him along the corridor. The figure either didn't hear or paid no attention, because he kept coming. Enda, fearing an attack, was on the point of lashing out with the golf club when some instinct stopped him. Even in the darkness there was a familiar shape to this person. He reached out to grasp him by the shoulders and brought him to a halt, realising immediately that it was Jack Daly, another member of the community.

'What's wrong?'

'For God's sake, don't go in. It's awful.' Jack could barely speak.

'What the hell are you talking about? What's awful? Pull yourself together, man, and tell me what's going on.' Enda was by far the most direct – some would say blunt – person in the community.

'Behind the door . . . Kevin . . . It's horrible. I think he's dead.'

And dead he was, no question about it. He was hanging from the rafters with his eyes bulging, his mouth open, and his tongue protruding. Kevin Dunne, one of the quiet members of the community, a man in his mid-fifties, had hanged himself.

Enda was quick to recover his composure.

'Come on, Jack. Help me get the poor devil down.'

Jack, who was at thirty-four the second-youngest in the

community, combined great talent in preaching and ministry with an athleticism that made the task in hand much easier. Once he had recovered from his initial shock, he went to work with a will, helping Enda to cut Kevin down, lay him out on the floor and spread the tablecloth over his body, mercifully covering the expression on the face.

'Why in the name of God would he do a stupid thing like this?' Jack wanted to talk. It was easier to deal with what had happened if they spoke about it.

'Living in this place would drive anyone to suicide. When you've spent as long in it as I have, you might feel like doing the same thing.' With nearly fifteen years of seniority over Jack, Enda was not above patronising the younger men in the community.

They had phoned for the ambulance and the gardai before they even thought of waking the Superior, Father Matthew. Neither of them had much regard for him, and they knew he would be overwhelmed by this situation, so they dealt with the immediate practicalities before they went up to his room to wake him.

Matthew had been Superior of the community for two years now. At first glance, he appeared to be an easy-going man, heavy and slow-moving on flat, plodding feet. But the laid-back gait was a cover for a strong sense of inadequacy and a deep underlying level of anxiety. The one thing Matthew wanted to avoid more than anything else was conflict. He could not cope with conflict, and Enda had often commented that when he was confronted with a difficult situation not only did he not face it, but he ran at a speed surprising for one so heavy in the opposite direction. In this way, he got through life, managing to avoid as many of the real issues as possible, while the world and the monastery were going through dramatic changes all around him. Like so many people in authority in the Church, he had been chosen as a Superior precisely because he lacked ability or originality. He was considered to be safe. But the problem he faced this morning, the dangling corpse, could not be avoided, and there was no way he could run away from it. When Enda broke the news to him at the door of his bedroom, his face sagged and his eyes began to dart about anxiously.

'Oh my God, what will we do?'

'The gardai and ambulance are on their way. They'll be here in a little while.' Jack was now back to his usual confident self. Not only was he good at his job, and far more self-assured than the uneasy Matthew, but he was also very good-looking, with long fair hair and regular features. Often people had commented to him (partly in jest) about the waste of having such a good-looking man in the priesthood, and what a fine husband he would make. Sometimes this was the expression of the feeling that celibacy didn't make much sense to them anymore, and they were wondering about the point of it, but more often it was a simple compliment on his appearance. He took pride in his athleticism, still played as much sport as he could, and went jogging most days. All of this contributed to the overall impression he gave of being the most approachable and effective priest in the monastery.

When Matthew informed them that he was going to dress himself and go to his office to look up the files on Kevin's next of kin, Jack and Enda returned to the community room to keep vigil beside the body.

'How did you come to find him?' asked Enda, when they had settled themselves at a reasonably comfortable distance from the grotesque figure underneath the tablecloth.

'I was coming in about half an hour ago . . . ' Jack began.

'Three o'clock in the morning! What were you doing out till that hour?' Enda was endlessly curious about the lives of the other members of the community. And since he was not inclined to pass moral judgements, he tended to hear more than most.

'That's none of your business. You're not my Superior, you know. How can you be so casual after what has just happened?' Jack smiled as he spoke, taking the harshness out of the words. He admired Enda's ability to deal practically with a situation, and apparently keep his distance.

'Visiting your latest dolly-bird, I suppose!' Bantering with each other was as good a way as any of coping with the extraordinary situation they found themselves in. But Jack was not going down that line. Even though Enda already knew a little about himself and Olivia, the woman he had been with, he was in no mood to talk about the hours he had spent with her earlier that night. It had been such an intense and emotional experience that he needed time to sort it out first. He continued with his account of the discovery.

'When I came in, I was more conscious of the possibility of meeting George than anything else. You know how early he gets up, and how much he disapproves of us younger ones being out late. I came in here to have a look at the paper. I hadn't had a chance to see it all day. I was surprised to find the light on, but just presumed that someone had forgotten to turn it off. I sat down over there at the table. But I got the weirdest feeling that there was someone behind me. I told myself not to be stupid, because often this place gives me an eerie feeling late at night.'

'It does the same to me,' agreed Enda.

'Anyway, after a minute or two, when the feeling didn't go

away, I looked over my shoulder. I suppose I was already very uptight, and at the sight of Kevin hanging from the rafters, I completely flipped. I must have fainted, because the next thing I knew I was getting up off the floor and heading for the door. I can tell you, I was glad to see you coming. How did you happen to be on the scene?'

'You did more than faint. You let a blood-curdling scream out of you that lifted me out of the bed.'

'Oh, did I?' said Jack, and he paused for a moment, clearly surprised at this bit of information, but then got back to the subject of Kevin. 'Isn't this weird? Did you know him well? Have you any idea why he might have done something like this?' Jack had had very little in common with Kevin, as he was about twenty years younger than him, and hadn't known him very well, so he had no great feeling of personal loss at his death, just bafflement as to why he had done it.

It was different for Enda, who had been closer both in age and in friendship to Kevin, but Enda was not the sort of person to show his emotions easily. He spoke in a matter-of-fact, almost casual, way.

'I suppose I knew him as well as anyone could know him. Do any of us know each other in this monastery? I knew enough to know that he was badly screwed up.'

He paused for a moment, and then continued: 'So screwed up, in fact, that I suppose it really isn't any great surprise. I couldn't say that I saw it coming, but now that it has happened, I can see that the warning lights might have been flashing. If only we could have seen them – but then, we aren't very good at seeing thing like that, are we?' Enda liked to throw in comments showing his detachment from, and general disdain for, life in the monastery.

'Oh?' said Jack, surprised. 'What do you mean by warning lights? What signs were there? I was never close to him.'

'Indeed you weren't. You're too busy trying to get close to your lady friends to have time for the rest of us.' Even though Enda's voice sounded sharp, his smile took the harm out of what he was saying. He returned to the topic of Kevin. 'He was gay, for starters.'

Jack had often wondered about this, but it was the sort of thing that was not discussed in the monastery.

'And he had never come to terms with it. Or to put it bluntly, he could never tell his mother, and she was the biggest person in his life. She's still alive, though I think she is very old and feeble at this stage. Alzheimer's, as far as I know. It will be a mercy if she has completely lost her marbles by now. If she still has her senses, Matthew will have some task breaking the news to her. I'm sure he's already pissing his pants at the thought of that.' And Enda, with that ability to stand outside everything that was going on around him, even something as dreadful as Kevin's death, gave a little laugh and a rueful shake of the head at the thought of Matthew trying to work himself up to deal with this one. 'I think he told his sister not so long ago, but I believe she responded by warning him not to dare tell his mother under any circumstances in case it would be the end of her. I know he was taken aback by that, and as a result he couldn't get up the courage to tell his brother. The brother is a successful businessman and a bit of a prig, by all accounts.'

Enda paused, looking over at the cloth covering the body for a while, and then came out with one of those statements that Jack liked. The irreverence of Enda appealed to him.

'That's what was behind his vocation to the priesthood, you know. When he discovered that he was gay, he took fright and looked for a way to escape, and he thought that religious life and the priesthood would provide it for him, that it would give him shelter and respectability – a life spent with other men without any social opprobrium attached to it. But he learned otherwise. He found that it made things more, rather than less, complicated. The poor devil.'

Jack was surprised that Enda knew about Kevin at all, and that he could sit here talking about him in an apparently casual fashion. He wondered, as he often did, why Enda himself had become a priest. He seemed to go through life without ever getting seriously engaged with any person or situation. Jack liked him in a lot of ways and found him entertaining, but he wondered if Enda had any emotional life. Or was this the way that he had coped with the demands of celibacy and living the religious life? And yet he was fascinated, and listened closely as Enda continued.

'It got harder for him as he got older. Nothing very unusual about that, I suppose, but it was certainly true in his case. In his early days, he never admitted it to anyone. He thought that if he lived like a good religious it would somehow go away. But of course that didn't happen. And, in more recent times, he began to face the issue, and to become a bit daring about exploring his sexuality. He had started going to some of the gay clubs in Dublin any time he was up there. But he was losing the grip of himself too. I know that in the last year or so he tended to do some cottaging, especially at the local railway station.'

'Cottaging?' Jack frowned. He had never heard that term before.

'It's what they call prowling around public toilets looking for willing partners. Not to be recommended, from many points of view.'

Jack knew very little about the homosexual world. He himself was definitely heterosexual, and thoughts of the hours he had spent with Olivia earlier on in the night flashed through his mind. He dragged himself back to the subject in hand, with some difficulty.

'Kevin, going to gay clubs, and hanging around public toilets? I can't imagine it! He was always so . . . ' He was trying to find the right word to describe the Kevin Dunne he had known. Because of the age difference, he had always seemed very much part of a different generation to Jack. He had appeared to be fairly stiff and uneasy in himself. In conversation, he was traditional and conventional. You could depend on Kevin to give out the official line on most things. So Jack, who increasingly questioned the official line on everything, tended to avoid having any serious conversations with him. And he always had a feeling that there was something insincere about Kevin, that what he was saying did not fit very well with his personality. He remembered the time – not long ago – when Kevin's class had celebrated the silver jubilee of their ordination, and Kevin had given the talk at the Mass. When Jack sat back to listen to him, he had hoped for something interesting, some reflection on the extraordinary time of upheaval they had lived through. The famous Vatican Council, held in the sixties, had been in session around the time when he joined the Order. Religious life was booming: the seminaries were overflowing with candidates. Now it was in what appeared to be terminal decline. In the twenty-five years of his priesthood, the country had changed from being a largely traditional, simple and rural society to become a modern, industrialised, urban and liberal one. In more recent years there had been numerous damaging scandals in the Church, and a fall-off in religious practice. This was surely an exciting time to have lived through. But Jack's expectation of a reflection on some of these major events had been disappointed. Kevin's talk had been pious in the extreme, thanking God and the congregation for the great gift of his vocation, and saying what a privilege it had been, and praying that he would live it faithfully until the day he died. No one else there had suspected how soon that day would come. 'He was always so correct,' Jack concluded. And then he smiled as he realised the irony of what he had just said. Hanging yourself from the rafters, especially for a priest, was hardly the most correct way to bring your life to a conclusion.

'So you would doubt if he ever had a vocation?' he asked Enda.

'No doubt at all about it. Of course he never had a vocation. Not that I'm sure what any of that means any more. Do any of us in here have a real vocation?'

As if suddenly realising the situation they were in, Jack looked over at the body and said, 'Isn't it strange, us sitting here and chatting away as if nothing had happened. We should be in a state of shock and upset.'

'Not at all,' replied Enda. 'This is the reality of religious life. We live together in the same house, and all the books say that we are a family. But in fact we're not. We're more like ships in the night. We pass each other by each day without any real interaction. Did you ever see the monks shedding tears at the funeral of one of our own? In all my years I only saw it once, and that was for an exceptional man who died young and suddenly. No, we don't love each other in any normal, human meaning of that word. Maybe that is the only way it can be. If we tried to be really close, we might end up killing each other. I'm sorry for Kevin. I liked him in a way. But it is not as if my brother or sister had died. Nothing like that.' Then Enda's face took on a worried look.

'But that's not my main concern right now. I don't like the look of this. I just hope there isn't more to it than meets the eye.'

Before Jack had a chance to ask him what he meant, the door opened and Brother Bartholomew, the oldest member of the community, wandered into the room. Bartholomew was small of stature and white-haired, with a closed, tight face. He seldom smiled, and was laconic by nature. Perhaps his general disillusionment with life sprang from spending the greater part of his life as a brother, a role that, until the Church began to modernise itself, was essentially one of service to the priests. In any case, whatever he said tended to be negative. He had lit the fires in the priests' rooms in the days before central heating, and dutifully polished their shoes, which they would leave outside their doors each night. The role of the lay brother was always presented with a strong religious gloss: the homemaker who shared in the work of the priests by his prayers and penance, but the reality, in his experience, was modelled on the position of the servant in aristocratic houses of the nineteeth and early twentieth centuries. The scars the system had left on Bartholomew were very evident.

He and George Forde were the only two who still got up at the very early hour which used to be mandatory. When Jack and Enda saw him come in, they presumed he didn't know of the events of the night, and they both jumped up to prevent him seeing what was in the corner behind the door. But he stopped them with the words, 'Where's the body?' He had obviously met Matthew outside, and heard the news.

The others watched as he slowly walked over to where Kevin

was lying. He lifted the cloth, and exposed the horribly twisted face. He stood looking down for what seemed a long time, not moving or saying anything. Then he slowly replaced the cloth, and turned and walked towards the door. There he stopped, and stood facing the two of them. His face had the same slightly disgruntled, disapproving look that it always had.

'That was a terrible thing for a religious to do. May the Lord forgive him. Though I doubt if He will.'

And then he slowly made his way out the door, leaving Jack and Enda speechless behind him. Enda was the first to react.

'The self-righteous little bastard! Judged and condemned straight away. I wouldn't like to have to face him at the Last Judgement.'

'Be easy on him,' said Jack. 'It must be very hard for a person of his age to come to terms with something like this happening in the monastery. For most of his life they were sheltered from the type of problems that led to suicide.'

'But the way he stood there looking down at the body. You would almost think he was getting some pleasure out of it.'

Enda unconsciously used one of the great phrases of the traditional sermons on sex. The big sin was to take pleasure in things.

Both men almost jumped out of their skin when they heard a knocking at the window behind them. On looking around, they glimpsed two eyes staring in out of the dark; a wide leering grin on the face. It disappeared almost as soon as they had seen it, and they heard a cackle of laughter, along with the sound of running feet. Enda ran over to the window, but by the time he had managed to open it there was no one in sight. Jack raced around to the back door of the monastery, but all he managed to see was a tall figure, dressed in a dark anorak and with a hood over his head, disappearing round the corner at the other end of the street. The feeling of uneasiness which he had had all night since he returned home, before he had discovered the body, was still weighing heavily on him, so he quickly dismissed the thought of chasing after the rapidly receding figure. A deep weariness descended on him. He could hear the ambulance and the gardai arriving in the monastery behind him. He decided to leave all the formalities to Matthew and Enda. He slipped quietly up the back stairs to his room, threw off his clothes and collapsed onto the bed. So much had happened in the hours since he had returned from his missionary journey that afternoon. A beautiful but disturbing time with Olivia, followed by the horror and drama of the last few hours. So many questions to be answered. But Jack had a fairly highly developed ability to switch off, to put things aside for another time. With some effort, he decided to think everything over the next day. Before long, despite all that had happened, the weariness overcame him, and he slipped into a deep sleep.

CHAPTER TWO

'Just as well he didn't do it in the oratory. If he had, he wouldn't have been found for days.' George Forde was the speaker. It was half past seven on a late autumn morning in the monastery of St Carthage. In the century-and-a-half of the monastery's existence, the life lived by its inhabitants had remained, for the most part, unchanged. Each succeeding generation faithfully followed the same rule and way of life. But the last twenty years or so had seen that whole system dismantled. Now the rules were largely gone, and with them went most of the uniformity of the old way of life. Each member of the community lived fairly much as he himself chose. George, at eighty the second-oldest member of the community, was even more disgruntled than usual as he sat at breakfast in the large refectory, with its highly polished timber floor. In his own mind he had very good reason for being disgruntled. Apart from the general malaise that affected him at this late stage of his life, he had just been informed that a member of the community to which he belonged, and in which he had lived all his life, had hanged himself during the night. To say that this was a shock to George would be putting it mildly. In more than fifty years of religious life he had never seen anything like it. The monastery of St Carthage had a long and honourable history of service to the town and surrounding areas. The people had responded with warmth and enthusiasm to the recent anniversary celebrations, showing how much they appreciated the presence of the monastery and the monks. But now those days seemed to be coming to an end. George often recalled with fondness the time when the monastery was full to bursting with members, and more young people than could be accepted wanted to get in. The seven surviving members seemed to him like a pathetic remnant of what he had known. But not everyone felt like him.

'Well, God blast you, anyway. Would you shut your mouth,' Enda barked at him, in his most impatient tone. He hadn't gone back to bed after the events of the night. By the time he had answered all the guards' questions, and got permission for the ambulance to remove the body to the hospital, the light was already beginning to appear in the sky. Some instinct had warned him to be cautious, so he hadn't told the guards about the knock on the window, or the strange apparition peering in at them. In the midst of all the tragedy there was the good name of the community to be thought of, so he had to think twice before telling them anything they didn't need to know. And anyway, there might be nothing to it. Monasteries were places that tended to attract all sorts of weird and unstable people. Maybe it was somebody who just couldn't sleep and was wandering around. Whoever it was, Enda hoped he hadn't seen much, and that whatever he had seen, he would keep quiet about. By the time everything was done – the body taken up to the hospital, and the guards departed for the present – it was almost breakfast time, and any possibility of sleep had departed. After a short walk he joined the other members of the community at the breakfast table, but he was in no mood for listening to the judgmental rantings of George.

'Could you not lay off for this morning, at least? It wouldn't matter where you died. We'd get the rotten smell of you straightaway because you are all eaten up with bitterness and discontent. Give us a break, and say no more.'

Enda Staunton was the one person in the community who intimidated George Forde. It was his directness that George couldn't cope with. During all those years when the rule was properly observed in the community, people spoke more carefully to each other. But then, in those days life generally in the monastery was much better. He lapsed into silence. This morning, more than ever, he was showing the signs of his age. What had been for a long time a marvellous head of black hair was now reduced to a little rim skirting the edges of his shiny skull. His face was deeply lined, especially around the sides of the mouth and eyes, and he had developed drooping jowls that gave the impression of sternness and discontent. And indeed that was how George was feeling at this time in his life. He had loved the old system, observing its rules and regulations to the letter, and he had hated to see it collapse. If truth be told, though George would never admit it, even to himself, it was precisely that system that had kept his life together, and given it shape and meaning. This morning, eating his porridge in that big, cold room with the ill-fitting windows allowing in sharp draughts of autumnal air, and with the heating system, for what little it was worth, only beginning to crank on, he somehow felt justified and vindicated by the news of the night. If you dismantle the very structures that are holding a way of life together, if you recklessly throw out the rules and ways of life that have been sanctified by generations of religious, then you should not be surprised if the consequences are serious. There was one thing he was sure about. Something like this would not have happened in the old days. Besides, he had not particularly liked or approved of Kevin Dunne, and had no feelings of warmth towards him.

Nobody else around the table was in the mood for talk either this morning; everyone was still trying to come to grips with what had happened, so a heavy silence settled on the group. They sat around a long table. The older ones had large black cloaks wrapped around them. This was the official garment of the Order, and it also served to keep them warm. The younger ones had long ceased to wear the cloaks except on ceremonial occasions, and were mostly dressed in sober jumpers and trousers, in shades of grey and navy in most cases. The silence was broken by the arrival of Matthew.

'Have the gardai gone yet?' asked Michael. Michael Moran was the youngest member, new to the community, and only slowly finding his feet. He was one of those dressed in grey trousers and a jumper, with a clerical shirt open at the neck. It annoyed George immensely that he did not wear the religious habit. Michael had been trained in the new way of thinking, and while he was quiet by nature, his views were strongly held.

'Yes, and the body has been taken to the hospital for a post mortem,' Matthew answered.

George had recovered from his earlier telling off and now spoke out strongly, in the tone of a man who was dealing with a child in need of some urgent direction. Like Enda and Jack, he didn't regard Matthew as a good Superior of the community, certainly not of the calibre of the great men of the past. He had seen many superiors come and go in his time, and he especially liked to think back to what he saw as the halcyon days, when Charles Walsh, a big, strong, autocratic man, ruled the community with a rod of iron. Matthew, by contrast, was weak and indecisive. But George kept his opinions on this matter to himself. He was the only one in the community who remembered Walsh with affection, the others who knew him considering him the epitome of everything that was bad about those times. And anyway, George had too much respect for the office of Superior to undermine Matthew in any obvious way.

'Ring up Dr Smith, and he will deal with the matter discreetly,' he said firmly.

'I've already done so.' Matthew was even more anxious than George to keep the whole thing quiet. The thought of the media asking awkward questions and exposing the monastery to public scrutiny terrified him.

'Good,' said George. 'Whatever about ourselves, nobody outside the monastery must know what has happened. It would ruin our reputation if the truth emerged.'

'Has anyone seen Brendan yet?' asked Matthew.

'He's up,' Timothy answered. 'I saw a light in his room when I was coming down. He'll be here in a few minutes.' Timothy Brown, small but thickset and strong, could always be depended on to know about Brendan Quinn. He followed him around, almost like a servant, and tended to all his needs. He seldom expressed an opinion of his own, but tended to parrot what Brendan would say.

'I wish he would hurry up. We need him at a time like this.' Matthew's tone sounded almost whining, and Enda felt the contempt rising inside him. It isn't we who need him, he thought. It is yourself. You cannot go for a pee without the approval of Quinn.

Everyone in the community knew that while Matthew was the official Superior, Brendan was the man who wielded the real power.

George persisted, not allowing himself to be deflected from his particular line of thought. 'We must have a full burial ceremony, as we would for anyone else. Otherwise the story might get out.'

It only slowly dawned on Michael, the only young man sitting at the table, what George was talking about. He was thinking back to the days when people who committed suicide were refused both the funeral Mass and burial in a Christian cemetery.

'Thanks be to God, those days are gone, anyway,' Michael said. 'And may the Lord have mercy on the poor man's soul.'

'Waste of time. Prayers are no use to him now,' snapped George, with what sounded almost like a note of satisfaction to Michael.

'What do you mean?' he asked.

'When he tied that rope around his neck, he turned his back on God, and on any hope of salvation. That is, of course, unless he repented at the last moment, as he hung from the rafters, and appealed to his Saviour for mercy.' The fact that George had never really liked Kevin, that he had no feeling of warmth towards him, was now very obvious in the way he spoke. But then, George had had few feelings of warmth in his life towards anyone. Sentiment played no part in his assessment of himself or others. His view of Kevin's death was that it was an inevitable result of all the laxity and worldliness that had been allowed into the monastery, and that Kevin had allowed into his own life. It was as simple as that.

'God, you are something else. You're so narrow-minded, so selfish.' Enda had roused himself from his tiredness, and was holding nothing back in his assault on George. 'All you care about is the good name of the monastery. You don't give a damn for poor Kevin. So he has gone to hell, has he? Well maybe he's better off, if heaven is going to be full of the likes of you. It is the Church that should be condemned for the way it has treated people who committed suicide, and their families, in the past. Christianity, how are you.' Enda didn't often make a public attack on the Church like that, but this morning his usual caution in theological matters was thrown aside.

'And I don't believe that God will send Kevin to hell for this.' Michael's voice was quiet, but definite. 'Anyone who commits suicide must be so desperate. He will not be held responsible for his actions. Maybe we will be judged more harshly because of our failure to notice how desperate he was.' He paused, hoping that somebody would respond, but his opinion was greeted with silence. He decided to be a little more provocative. 'Anyway, for some people, suicide might be the right spiritual option.'

'Oh, I couldn't agree with that.' Matthew felt that, as Superior, it was his duty to refute anything that sounded like heresy, especially coming from a younger member of the community. 'I would agree that we should not pass judgement on Kevin. Let us leave that to the good Lord. But we can never be seen to approve of suicide. It goes against the plan of God.'

'How can you be so sure what the plan of God is?' Michael was not letting go of his point easily. 'He gave us free will, and we are encouraged to take responsibility for our own lives. Maybe sometimes a person's life is so hopeless, so impossibly destructive, that they have no other way out.'

Matthew wanted to avoid an argument. He had no confidence in his ability to match this bright young man with all these new and disturbing ideas. Matthew still depended on the old theology that he had learned as a student many years before. He knew he should be reading some of the modern stuff, but he was never much of a reader, and anyway, the small bits he had read were so upsetting that he was afraid to continue. He was relieved when Brendan came in behind him.

Brendan Quinn was tall and stately, and while Matthew was lacking in confidence and afraid of conflict, Brendan was strong and assured, and carried a natural sense of authority. People generally looked up to him, especially outside the monastery. Within the community there were some – and Enda was one of them – who saw him as autocratic, a control freak who was unable to work with anyone who had a mind of their own. He had missed out on the crisis of the night, and was just now picking up on the fact that everything was not as it should be.

'What's wrong? Has somebody died or something?'

'I'm afraid you're right,' said Matthew, and quickly explained the situation. He had begun to relax a little after Brendan's arrival. Brendan was the high-profile figure in the monastery, the one renowned for his preaching, which was always direct and easy to listen to. He had been in the community for many years, and the townspeople knew him well. He held the position of director of the sodality. The sodality was a devotional movement over a hundred years old which was set up in order to enrich people's spiritual lives. Each member of the sodality attended a church service, consisting of prayer and a sermon, once a week, on a particular evening, over and above their attendance at Sunday Mass. Since this sodality was a large and famous one, the position of director was important. Indeed, after the bishop, it was the most significant religious position in the town. Brendan was also the bursar of the community. He was known to be a genius with money, and about two years previously had been appointed to the management body that looked after the finances of the whole congregation worldwide. This had been a great honour, not only for himself, but for the entire community. Along with all of this, he was friendly with the people of influence in the area. He had always regarded this as important, and all his life he had cultivated the friendship of significant people. Indeed, if you asked anyone outside the monastery who was the boss, they would automatically have said that Brendan was.

Now he immediately switched into his efficient, managing role. He would get on to the CEO of the local Health Board at his home before he left for the office. It was typical of him to have access to the home numbers of people like that. He would see that everything was done to cover up the situation as far as the medical records were concerned. Then he'd talk to the superintendent in the barracks, and fix things up at that end.

'Have the family been notified yet?' he wanted to know.

'I was waiting until daytime. I didn't see much point in disturbing them in the middle of the night with that sort of news.' Matthew, as usual, found himself explaining his actions to Brendan.

'How many are there in his family?' Michael inquired.

'His mother is still alive, but she's old and senile, and confined to a nursing home. He also has a brother and a sister, both married.' Enda, showing off that he was a mine of information on each member of the community and their pedigree, gave the answer before Matthew.

'What will we tell them?' Matthew appeared to address his question to everyone, but he was really looking to Brendan for the answer.

Brendan did not disappoint him. He responded immediately. 'Just ring them up and tell them that he has taken a bad turn, and ask them to come as soon as they can. It will take them a few hours to get here, and that will give us a chance to square things with the authorities, and put a lid on the whole situation. Then we'll have a better idea of how much we need to tell them.'

Enda eyed Brendan. His hackles were rising at the way Brendan was taking over the whole affair, and he resented the power he held in the community. He'd take the wind out of his sails. It wasn't often he was in the position of being one ahead of Brendan in the latest crisis, so he was determined to make the most of it.

'Put a lid on the situation, is it? Forget it. The guards have been here already. Jimmy McCormack was one of them, and you know what he's like. Half the town will know about it at this stage.'

'Don't speak like that about our garda force.' Brendan's tone was superior. 'Garda McCormack is a good man, and a good garda officer. I'm sure he will exercise discretion in this matter, as he has been trained to do.'

'He will like hell. You just wait and see.' It was hard to argue with Brendan, and Enda wouldn't risk telling him to shut up, as he would with the others. He was tempted to mention the strange incident of the person knocking at the window, to use it as a way of highlighting the futility of Brendan and Matthew's plans to keep everything quiet, but he decided against it. The more he thought about it, the more he had an uneasy feeling, and he wanted time to talk it over with Jack and see if he could get to the bottom of what was going on before he involved anyone else. But there was another line he could take that would make things difficult for the pair of them.

'There could be more to this than meets the eye. You mightn't find it quite as easy to cover it up as you think. Kevin was homosexual, you know.'

'Stop that filth!' said George.''Tis an awful thing to say

about anyone. Bad enough to have him end his life as he did without slandering him entirely.'

Timothy Brown began to snigger quietly. 'Did you hear the one about . . . ' he started.

'Keep quiet, Timothy. This is not the time for your jokes. Let the man rest in peace now. We must say no more about this, and we must not judge.' Brendan was occupying the moral high ground.

But Michael took a different approach to the issue. 'Are we saying that there is something wrong with being homosexual?'

He was always on the lookout for intolerance in any of its forms: racism, homophobia or whatever, and he made no secret of the fact that he was disgusted by a recent statement from the archbishop. The previous Lent, the archbishop, following the line of the current Pope, had come out with a hardline pastoral letter saying that homosexuality was a disorder, that all gay relationships were seriously sinful, and, most controversial of all, implying that homosexuals could be discriminated against in certain professions, especially those to do with caring for the young. Michael was a strong believer in the equality of all people, and the right of every person to live their lives as they wished.

'Of course we are not saying any such thing,' said Brendan. 'Though the less said about any of this, the better. Let me hear no more on this subject until the man is buried.'

'But I am saying that there is something wrong with it.' George could not let go. 'I have heard it all now. A member of the community commits suicide, and then I'm told he was a pervert. I'm sorry I lived to see this day.'

Enda was a little sorry that he had brought this up. He felt that maybe he had gone too far, considering the situation, so he decided to try to deflect the conversation.

'Being homosexual is one thing.' he said. 'I have no problem with that. Live and let live, that's my motto. But trying to keep this quiet is another matter entirely. Whatever about Dr Smith's discretion, or calling on the auspices of the superintendent, the guards have raised all sorts of questions, and they want to interview every member of the community – every one of us. We will all have to sit and answer questions.' There was an unmistakable hint of glee in Enda's voice as he announced this.

'Interview us? Surely not!' George clearly considered the idea preposterous. What would he have to say about Kevin's death, except that it was the inevitable result of sinful living? He knew the guards wouldn't exactly be interested in that line of thought.

'What do they want to know?'

'It seems they think that there was a possibility that someone else might have been in the room with Kevin last night.' Enda was being deliberately provocative. 'They want to make sure that it was actually suicide.'

'Are they suggesting it might have been murder?' Even Michael's normal quietness was shaken by this news, and there was an unusual degree of urgency in his voice.

'They aren't saying anything at all. It's normal practice after this type of incident to make some inquiries. That's all they're doing.' Matthew tried to defuse the situation, to counteract Enda's efforts at scaremongering. But George was not reassured.

'Glory be to God,' he said, 'that's all we need. Murder in the monastery. We'll never live this one down!'

'The newspapers will report that we are helping the gardai with their enquiries.' Enda was beginning to enjoy himself.

'Ah, shut up!' George caught himself saying, but he checked himself. There was a danger he'd begin to talk like that scut Enda.

CHAPTER THREE

Jack was woken from a deep sleep by a loud knock on his door, and before he was fully aware of what was happening, Enda was standing in the middle of the room.

'Time to get up. There's a lot we need to talk about. Anyway, I can't understand how you can sleep after last night.'

Jack sat up. 'I'm lucky that way. It takes a lot to come between me and my sleep.'

The events of the night had come flooding back into his mind, and he began to pay attention when Enda said to him, 'We'd better decide what we are going to tell the guards. They're interviewing everyone in the community today. Old George is in with them right now.'

'We'll tell them everything, I presume. Why not? There's clearly something shady going on here, and they're the people to investigate it.'

'I'm not sure,' said Enda. 'You know me. In spite of all my giving out, I have a great fondness for this monastery. After all, it is my home. I don't have women in my life, like you, so I don't have any little cosy nests to be going to. Besides, I'm not sure if I really trust those guards. I'd like to know a bit more about it all before we tell them too much.'

'You could be up in court for obstructing justice, withholding information. Not to mention slandering my name with all this talk of women. I'll go to visit you when you're in jail.'

Enda smiled, but his mind was on other things. Suddenly he got serious.

'Something strange happened this morning. You know how two-faced Brendan can be. At breakfast, when I suggested that Jimmy McCormack would tell the whole town about the suicide, he lectured me about what a good man and a good garda officer he was. But I was barely back up in my room when there was a knock on my door, and it was Brendan. He got straight to the point: "Be careful what you say to that crowd." It took me a while to cop on, if you'll excuse the pun, what he was talking about. "Remember," he said to me, "the less they know the better. Our loyalty is to the community. This is our family, and what goes on in here is nobody else's business." He was really into his preaching tone at this stage, talking down to me. Needless to say, I was mad. He finished his lecture by saying: 'Don't dare to say anything to them about the sodality, and Kevin Dunne leaving the team." He was turning on his heels and going out the door, but I stopped him in his tracks when I said: "And what are you trying to hide?" I could see by the look on his face that he knew he had gone too far, but he had no way back. So he gave me this real cold look as he stood with his hand on the handle of the door. "I'm warning you," he said to me. "I might know a thing or two about you." And he backed out and closed the door.'

'The plot certainly thickens,' said Jack. 'Have you any idea what is going on? I'm away from this house so much that I'm out of touch with a lot of the real stuff that's happening.' Jack was a travelling missioner. He went around to the parishes, preaching missions and retreats. He had only just returned from a few weeks up north. 'And what is it that he might know about you?' Jack wouldn't have minded having a bit of juicy gossip about Enda, to have something to throw back at him when he brought up Olivia. But he suspected Brendan was bluffing. Enda was much too careful to give anyone anything to use against him.

Enda began to fill him in: 'Well, I know that there was a fair bit of tension between Brendan and Kevin over the sodality. Kevin wasn't long on the team, but he never really became one of them. For someone who was almost timid by nature, I was surprised at how much he disapproved of the way Brendan ran the sodality, and how strong his opposition became. Of course, he hadn't a hope. When you take on Brendan, you take on Timothy too. And that fellow is sly. My guess is that he could shed some light on last night's happenings, but he'll only say and do what Brendan tells him to. And, in answer to your question, and sorry to disappoint you, they have nothing on me. That was only bravado talking, trying to frighten me.'

'What did Kevin object to about Brendan and the sodality?'

'Two things mainly: his preaching and the way he ran the team.' Enda was one of those people who loved to talk, and, even though there was so much happening around them, he would happily sit all day long talking to Jack. 'If you are a member of Brendan's team you have to do it his way. He has to be in charge. He can't cope with anyone who has a mind of their own. That's why Timothy is such a perfect companion for him, and why he's so happy to have somebody as spineless as Matthew as Superior. I thought that Kevin would adapt easily enough to the situation. But he showed a surprising degree of resistance to being told what to do all the time. And he used to get so mad about Brendan's preaching. He used come in to me some nights after the sodality services, boiling with anger over the things that were said. Have you ever heard Brendan in full flight, preaching to a sodality meeting?'

'No,' answered Jack. 'The sodality wouldn't be high on my list of places to go if I had a night off. I used to listen to him a bit in my early years. It embarrasses me now to think that for a short while I thought he was someone I could model myself on. But I quickly learned. More recently, I've only heard him once or twice, doing Sunday homilies, and they were innocuous enough. A very traditional style, but nothing too objectionable.'

'He keeps the best for the sodality,' Enda explained. 'He has an old-fashioned group there who love when he attacks people, so they encourage him. I heard him a few weeks ago on single mothers. It was one of the sermons that really upset Kevin. It went something like this.' And Enda stood out in the middle of the floor, hauled himself up to his full height, and began to do an uncanny imitation of Brendan:

'"My dear brethren, this evening I want to talk to you about a very serious matter; a matter that I would go so far as to say is a cancer on the otherwise healthy body of this nation. I am referring to single mothers, those young women who have so little respect for themselves that they go out and mate with whoever comes along, and then bring an innocent child into the world. A child that has no chance of being reared with any respect for God or man. Do you know what these women are like? I'll tell you what they are like."' At this point, Enda's voice rose to a crescendo, and Jack was afraid the whole house would gather to see what was happening, but he was enjoying the spectacle too much to interrupt. '"They are like rabbits. They breed without shame and without morals. They are no better than animals. They hop in and out of bed with every Tom, Dick and Harry. They are destroying the moral fibre of our society; they are undermining the holiness of family life. Things weren't too bad until the government began giving them money, a weekly allowance. A handout, if you don't mind. Payment for sin. Payment for tempting men. Whipping should be their payment."' Enda paused, and the two of them burst out laughing. The imitation of Brendan had been superb. Enda returned to his chair.

'Why do you go out and listen to him?' asked Jack.

'It's the best entertainment of the week around here. I wouldn't miss it for the world. Of course, the old biddies who follow him love his sermons. They think all our problems today are the result of preachers not laying down the law, not preaching the Ten Commandments. When he had finished that sermon they broke out into applause. But I could see the face of Kevin up on the altar, and I knew he didn't feel like applauding. He said to me afterwards: "From where I sat, I could see at least three single mothers down in the church, each of whom is living in a little flat, trying to bring up her child on the lone parent's allowance. It was great to see them at the sodality. What he was saying about them was so unjust."' By now Enda was really in flow, and again he jumped up and took his position in the middle of the floor.

'There was the other day recently when he launched again into his favourite topic, abortion. He was screaming: "Abortion is murder, and anyone who has hand, act or part in performing an abortion is a murderer. God will punish them. He will thrust them down to hell, where they will burn forever. And in the midst of the flames they will forever hear the screams of the innocent babies they have killed. There will be no escape."' Enda was presenting the sermon with all the appropriate hand gestures and facial expressions. He paused for breath, and then said: 'I always think when he preaches like that he takes great delight in the thought of people burning in hell. He works himself into a state that is almost orgasmic. A sadist, that's what he is. Kevin came to me after that sermon too. He said he was aware of some women attending the sodality who had had abortions, and he felt sorry for them, and felt that pouring more guilt on them was the last thing they needed.'

'Did he ever go and confront Brendan about his preaching?' Jack wanted to know, when Enda paused long enough for him to get a word in.

'He did, and I think it was what brought about the bust-up that led to him being dropped from the team.' Enda thought for a moment. 'Brendan is a tough character. Maybe I do need to take this morning's warning seriously. What he said to Kevin, when Kevin tackled him about his preaching, was "My dear man, when you can fill a church with people in the way that I can, and get a round of applause at the end of your sermon, then you can come and talk to me about my preaching!" Poor old Kevin was never much of a preacher, as you know, so he had no answer to that.'

Jack began to haul himself out of the bed.

'I must get up. So what will we tell the guards? Maybe we should say nothing for the moment about the knock on the window last night. It was weird, wasn't it? I just caught a glimpse of him as he rounded the corner of the street: a big fellow, with a loose anorak and a hood over his head. I was so exhausted at that stage that I decided to go straight to bed, and leave everything till this morning.'

'And leave me with the mess, holding Matthew's hand. But yes, it was weird. I've been asking myself was it the timing of it that made it so weird. There might be a very innocent explanation. You know the sort of weirdos who gather around monasteries. Most of them are harmless. I think it is a good idea to say nothing for the moment. We can fill the guards in later if we need to.'

As Enda was opening the door to leave, Jack threw a parting shot at him.

'Brendan did say he had something on you. I must let my imagination work on that one.' All he heard was a loud 'Shut up' as the door closed.

Enda, standing in the corridor outside Jack's room, looked at his watch and realised that the main weekday morning Mass in the church was just ending, so he made his way out to the yard to see if the locals had any news of the events of the night. The first person he met was old Dolly, one of the regulars who never missed her daily Mass and all the latest gossip that went with it. She came straight up to him.

'Terrible news about Father Dunne! I was so shocked when Father Timothy announced it at Mass, and asked us to pray for him.'

'Indeed it is.' Enda tried to sound as ordinary and non-committal as possible.

'Dying just like that without any warning. God save us all, but you wouldn't expect it to happen to him, of all people. He seemed so healthy. Was it some type of heart attack, Father?'

Enda could see by the look on her face that she knew more than she was admitting.

'Yes, Dolly, a heart attack. It could happen to any of us at any time. That is why we always need to be prepared to go.'

'You are right there, Father. I feel I am ready, thanks be to God, because I never miss my daily Mass. The greatest possible preparation for death. But there is talk going on around the town, Father.'

'Talk?' Now it was Enda's turn to do some fishing.

'Bad talk, Father. People will say anything about the priests nowadays.'

And none quicker than yourself, you pious old fraud, Enda muttered to himself as he walked away. So the rumours were already out, and would by now have gone around the town like wildfire.

When Jack had showered and dressed himself, he decided to slip down the road and visit Joan rather than get caught up just yet with the guards and their questions. He remembered Enda's comment about him having women in his life. Joan would hardly fit into the category that Enda was alluding to. She was almost twice his age, a widow with her family gone about their own lives. She was crippled with arthritis, and was unable to go out of the house except in a wheelchair. Both her family and the neighbours were good to her, and she managed to live as independent a life as possible in the circumstances. For Jack, whose mother had died when he was very young, she had become like a second mother. He thought that she was an amazing person. There was a peace about her, and an ability to laugh at life and not take it too seriously. You could say anything to her, and Jack had gradually got into the habit of discussing all the different aspects of his life with her. Though she was a committed Catholic, she had developed independence of thought over the years, and she now viewed the workings of the Church with a fairly sceptical eye. She was sitting at the fire when he let himself in.

'Welcome back from your travels, Jack. It's good to see you. Make yourself a cup of coffee there, and come and sit by the fire and tell me all about yourself.'

When Jack had settled himself with the coffee, having given Joan her usual cup of warm water with a squeeze of lemon, he felt at home and relaxed. Clearly Joan hadn't yet heard about Kevin, and he decided he would leave that bit of news for a while.

'Tell me about your trip to the North.' said Joan.

Jack had just come back from working on a mission in a poor urban parish in Northern Ireland. Though the people there were not the best at going to church, they responded to what himself and his fellow missioner, a member of the Order from another community, were doing, and they had a great few weeks. He told Joan about the close of the mission.

'Because the crowd was so big, we decided to have an open-air event in the car park of the church.' Jack got a lovely, warm feeling as he remembered it. 'It was amazing. The people, men and women of all ages, sang and prayed their hearts out. And when it was over, they queued up to say goodbye, and to get our autograph on the little mission book we had been using. For an hour and a half we stood, with our backs to the outside wall of the church, as streams of people came up to us. I shook hands with the men, embraced the women, and patted the children lightly on the head, while I signed their books and said goodbye to them all. I felt like a pop star.'

'What were the people like?' asked Joan. She was delighted to have Jack with her, and would happily sit and listen to him. Since she got sick she was so confined, it was great to get some taste of the outside world.

'They have hard lives – poor, with very little opportunity. And yet there was a spirit about them. Do you know what I admired most about them? There was a sort of casualness. They didn't take any authority or system, either Church or State, too seriously. They could take them or leave them. So many of them, for instance, had few hang-ups about sex. They were in all sorts of irregular relationships, but they made no big deal about it. What bishops or even popes had to say was not important to them. They saw all of that as belonging to another world, one that they did not inhabit. I liked that about them; it is such a different attitude to the one I was brought up with. And even their attitude to God. They didn't seem to feel the need to placate God, or to keep Him humoured. He was there when they wanted Him, but they weren't going to pester Him excessively. Now and then, when sickness or some trouble came along, they would come to God looking for help, and having no doubt that they were perfectly entitled to it.'

'Hold it,' said Joan. 'You're going too fast for me there. Why did that attitude to God appeal to you? After all, aren't you supposed to be the one who is trying to get the rest of us to take God seriously?'

'I don't know how much of that I believe any more, Joan. The God that I grew up with was such a hard taskmaster. It was almost impossible to please Him. I'm trying to get rid of that notion.'

'But surely you shouldn't be approving of their casual attitude towards sex and marriage.' Joan was teasing him. 'You should be keeping us in line. Belting the Commandments down our throats.'

'When word of what happened last night gets out, we won't be in a position to belt anything down anyone's throat.'

'What do you mean?' asked Joan.

'Kevin Dunne hanged himself, from the rafters in the community room. I was the one that found him.' He went on and told her the whole story. When he had finished, she said, 'I'm sorry for poor Kevin. I didn't know him well, except for seeing him up on the altar, the few times I managed to get down to Mass. But in a way, it doesn't surprise me. It's a strange way of life that you live in that monastery. I've seen it now over the past forty years, and I have come to the conclusion that it isn't natural.' Jack had noticed that more and more people were saying things like that to him. It was such a change, even since he first joined the Order. Then people were congratulating him, and telling him he was making the best possible choice in life.

'Why do you say that, Joan?'

'Ah, I don't know: a group of men living together! Men are poor at closeness, at talking about the real things in life. Every man needs a woman to talk to, to learn how to be gentle, to have a bit of intimacy. Life without intimacy isn't worth living.'

And then she threw out the sort of question that was typical of her, that nobody else would ask him. But he didn't mind her asking, he could trust her, and knew she would accept him no matter what. 'How do you manage, Jack? For someone to talk to, to be intimate with – for sex?'

Jack hadn't yet told her about Olivia. 'I have got close to a woman,' he admitted.

'Well now. Isn't that news?' she said, beaming. 'Tell me all about her.'

'She's lovely. Almost my own age. We can talk about anything. I love being with her.'

'Have you been to bed with her yet?' Joan was smiling as she let her curiosity run free.

'Oh God, no. Nothing like that. Don't you know that would be against my vow?'

'Of course I know all that,' said Joan, 'but I know human nature too. Is she pretty?'

'Very. I think she is beautiful. You know, Joan, the modern attitude to celibacy is that we should have friendships with people of both sexes. The old notion of keeping your distance from women as a way of observing your vow is no longer recommended. The books tell us that our emotional lives will be stunted unless we are close to women as well as men. Just what you were saying yourself, that we need intimacy.'

'That's true, anyway. But how are you supposed to manage it?'

'Non-sexual friendships between the sexes. That's how it's supposed to work; you are close to somebody, but with no physical contact except maybe a hug, or a peck on the cheek.' As he spoke he could see that Joan had a sceptical look on her face. 'You don't believe that works; I can see that from your expression.'

'Well, how is it working with you and that pretty girl you love being with?'

'With difficulty, and getting harder all the time.'

'That's what I thought. But anyway, I don't believe in celibacy for priests, and certainly not in making a law out of it and imposing it on everyone. The sooner you are allowed to marry, the better.'

'That's not likely to happen in my time, I'm afraid. The Church is a big organisation, and moves very slowly. It wouldn't be wise for me to sit around and expect that to come about, to get me off the hook.'

'So, what are you going to do? Are you going to keep seeing this pretty girl?'

'I've no plan to give her up at the moment, anyway. I don't know if I would be able to, even if I wanted to.'

'So you have it bad, by the sound of that. What will you do

when the attraction gets too strong, and it goes beyond these chaste hugs and kisses on the cheek?'

'According to the books, that's not supposed to happen.'

'I don't know if that would be much fun for her. I imagine she might want more in the long term than just nice conversation.'

'Oh, Joan, don't confuse me. Let me just enjoy this for the moment. Haven't I enough problems, with people hanging themselves off the rafters? Am I not entitled to a little bit of enjoyment?'

'I agree with you on that. You are. But I don't imagine the Pope would.'

'And we'll certainly leave him out of it. Look at the time! I must rush. Thanks for the coffee, Joan. I'll call up again tomorrow, and keep you informed about what's going on.'

Joan smiled wryly. There was a lot to be kept informed about.

CHAPTER FOUR

George Forde couldn't rest, and the day dragged interminably. Though he was the oldest of the priests in the community, and now officially retired, he was in good health. And he belonged to the generation that did not believe in retirement. He had been taught as a young religious that time was so precious, it was a sin to waste even a moment of it. Every minute must be used to work on your salvation. So he was available to do any work that came his way, and plenty did. Whenever a request came to say a Mass, represent the community at a funeral, or anything of that nature, Matthew came knocking at his door and George was glad to oblige. He also attended a few prayer meetings each week, and gave benediction every evening for a convent of contemplative nuns who lived nearby. He was a good reader, though narrow and confined in his taste, and whatever spare time he had, he sat in his room and read books. He hardly ever watched television. He said that it came between him and his prayers. Apart from saying Mass, and joining in the prayer of the community, he always set aside an hour for quiet personal prayer each day. But today he couldn't do any of these things, least of all sit in his room and read. Part of the reason he couldn't rest was the thought that he would be interviewed by the guards. They were in the monastery all day, conducting interviews with every member of the community about the events of the previous night. He had never been interviewed by a policeman in his life, and he was not looking forward to it.

Luckily, he was one of the first ones called, and well before lunch he was summoned to the room where the interviews were taking place. It was the large parlour where, in the past, the priests entertained members of their own family when they came to visit. It had recently been renovated, along with the rest of the house, something of which George disapproved. Comfort, he believed, was a sign of laxity. When he entered the room he saw that the two officers had rearranged the furniture. There was a table in the centre, and they were sitting behind it, with their notes in front of them. An empty chair awaited him on the other side. He knew Sergeant McCormack – a regular attender in the church – who welcomed him with warmth and politeness. The younger man, whom he had never met, introduced himself as Noel Bluett, and it was he who did most of the questioning. Immediately George took a dislike to this man. He was bright, efficient and clinical in his way of asking questions. George quickly concluded that at the very least he didn't attend church, and that perhaps he was not even a believer. He did address him as 'Father' but in a very formal way, and, apart from that, the fact that he was a priest clearly made no difference to him. The effect this had on George was to make him very uncomfortable. The line in the Gospel about people who were not with you being against you had always made sense to him. And he had considerable disdain for the new generation of people in the country who no longer went to church and who, as he saw it, turned their backs on the faith of their fathers. What Cromwell had failed to do, the modern generation were doing of their own accord.

'How well did you know the deceased?' asked Noel Bluett.

Immediately he was faced with a dilemma. How could he answer this? The main thought on his mind was the good name of the community, and the need to avoid saying anything to these two outsiders that might reflect badly on life within the monastery. Even in the face of this awful situation, he must preserve the illusion that everyone got on well, and that there was peace and harmony among them all. Despite all that had happened in recent years in the Church, the issue of not giving scandal to the people by letting them know that human weakness was as prevalent in the monastery as elsewhere was very important to him. So he would tell them as little as possible.

'Yes, I knew him very well. Of course I did. Haven't I lived with him for many years? He was a good priest. He worked hard and said his prayers. I cannot understand why this happened.'

'Did you notice anything unusual about him in recent times? Was he in bad form, depressed, under particular stress in any way?'

Under stress! The very language irritated George, never mind the question. He had no patience with all this modern jargon about feelings and personal stuff: it was both selfish and soft. If he were to be honest, he would have had to admit that he had no idea what form Kevin had been in – or anyone else, for that matter. People should get on with their work, say their prayers, observe the rule and follow their vocation. Then they would have no problem. Feelings had nothing to do with it, and it was precisely because Kevin worried too much about how he felt that he had ended up the way he did. But George was certainly not going to say any of that to these interrogators.

'No, I didn't notice anything at all. He seemed to be fine.'

'Have you any reason to suspect why he might have done this?'

Reasons, George thought to himself. Of course I have my reasons. The man was a bad religious, that's the reason! He had become lax in his way of life. He was too selfish, and he didn't observe the rule properly or say his prayers as faithfully as he should!

But he said nothing of that. 'No reason at all,' was the answer he gave.

'Did you know that he was gay?'

What could they possibly mean by that question? What had being gay got to do with it? If anything, Kevin tended to be dour and reserved, not gay. His perplexed look told Bluett that George did not understand the question.

'Did you know that the deceased was a homosexual?'

'He was not. He was a good man, and he would never have got up to anything like that.' How dare they suggest that such perversion was prevalent in the monastery.

But the garda pressed on, not conceding his point. 'We have known about him for some time, and we have known that he was in the habit of frequenting the places where homosexual people meet.'

'I have never heard anything so preposterous in all my life . . .' But George's voice trailed away at the end. So Enda had been right in what he had said. But the fact that George had first heard this earlier on that morning didn't make it any easier to deal with, especially in front of these two outsiders. To be homosexual was a dirty and sinful thing to his way of thinking. He fell back on his usual explanation for anything he didn't approve of. The changes! If things had remained as they had been in the past, this sort of behaviour would not be going on.

If there had been homosexuals in the past, and he doubted if there were, they kept very quiet about it. And that was the only way of dealing with something like that. Shameful things should not be brought out into the open.

Jimmy McCormack, realising how shocked George was, and angry with his fellow officer for what he saw as a lack of sensitivity to an old priest, intervened at this point.

'We have no more questions, Father George. Thank you very much for your cooperation, and please accept our sympathies over the death of your fellow priest.'

George got up and left the room. As soon as the door closed, Noel Bluett turned on Jimmy McCormack angrily, saying: 'What do you mean by interrupting my interview in that fashion?'

'You should have more respect for a poor old man who has lived a sheltered life,' McCormack replied. 'Why did you have to bring up Father Dunne's sexual orientation? That had nothing to do with old Father George, or what he thought about him.'

'But it may well have had something to do with Kevin Dunne's death,' Bluett said. 'You might have seen that old man as innocent and naive, but I saw him as someone who was evading my questions, and not telling the truth. Why should I treat him any differently because he has a collar round his neck? And anyway, did the Super ask me to conduct these interviews or did he not?'

'Yeah, he did. But he asked me to come with you, because I know this community so well.'

'I would appreciate if you wouldn't interfere again.' A cold tension settled in the room between the two guards as they continued their work.

Michael Moran was soft-spoken, but they quickly realised that they were dealing with a very different type of person to George. He was young, open, and he spoke his mind clearly, in a very earnest voice.

'Kevin was not easy to get to know,' Moran said. 'He was friendly, in a casual sort of way, but it was impossible to get near the real person. He was tense and highly strung by nature; he had a forced, artificial-sounding laugh that came from his mouth but was not reflected in his eyes. I would say he was never very happy in himself.'

'Why do you think he committed suicide? Were you surprised when it happened?' Garda Bluett was immediately impressed by this young man, but he asked his questions in a more careful tone than he had used with George, conscious of his disapproving companion beside him.

'Of course I was surprised. You don't expect a priest to hang himself from the rafters in his monastery. We are presumed to have a better grip on our lives than that. And yet, as I am getting over the initial shock of it, maybe it isn't that surprising. The life that was lived in places like this in the past was so impersonal; people were discouraged from being close to each other, or to anyone outside the monastery.'

Michael fell silent as he pondered the life they lived. He suspected that a lot of his colleagues, especially the older ones, didn't really know how they felt. Because of the nature of their training, they weren't able to recognise hurt, anger, relief, sadness, joy, loneliness – yes, loneliness, that was the one that killed the spirit, sapped it slowly of life. Aloud, he said: 'Maybe it isn't any wonder that every now and again somebody cracked up and couldn't cope any longer.'

The young officer was clearly interested in this insight into monastic life. And after his session with George, he was relieved to have someone with whom he could relate. He found himself forgetting about Jimmy McCormack and relaxing into the interview.

'And how do you manage?' he asked.

'It's different for our generation,' Michael said. 'We have been trained to deal with our feelings, and not to be afraid of getting close to people, male or female.'

'Women? How can you do that? What about the vow of celibacy?' Bluett decided to ignore the cough that came from beside him. This was interesting.

Michael became even more earnest. 'That doesn't prevent us from having close relationships with women, as long as they aren't sexual in nature.'

The policeman thought of his own girlfriend, and what it would be like for him if their relationship was non-sexual. He was glad he had met a girl who had no hang-ups about sex, and he suspected it had a good bit to do with the fact that she didn't go to church. For him, religion was an oppressive influence which tried to take the fun out of life. He was surprised that only one member of the community had committed suicide. How could you live like that?

'Good luck to you, anyway. It surely wouldn't be my way of doing it.' He knew by the look he got from McCormack that he was overstepping the mark again, and that he had better get back to business, so he asked, 'Do you think that the fact that this man was a homosexual had anything to do with his suicide?'

Michael thought about this for a while.

'The only answer I can give to that is that I don't know. Maybe it was a factor. Of course, a subject like that is never discussed in here, and Kevin would never have mentioned it to any of us, as far as I know. Most of us suspected it, except some of the older men, who don't think along those lines. You see, the Church doesn't handle the whole gay issue very well. In my experience, most gays feel rejected and condemned by the Church. And the ironic thing is that a great number of my age group of young priests are themselves gay. Who knows what struggle went on in Kevin over it all?'

Again the young policeman was very interested in this reply, and it raised a number of questions which he would have loved to ask. For instance, why was it that many young priests were gay? But he was conscious of his older, more strait-laced colleague, and he decided to keep to the job in hand.

'Were you conscious of any particular source of stress in his life in recent times?' he asked.

'To be honest, we were not very close, and as I said, he was hard to get to know, so he could have been in trouble and I wouldn't have known about it. I'm sure that is not a good admission to make for someone who is supposed to be living a life of Christian love. But it's the reality of the situation. I'm sorry I can't be of more help.'

'And our sympathies to you over this sudden bereavement.' These were the first words the older man had spoken, and with them the interview ended.

'My good man, if you had seen as much of the world and of life as I have, you would know that these things happen. There is no need for any of this investigation. Are you suggesting that we strung him up ourselves?' Brendan Quinn's laugh was derisive and dismissive.

The young officer took an immediate dislike to him. How dare anyone call him 'my good man'! This big bully of a priest was not going to talk him down, no matter what Jimmy McCormack, who clearly was a friend of his, might think.

'I am not suggesting anything. I am merely asking why a member of this community was found hanging dead from the rafters last night. Can you explain that to us, please?'

'In my work I come across suicide cases practically every day. Don't you know that suicide is now the major cause of death among men?'

'Among *young* men,' the guard said coldly, 'not among middle-aged clergymen.'

Brendan turned to Jimmy McCormack, obviously ignoring Bluett.

'We must keep this quiet for the sake of his family. He has an invalid mother as well as a brother and a sister who are due here this afternoon. What are we supposed to tell them? We can't say that he hanged himself. So we are going to tell them that he died of a heart attack. It's crucial that the whole thing be kept quiet. I'm sure you understand and will be able to cooperate with us.

But Brendan had made a mistake. The younger man quickly informed him that, despite his age, he was higher in rank and was in charge of this particular investigation. And before McCormack had a chance to say anything, he continued: 'I don't think it will be quite that simple. There are questions to be asked, and motives to be established.'

Brendan stood up, drawing himself up to his full height.

'My young man, there are more important things in life than your questions. And in this case, the feelings of the family and the good name of the community are the really important issues.' And then he swung his body around dismissively and faced McCormack again. 'Can we get on to discussing how to deal with this situation sensitively?'

'Please sit down, sir,' the young man said. 'May I suggest to you that the reason why a resident of this house hanged himself from the rafters might be more important than the things you are concerned about? I have a few more questions to ask.'

Brendan had never once been addressed as 'sir' since his ordination. He was a strong believer in proper titles, and always insisted on being called 'Father', even by his friends. He remembered the tension in his own home, one day not long after his ordination. He had been sitting at the head of the table, when his younger brother had called him 'Brendan'; he had corrected him. 'I am "Father Brendan"; please remember that from now on!' Things had never been the same between his brother and himself from that day, and now they only met at major family events. But his mother, who was so proud of him, gave him due respect, and called him 'Father' until the day she died.

'"Father", to you, if you don't mind, Officer Bluett.' He spoke curtly.

Jimmy McCormack was clearly very uncomfortable, but he kept his peace.

'I understand the deceased worked in close association with you for a period of time. Is that correct?' asked Bluett.

'Yes, that is correct.'

'But this association came to an end quite recently.'

Who the hell told him all this, Brendan wondered. That fool Matthew? Or Enda, trying to make trouble? How much more has he been told?

'Yes,' he replied.

'Could you explain to us why the association ended?'

'He was appointed to a new job by the Superior.'

Brendan smiled to himself. The notion that the Superior would dare to interfere with his team of helpers on the sodality without being instructed to do so by him was laughable. Brendan had long ago realised that you had to take charge of your own life. Most of the superiors he had known in his time were fools, and if he allowed them to dictate to him, he would have been walked into many a mess. But as he also learned a long time ago, there were occasions when it was useful to hold to the official line, and take cover behind it.

'Had there been any tension between the two of you before his departure?'

'None at all. As I said, he was simply asked by the Superior to do another job. I was sorry to see him leave the team, but in our way of life we learn to accept the will of the Superior.'

'Are you sure?' Bluett spoke with heavy sarcasm. Accepting the will of anyone but himself would surely not come easy to this man.

'My good man, of course I am sure.'

'Thank you, reverend sir.' Again the sarcasm was loaded. 'That will be all for the present.'

'But not the last you will hear about this, I assure you,' Brendan said coldly, as he walked to the door.

Brendan left the room and went straight to the phone. He rang through on the direct line to the Commissioner's office. The Commissioner himself answered the phone.

'I have never been so insulted in all my life. The impertinence of that young man you sent up here to question us. He has no respect. He even went so far as to call me 'sir'. He has no understanding of how to handle a situation like this. I want him taken off the case straightaway, and then I want the whole thing handled quietly and with sensitivity, so that it will appear as if Father Kevin Dunne died of natural causes.'

The Commissioner was embarrassed. He did not want to antagonise Father Brendan Quinn, who was, after all, a very influential person in the locality, and who was a man who tended to assume power in most situations. And yet he trusted this young garda he had asked to deal with this case. He was not surprised that there had been a clash between him and Brendan. He had observed Quinn for many years, and knew him as a man who was used to getting his own way. But Noel Bluett was good, and had a mind of his own. This would inevitably bring him into conflict with Quinn, who had surrounded himself with submissive people who looked up to and admired him.

'I'm afraid, Father Brendan,' he said, in his most conciliatory voice, 'like yourselves we have had to endure big changes. The day when I could order the younger generation around is long gone. But I promise I will have a word with him.'

Jack returned to the monastery just in time for the midday meal. There was a long, wide corridor leading to the refectory. It was tiled and newly painted, but as always, it appeared to him to be cold and severe. Whenever he said this to one of the older men, they reminded him that there had been a time when the surface was cobblestones rather than tiles, and there was no paint on the walls. That was before the heating system had been installed in the monastery. Jack couldn't even begin to imagine what life was like in those days.

The first person he met on the corridor was George, limping along slowly towards the refectory with his rosary beads in his hand. In spite of everything, he liked George. Even though they belonged to different generations and had radically different views on most things, they got on well together. They tended to carry on a line of banter with each other that had something of an edge to it but was basically good-humoured. But today George was in no mood for humour. He looked shocked, white-faced.

'Do you know what "gay" means?' George asked.

Jack immediately understood what he was getting at, and while he smiled in response, he was angry, and wondered who had told him about Kevin.

'Yes, I do.' His voice was quiet and gentle. This was not a time for flippancy. 'Why do you ask?'

'I'm learning a lot today, God help me. And that is one of the things I have learned. The guards said that Kevin was gay, and Enda talked about him being a homosexual earlier in the morning. Surely it can't be true?'

'Yes, it is. Kevin was a homosexual.'

Jack could see that George was paying the price for having lived a very confined life and having restricted his reading to books of a religious nature. He was struggling with this new idea, and trying to get his mind around it. Jack felt sorry for him.

'Does that mean . . . ' and the question was almost funny coming from this old man, dressed in a large black religious cloak with rosary beads in his hand, ' . . . that he went around sticking it into other men?'

Jack was both amused and saddened by the naive bluntness of the question, and all the pain that this represented for poor, innocent old George, and he thought that it was strange that someone could live for so long and yet be so unaware of the realities of the world around him. George's question reminded him of the joke that Timothy liked to tell, the one Jack once thought funny, but now found coarse, maybe because now he knew that sexual depravity could exist among so-called 'holy' people also. But now he chanced telling it, in the faint hope of getting George to see a funny side to the whole situation.

'Did you hear about the fellow that went to Confession, and said to the priest: "I stuck it in a sheep, and I stuck it in a hen." And the priest answered him: "And for your penance, go and stick it in a beehive!"'

But George didn't laugh, and Jack, immediately regretting his attempt at humour, tried to answer the question seriously.

'No, it doesn't mean any such thing. It is more about his sexual orientation than his lifestyle. He was attracted to men rather than to women. That is the way he was made. But he had his vow of celibacy like the rest of us, and I'm sure he kept it as best he could.'

'But the gardai told me that they had known for some time that he mixed with the homosexuals down the town.'

Jack was annoyed. What business had they telling any such thing to George? What was the point of it? It was only last night he had heard from Enda about Kevin frequenting the gay bars in Dublin, but Jack was of the belief that everyone should be allowed to live their own lives, and he was glad that the old rules, with all the moralistic oppression involved in them, were gone. He would never have seen it as his business to worry about or interfere in the way Kevin chose to live.

They had just reached the door of the refectory, and the rest of the community were assembling for their lunch. As a final comment to George, Jack said: 'I know nothing about him associating with homosexuals. But Kevin was a good man, and he did a lot of good in his time. I'm sure God will be merciful to him, as I hope he will be to us when our day comes.'

But he saw the look of scepticism on George's face, and he remembered that George would have a very different view of suicide. For him it would be the ultimate mortal sin, and he would believe that unless Kevin had repented of his sin in the moment between the act of hanging and his death, he would be lost for ever. He was grateful that he had learned a different understanding of God, and didn't think of Him as somebody who was waiting to catch him out and punish him. By now they were mixing with the rest of the community, and the conversation ended.

The interview between Enda and the two guards took place immediately after lunch. It did not turn out to be as easy as Enda had thought it would be. Bluett questioned him closely on Brendan.

'I believe there was a big falling-out between Father Kevin and Father Brendan just a few weeks ago. What exactly was it about?'

'Kevin didn't agree with the way Brendan was running the sodality, and with the type of sermons he was preaching.'

The young garda was learning a lot about monastic life in the course of the day, and he found it very interesting. He was lamenting to himself the fact that he had been shackled with McCormack. There were all sorts of interesting questions he wanted to ask.

'Do priests fight over things like that? That's interesting.'

'Of course we fight over things like that. It's our job, and it's important to us that it's done well.'

'What did he object to?'

'Brendan is too autocratic, too dictatorial. He makes all the decisions himself, and, while he makes a show of consulting the other members of the team, in reality he listens to nobody.'

That fits, thought the young policeman, who had regarded Brendan as by far the most arrogant of the men he had interviewed that day, and he wasn't surprised that the suggestion was emerging that working with Brendan might have been a factor in driving Kevin to suicide. But if that was a crime, many of the bosses he had known in his relatively short career in the gardai would be in jail.

'And what about his preaching?'

'Kevin felt that it was too moralistic, and there was too much condemnation of people, especially in the area of sex.'

'But couldn't that be said about the Church as a whole?' Once again he heard the cough from his partner, to let him know that he considered he had yet again gone beyond the bounds of what was permissible. He continued without waiting for the answer.

'Have you any reason to believe that there might be more to this than just an act of suicide?'

Enda made the mistake of hesitating slightly before he answered.

'No. I don't know why Kevin did this, but I have no reason to suspect anyone.'

The questioner immediately noted the hesitation, and said, 'Do you know, for instance, of any excessive pressure that might have been put on Father Kevin, any effort at blackmail or intimidation?'

'None that I know of.' This time he made sure that he sounded more definite.

He could see that the policeman was unconvinced, but that he felt he could not push it any further just now.

'Did you know that he was homosexual?'

'Yes.'

'Had that anything to do with his death?'

'I don't think so.' Enda had decided to say no more, and

bring the interview to an end as soon as he could.

'Will you be available if we wish to ask some further questions at a later time?'

'Yes,' said Enda, and that was all. He had an uneasy feeling leaving the room – a feeling that he hadn't handled himself very well.

'Another man not telling us the truth,' was Bluett's comment as the door closed behind Enda. But McCormack pretended he hadn't heard it.

The last interview was with Timothy Brown.

'Good evening, Father Brown,' said Garda Bluett in his most conciliatory voice, intended more for his companion than for the man on the other side of the table.

'Good evening.'

'Did you know Father Dunne well?'

'No!'

The brevity of Father Brown's answer took Bluett by surprise, and there was a moment's silence before he continued.

'Have you any idea why he might have committed suicide?'

'No! None!' Timothy was sitting with his head down. He would not look up at either of the two guards, and he constantly fidgeted with his hands.

'You lived with this man for years, and yet you have nothing to say about him committing suicide?' Bluett was getting impatient.

'Nothing at all!'

Bluett did not like the look of Timothy, and was about to warn him about withholding information, but one look at McCormack told him that it would be better for the present to end this interview and cut his losses.

'Thank you, Father Brown. You may go.'

CHAPTER FIVE

Jack's interview with the gardai had taken place immediately after lunch. It did not last long, and had gone well from his point of view. As an experienced public speaker, he knew how to keep talking in a pleasant, easy way. He explained to them that because of the nature of his work, he was out of the house a great deal of the time, and really knew very little about Kevin Dunne's personal life. What he did know was that Kevin had had a confrontation with Brendan, and that as a result he had been dropped from the sodality team, something which had upset him very much. But he had had no idea that Kevin's distress had been so deep as to cause him to commit suicide, if that was the reason why he'd done it. He said that the community was not particularly surprised that Kevin's time working with Brendan had come to a sudden end. If you worked with Brendan, you had to learn to do it his way. 'Be reasonable, and do it my way' was one of his favourite sayings. So in a sense, Jack hadn't felt any sympathy for Kevin. He should have known what he was taking on when he joined the sodality. If you go into the kitchen you had better be able to stand the heat, and that sort of thing. Now, of course, he saw it differently, knowing the toll it had taken on Kevin, but it was a bit late to learn that. In this way he kept the conversation going while not mentioning the strange event of the knock at the window, or the warning that Brendan issued to Enda. He was confident that he hadn't raised the guards' suspicions about him. But Bluett was well trained, and, despite his years, he had a lot of experience. When Jack left the room, he said, 'I can't understand these people. They are all trying to hide the truth.' But by now the tension between himself and McCormack was so great that his remark was greeted with a stony silence.

When the interview was over, Jack had a chance to think about Olivia, and where he stood regarding her after the intimacy of the previous night. Having come home the day before from his few weeks up north, he had dropped his cases in his room and gone straight out to visit her. It was three o'clock in the morning when he had left her house and, entering the monastery, made his gruesome discovery in the community room. Now he picked up the phone and rang through to her office, but she was in a meeting, and he couldn't speak to her. He had known her for about six months. She was in her late twenties, about five years younger than himself. She was a solicitor, attached to one of the big companies in the town, and had recently bought her own house. They had met at a wedding.

Jack avoided weddings as much as possible. He was not particularly sociable by nature – more at ease with one or two people than in a crowd – and he didn't dance. It was one of the good things about not being a parish priest. Going to weddings was a regular part of their duty. But for him, it was only something he did occasionally, and this one was the wedding of the daughter of one of his father's closest friends, and she had specially requested him to officiate at the ceremony. He couldn't refuse. And anyway, it wouldn't be too bad, because his own family would be there, so he wouldn't have to make forced conversation with people he had never met before, and probably would never meet again. He really felt very awkward about the way that the priest was usually placed at the very end of the top table. With nobody on his right-hand side, he had no choice but to talk to the father of the bride, who sat on his left, but this man was under pressure to keep conversation going with the mother of the groom, who was on his other side. It was seldom – if ever – a relaxed situation, and he was always glad when it was over. And then the speeches! They were often so painful, embarrassing and cringe-making. But the worst part of all was when the best man started reading out the usual off-colour jokes, and everybody looked at him to see if 'Father' was shocked. In fact, he often felt that part of the purpose of the exercise was to see if they could shock 'Father'! He considered it all fairly adolescent stuff, but then by that stage of the meal most people were usually well-oiled and capable of seeing humour where little or none existed. He had to play along with it, but pretending to enjoy himself in these situations did not come easily to him.

This particular wedding passed off nicely, and when the meal was over he removed his collar, slipped off to the bar quietly, ordered a pint and sat in a corner waiting for one of his brothers or sisters to join him so that they could chat about things that had nothing to do with church or religion. He had just taken his first sip from the pint, stretched out his legs under the table, and relaxed into the seat, when he heard a voice address him: 'That was a nice ceremony, and you spoke well. But do you really believe what you were saying?'

When he looked up, what struck him first was not so much the beautiful dress, but the way it accentuated her tall, slender figure. Jack didn't know much about women's fashions, but the dress looked expensive and elegant, much like the woman wearing it.

Thinking back now, the other thing that stood out in his memory was the brightness of her eyes. They were sparkling mischievously, and lit up her whole face.

'I'm Olivia Lenihan. May I join you?' And she held out her hand, to give him a firm handshake. He moved over and she sat beside him.

'Well, do you believe it?' She repeated her question, smiling quizzically.

Jack felt that belief was a difficult and complex thing at the best of times, and he never minded admitting it. He wasn't of the generation that considered that a priest should always present an image of complete and certain faith.

'I believe in some of it, some of the time.'

'Well, I don't believe in any of it, any of the time.' She smiled at him, to take the sharpness out of her words. Even though she was speaking strongly and challenging him, there was a warmth to her voice that attracted him and made him feel at ease. She continued.

'All this stuff about marriage, for instance. I don't believe that marriage has to be for life. Lucky for you if it works out that way. But if it doesn't, a person shouldn't stay in a situation where they are miserable.'

'Would you allow the same freedom to my profession?' Jack asked.

'Definitely,' she responded. 'I don't know how anyone could stay a lifetime in your job without going at least partly mad.'

'I'm probably that already,' Jack said lightly. 'What else do you not believe?'

'That nonsense about not having sex before marriage. What world do you people think we're living in? I think that sex before marriage is not only good, it's necessary. How would you know you were sexually compatible otherwise? I wouldn't dream of marrying someone unless I had lived with him first, so that there would be no surprises.'

This was the sort of conversation that Jack often found himself having now, especially when he worked with young people. And increasingly, he wasn't sure where he stood himself. As much to cover up his own uncertainty as anything else, he tried to bring the conversation onto a different level.

'Do you believe in God?' He could see that this was not a simple question for her.

'I don't know,' she said. 'I know that I don't believe in the God that I was taught as a child, but whether I have replaced him with another sort of God I am not sure.'

'You were brought up as a Catholic, I suppose.'

'Indeed I was.'

'And at what stage did you begin to reject it?'

'When I was about sixteen.'

'Was it teenage rebellion?'

'I'm not sure how much of a rebel I am really,' she said in a thoughtful manner. 'I still go to Mass whenever I go home to visit my parents for the weekend. And if I ever allow myself to think about it, it throws me into some confusion. There is so much about all that old religion that I find oppressive, and yet it is not easy to leave it behind you completely.'

'Once a Catholic, as they say.' He smiled at Olivia. Normally he hated this type of conversation at a wedding. When he relaxed, he liked to get away from all talk about God and religion. That was for work. But now he was happy to continue. He was just glad to have this woman beside him, and he would happily have talked to her about any topic under the sun. He was drawn to the warmth of her personality and he was also intensely aware of her body beside him. The rest of his family, seeing him so deep in conversation, and conscious that they may be interrupting something that was personal or important, left him alone.

Olivia and Jack talked for a long time that evening, and he still remembered it with a warm glow. He had always been aware of the sensitivity of women – how they can focus on you and get you to talk about yourself in a way that a man would seldom do, and in a way that never happened in the monastery. So before too long, the conversation had moved on from Olivia's difficulties with faith. She didn't have any great difficulty in the first place. She seemed to get on with living her life, and didn't worry too much about it. That was her way. She was so active, and she had a full and interesting life, as far as he could judge. But that day she had asked him many questions about himself. Why had he become a priest? What was the life like, and what did he miss most? She was particularly interested in the whole area of celibacy, and questioned him about the thinking behind it, when and why it had been introduced, and even probed him gently as to how he coped with it. He hadn't often spoken in such a personal way, especially not to a complete stranger. But that was the thing about her. After five minutes in her company, she didn't seem like a stranger at all. It was as if he had known her all his life. Their conversation flowed freely, back and forth, and an hour or more had passed without him realising it. He was sorry when eventually his brother came over.

'Sorry to interrupt, but could you come over, Jack, and meet your uncle Jim? He hasn't seen you since your ordination.'

So Jack reluctantly had to excuse himself from Olivia, and he spent the rest of the evening with his family. Once or twice their paths crossed, and she smiled warmly at him.

Though he had thought a great deal about her over the next few days, it was she who phoned him first. She was bright and easy. She asked him how he was, and if he had enjoyed the wedding. They chatted away, and almost before he noticed it happening, he had arranged to meet her for dinner that evening. That was the beginning of their relationship.

In six months it had developed quickly, and last night had seemed to bring it to a new level. It was this new level that preoccupied him today, over and above his attempts to come to terms with the suicide in the community.

Meeting Olivia at the wedding had brought home to Jack how much he was questioning the things he had previously accepted about life without really thinking too seriously about them. Even hearing her talking about the next life, he realised he was questioning that too. Would there be a reward in heaven at the end of it all? That belief had been the bedrock of most of the important decisions he had made: that we should do things, not for any reward in this life, but for the much greater and more enduring happiness that waited us in heaven. If he lost faith in that, then everything would be on shaky foundations. It was exciting to question, but it was also disturbing. And he was left wondering how much of the uncertainty was simply the result of Olivia having come in to his life. Here was the possibility of tangible, present happiness. To put his arms around her and feel her warm closeness, as he had recently begun to do, seemed to offer answers of a completely different kind, and at a different level, from anything he had ever experienced before. He hoped that Claudel was not right when he had said about a woman: 'She is the promise that can never be fulfilled, and that is just her charm'. He liked to think there was a great deal of promise in Olivia that could be fulfilled. Certainly, her coming into his life had been fairly dramatic. He hoped to get a chance to see her that night. They had a lot to talk about.

When the two guards returned to the station they were summoned to the Chief Superintendent's office. They had not spoken to each other on the short journey back from the monastery. It was obvious to Bluett that McCormack had become increasingly angry with him as the day went on, over the way he was conducting the interviews. They walked silently to the Super's office, where they sat on one side of the large desk, facing the head man.

'I have had a complaint,' the Super began. 'Father Brendan Quinn rang to object about the way he was interviewed. He wants the investigation discontinued.'

'That doesn't surprise me,' Jimmy McCormack said, leaping in immediately. 'I want to object in the strongest possible terms to the way Garda Bluett conducted the interviews.'

Bluett ignored McCormack's intervention and addressed himself to the Super. 'What exactly was the nature of the complaint? What did Father Quinn object to?'

'He objected to the general tone of the interview, and in particular to the fact that he was not given his proper title by the interviewer. Did you really call him "sir"?' Bluett thought he noticed the slightest sign of a smile on the Super's face. But Jimmy McCormack certainly didn't think it was funny.

'He did. It was no way to address a man of Father Brendan's position and dignity. And it wasn't only in that interview that he showed no respect. The way he spoke to Father George, a man of great years and wisdom, and the things he discussed with the young man, Father Moran, were also totally inappropr-iate.'

Bluett now turned to McCormack, clearly struggling to keep his voice calm.

'Did the young man object to what we discussed? He was as happy to talk about those things as I was. And it was not inappropriate. It was all part of my effort to try to understand the type of people I was dealing with, and the lives they live. I don't have the intimate knowledge of them that you do.'

'That's obvious. And you have a lot of understanding to do,' responded McCormack. They had temporarily forgotten about the Super, and were addressing each other directly. The pent-up feelings of the day were coming out. 'That monastery has been the most important place in this city for a hundred and fifty years. Those priests are highly respected, indeed revered, by the people.'

'I'm afraid I didn't see a lot to make me either respect or revere them. I thought they were a very strange group of people.' Bluett had held himself in check long enough. McCormack went on the offensive.

'That's because you don't go to Mass yourself. You are typical of these smart-alec young guards we are getting nowadays. Guilt is your problem. You are so guilty about not practising your religion that you are full of prejudice against these good men. And that prejudice was coming through in all the interviews. Wouldn't you think that this modern training we are hearing so much about would have taught you not to allow your prejudices to come between you and your work.'

The Super, who had been sitting back, content to allow the exchange of views to continue, decided that it was now getting too heated, so he spoke up.

'That's enough of that, men. The real question is, did you learn anything? Is there any reason for us to be concerned, or to involve ourselves further in the matter?'

'None at all.' Again, it was McCormack who spoke up first. 'How could we possibly have anything to concern us with those good men? It is just a sad incident. Poor Father Kevin must have been suffering from depression, and he told nobody about it. It got to be too much for him, and he decided to end it all. That's all there is to it. We must stay well away, and let them bury him in peace. Our presence around the place would only be a source of gossip, and provide ammunition for those who are trying to discredit the Church, and we know there are plenty of those today.'

But Bluett was still smarting over what he saw as an insult to his professionalism, and a slur on his character. He wasn't going to let that go without protest.

'I must object to the personal nature of the attack Garda McCormack has made on me, and his suggestion that I am not professional in the conduct of my work.'

The Super was not taking this dispute seriously. He had been in this city for many years, and he knew the monastery and the people in it very well, and was capable of a somewhat more objective assessment of them than either of the two guards.

'Let that be for now, and tell me about your impression of the interviews. Do you think we have any reason to be concerned?'

'I felt there were a great many unanswered questions. I had a sense of being fobbed off, and that most of them seemed to know more than they were willing to say. Whether that means that they may have some involvement in the situation, I can't say for certain. But I did get the distinct impression that Father

Quinn was covering up; and certainly Father Brown seemed to be determined to say nothing at all. I also wondered about that other man, the one called Enda Staunton. I got a different feeling from him than from the other two; but I suspect he is the one who knows more than anyone. Why should they be reluctant to tell us what they know?'

McCormack was ready to launch into another attack, but this time the Super cut in ahead of him.

'There may be a simple enough explanation for it. I know some of those men fairly well myself. They have traditionally put great store on privacy, on keeping the internal affairs of the monastery under wraps. It may simply be that you are running up against this. Be careful about jumping to the conclusion that, because they seem to tell you very little, they have something serious to hide.'

'And aren't they perfectly right not to let a disrespectful, prying young upstart of a garda know too much about them. If I was one of them I wouldn't tell you anything either.' McCormack wouldn't let go.

'That's enough of that now, men. I suggest that the two of you sort out your differences, and continue to keep an eye on this case. We won't close the file on it just yet.'

'Would it be all right if I interviewed one or two of those men again after the funeral is over? And this time, may I do it on my own?' asked Bluett.

'I object to that,' McCormack quickly intervened. 'That would amount to unnecessary harassment.'

'Yes, you may,' said the Super. And he turned to McCormack. 'A little bit of gentle harassment may be no harm in this situation.' Then he turned back again to Bluett. 'Just be careful. We don't want to draw the bishop down on us. And be especially careful of

Father Brendan. Arrogance is that man's middle name.'

He could see the look of shock on Jimmy McCormack's face as a result of the last sentence. But before he had a chance to reply, the Chief Superintendent ended the interview and dismissed them both.

It was about five o'clock in the evening, and Mary Anne Savage was in a thoughtful mood as she made her way up to the monastery. She hoped to meet that young priest whom she had heard preaching a few times in the church, the one who had a nice face. Maybe he would be able to help her. She was a woman in her forties, small and slim, with a pinched face, and the look of someone who felt that the world had treated her badly. Living in a flat and working at the checkout of a large supermarket did not exactly fulfil the dreams that she had had as a young girl. In fact, in her youth she had been a great one to dream. Some of her friends used to dream that they would wake up one day to discover that they were the daughters of some prince or other, but her favourite dream was simpler. All she wished for was that she would discover that her uncle was her real father. He was a nice man, tall and gentle, and always generous with sweets and gifts. Since he had never married and didn't have any children of his own, she knew from an early age that she was the apple of his eye. She wondered why he had never married. He would surely have made a better husband and father than his brother – her father – had been.

She used to love calling to see him in the evenings when she had her lessons done. Even when she was a little girl he gave her a great welcome and used to talk to her almost as if she were an adult. The fact that he was very wealthy was an attraction, compared to her branch of the family, who seemed to be permanently living from hand to mouth. Like so much of the rest of her unhappiness, she blamed this, too, on her father. If he hadn't drunk so much there might have been some chance for them. But with three in the family, and no money at all coming in on the weeks that he went on one of his binges, it was no joke. She realised now, with the benefit of hindsight, how difficult it must have been for her mother. Living with him had gradually turned her into a shrew, sour and bitter and constantly complaining, prematurely aged and dying before her time. Mary Anne herself had to leave school at fourteen, and start in the supermarket. Stacking shelves was where she began. You could hardly say she had made much progress, to be at the checkout thirty years later. But what could she do? Without an education you had no chance. Yes, life had treated her badly. And her uncle was not her father, and as time went by somehow she saw less and less of him. She supposed that he had eventually got tired of bailing her father out. And as soon as the children got to the age when they could be self-sufficient, he went his own way, and did not interfere any more.

The second big dream of her early life was that she would one day marry a rich man. If she didn't inherit money, and couldn't make it for herself, then maybe she could marry into it. But that hadn't happened either. Rich men don't mix with checkout girls. Or if they do, it isn't marriage partners they're looking for. It is something considerably more short-term. And she hadn't been blessed with good looks either. If there had been money, maybe something could have been done about it. If her parents had seen to her prominent teeth as a child, it would have helped a lot. What man would want to kiss a mouthful of buck teeth stuck under a head of mousy hair? She was definitely plain, Mary Anne told herself again. It seemed to be the right word for her. Plain Mary Anne. She had given up making any effort with her appearance at this stage. What was the point? You couldn't make a silk purse out of a sow's ear, after all. Yes, there were a lot of reasons why she should feel let down by life.

But now there was a real possibility that at least some part of her dream might become a reality. Her rich uncle's health was failing, and the doctor said that he might not have long to live. It was lucky he had never married, whether the reason was that he had been too busy working all his life to bother with anything like that, or for more personal reasons. She didn't know, but in recent years she found herself noticing aspects of his personality, and beginning to wonder about things that up to a few years ago she would not have thought possible. Nor did she know how much money he had, but it was believed in her family that he was very wealthy. Apart from what he made in the business, it was always said that he had invested wisely. Since she and her two brothers were the closest relatives, they had strong hopes that it might all come to them. What a marvellous thing it would be to have money. To be able to buy her own house! Never to have to check out other people's shopping again, and put up with their superior tones and demanding attitudes! To buy the sort of clothes that would give even someone like herself a touch of glamour! And maybe to go on a foreign holiday! She had been on only one journey in a plane. That was a few years previously, when she went on a pilgrimage to Lourdes. She remembered sitting in the plane that day and wishing that it would take her off to some exotic place instead of Lourdes – away from the boredom and drudgery of her life. But now there was hope. Even if her uncle only left her a few thousand pounds, it would be enough to give her a taste of the good life. And she felt now that even as little as that would make her happy. Deep down, she hoped to get much more. Hadn't her uncle's name been listed in the Sunday paper a few years ago as one of Ireland's richest men? He had vehemently denied it at the time, laughing at how preposterous it was. But she chose to believe it.

The reception room she was put into, after she had inquired in the office of the monastery for Father Jack, was a small, fairly shabby room, with four cheap armchairs and a coffee table in the centre with some old religious magazines. As Jack walked in he was struck by the tightness of her face, and her sharp features. Her hair was short, lying flat on her head: clean, but otherwise uncared-for. A long tweed skirt, thick tights and flat black shoes proclaimed a woman who expended very little time or effort on her appearance. Her face was familiar to him from attending the church. She stood up when he came in, and she had a surprisingly firm handshake.

'My name is Mary Anne Savage. Thank you for seeing me.'

'Hello, Mary Anne. Won't you sit down. What can I do for you?'

'Your colleague, Father Dunne, was very good to me and my uncle. It is awful what happened to him. Did he really commit suicide, as they are saying around the town?'

'How well did you know him?' asked Jack.

'Very well. He was a regular visitor to my uncle. And he was helping me out in trying to get my uncle to make a will, and to make it properly.'

Jack looked at her. A will. Where there is a will, there are relatives, as the saying goes. 'Yes, I'm afraid he did commit suicide. But tell me about your uncle.'

'It's simple. My uncle, Jim Savage, lives in John Street. He is only in his sixties, but he had a serious stroke a few months ago, and has never really recovered. A lot of damage was done, and he's too weak to have an operation. The doctor says he cannot live very much longer. We were hoping that Uncle Jim might leave his money to me and my two brothers, his closest relatives. Father Kevin was helping me in trying to get him to make his will. But now he's dead. He was a good friend. Which is more than can be said for some of the other people in this monastery. Father Brendan Quinn is his confessor, and he sends his sidekick, Timothy, to visit too. Excuse me for referring to your fellow priests in such a way, but I really don't trust them.'

Jack was curious and was somewhat amused by this story from Mary Anne. It was always fascinating to get a glimpse into the activities of other members of the community. There was a lot of questions he would have loved to have asked her, but he didn't know this woman well, so he decided he had better be cautious.

'That's all very interesting, Mary Anne, but why are you telling me this?' he asked.

'I was hoping that you might go up and talk to Uncle Jim, and encourage him to make that will.'

'Oh, that's something I don't think I should get involved in,' said Jack.

'But it's so important for us that we get that money. You wouldn't appreciate it. You have three meals put up to you every day, and you have no worry about keeping a roof over your head. But we have had to struggle all our lives. When you are reared poor, and come from the part of the town I came from, it isn't easy to get promotion. And then there's my brother Joe. You see, Father, he is not the full shilling, if you know what I mean. He is all right for now, but it would be great to know that there was a little nest egg to look after him in his old age. Will you help me?'

Jack felt caught in this one. He did not want to go to see any old man and talk about a will, but still, she was hard to refuse.

'I'll go up and visit him. But I don't promise you that I'll discuss his will with him.'

'Thank you, Father Jack. I must go now; since he got sick I try to call on him each evening if I can.'

They stood up, and Jack walked out with her to the main hall of the monastery. As he was saying goodbye, he noticed Timothy peering around the corner from the corridor with a look of disapproval on his face.

Chapter Six

'Have you seen Timothy anywhere?' Brendan was clearly in bad form, and Matthew knew well enough not to bother him at a time like this.

'I saw him out in the front hall a few moments ago, so he can't be far away.'

'He should be right here. This is not a night for him to be hanging around the front, watching who's coming and going.'

'Are you all set for tonight?' Matthew asked, being as conciliatory as possible. This was a big night in the church. The famous Irish-American healer, Father McSorley, was coming to do a healing ceremony. Brendan had been promoting this for weeks now, both in the church and in the media, and large crowds were expected. Indeed, they were needed, because this man was expensive. He and his entourage, amounting to six people in all, had to be flown over from the States, put up in a good hotel for the night and given a substantial fee. It was something Matthew himself would never have done. Too much risk involved. But Brendan liked to think big, and considered that it was good promotion for the church to have famous names appearing there. With falling numbers attending churches all over the country, he saw himself as being in competition with the other churches in the city. And anything that would raise the profile of St Carthage's would be to the good.

'We're getting things in shape. We have a problem with the

microphones, and that's why I'm looking for Timothy. He's the man to sort that out, if only he was where he should be.' Timothy was a genius with anything electrical or mechanical. He was generally good with his hands.

'What time are they arriving?' asked Matthew.

'In about a half an hour. Michael has gone to the airport to collect them.'

At that moment, Timothy appeared around the corner, coming from the front hall, and he and Brendan went quickly to the sacristy to repair the sound system. Brendan watched him as he worked, marvelling at his expertise and assurance in dealing with all this modern, highly technical stuff. They talked as he worked.

'How did you get on with the guards?' asked Brendan.

'I told them nothing.' Timothy was gruff and sharp in his manner. 'I didn't like the look of that young fellow, Bluett. A right little upstart, if you ask me. If he thought he was going to get information out of me, he had another think coming.'

'That's good. And if he comes up again, don't tell him anything.' Brendan was relieved. 'I wouldn't trust him. I complained about him to the Chief Superintendent, and that should be enough to get his wings clipped.'

'Good.' Timothy had by now taken the control box for the microphone system apart, and was examining it. 'I didn't expect that fool, Kevin, to go and hang himself. Maybe we should have left him on the team, useless and all as he was.'

'I have no regrets,' said Brendan. 'He was doing more harm than good to the sodality. And then when he started criticising my preaching! How dare he! And he couldn't put two coherent words together himself. But the last straw was when you discovered he was a regular visitor to Jim Savage. That was too much. We can't afford to have anyone messing up that situation on us, can we?'

'You're right there, boss. Now, test the mike and see if it's working.' Brendan walked over and tapped the nearest microphone, which echoed loudly.

'You're a genius.' Compliments from Brendan were important to Timothy, and he smiled at this one. When everything was back in place, he asked Brendan, 'What do you think of this fellow who's coming?'

'You mean McSorley, the healer?'

'Yes.'

'Not much, really. But the people will love him. Most people are gullible. And I believe in giving them what they want. Hopefully they will have a good experience tonight, and they will go away happy. Some of them are bound to feel better, and think they were cured. That's enough for me. Provided, of course, that they pay up well in the collection, so we can cover all the costs and have a tidy profit for ourselves.'

'So you don't think he really is a healer?'

'Not at all. I'm as much a healer myself as he is. But he's a shrewd operator, and runs a very professional show. You know, the young men who are joining us now haven't a clue. Michael was saying the other day that, instead of inviting healers, we should set up small groups and have people studying and discussing the Bible. How stupid can you get? He thinks the ordinary people can understand the Bible. I think I shocked him when I told him that I was a believer in the mushroom method of dealing with people. Really innocently, he asked me what that was. Keep them in the dark, and feed them loads of horse dung, I said. I had to laugh at the look on his face. Himself and his small groups! I went on to tell him the modern version of the parable of the Last Judgement from St Matthew's Gospel. You know, the one where it says that when Jesus turned to the people on his left, the people who were being condemned, he said to them, "Depart from me, ye cursed, and break up into small groups and spend eternity sharing."'

Timothy laughed, in his strange, high-pitched way that came out as a half-strangled sound.

'Michael walked away from me at that point,' Brendan concluded. 'Bad and all as Kevin was, if we had that young fellow on the sodality he would quickly empty the church. Small groups, how are you! But at least he was willing to go to the airport to collect them for me. Let's go in. They must be nearly here by now.'

Enda didn't have anything to do with the sodality, and was in no way involved with the healing ceremony. In fact, he thoroughly disapproved of it, and was angry that the community hadn't been given a say in the decision to invite this man. But Brendan would never allow himself to be constrained in his decision-making by involving the community. Still, Enda was, as usual, curious. And he made it his business to be hanging around, and observing what was happening. At six o'clock, McSorley and his entourage arrived. McSorley himself wasn't a particularly impressive individual: small of stature, slightly scruffy and, Enda was surprised to notice, almost a chain-smoker. Not the best image for a healer, he thought. But the manager was impressive. Impeccably dressed, with an air of authority, he immediately took command and began to give orders. He was precise and meticulous about everything that was needed in the church for the ceremony, and he checked it all to see that everything was in place and working properly.

Nothing was left to chance. Even more surprising to Enda was the fact that there was a woman in the group. She was dressed in a business suit, and seemed to act as secretary to McSorley, though Enda did notice a familiarity between them that seemed to suggest that she was more than just a secretary. The other three members of the party were very similar in appearance to the type of secret service men he had often seen on television accompanying the American president – the ones known as heavies. They were strong, well-built men with very short hair, dressed in grey suits. They spoke very little, but were a significant presence in the place, a guarantee that everything would go exactly as McSorley and his manager wanted it. It would not be at all wise to try to oppose them in any way. When they had seen that everything was in order for the ceremony, Brendan brought the whole party of them into the refectory for tea. Enda made it his business to be hanging around the kitchen, apparently busy, so that he could overhear what was being said. He almost laughed out loud when he heard the version of Kevin's death that was given to the visitors by Brendan. They were told that a member of the community had died suddenly, but no hint was given of the circumstances. Instead, the clear implication was that he had died naturally, and was greatly lamented. Apart from that, he kept the conversation to the preparations for the evening ahead, and was as businesslike as they were.

The crowds came in enormous numbers. The church could not hold them all, but Brendan had anticipated this, so all the rooms off the church and on the ground floor of the monastery were connected up with closed-circuit television, and a speaker had also been installed outside the church for the many hundreds of people who could not get in and who gathered in the yard. Luckily it was a fine evening. Enda took up a position in the organ gallery with a perfect view of the whole church, so that he could observe exactly what was going on. The woman in the business suit was the first to come out; she went up into the pulpit with the air of a person who was completely at home in this environment, and began to warm the people up. Enda hoped that George wouldn't be too busy in the Confession box to observe this. A woman in the pulpit in the church of St Carthage would be enough to give him many sleepless nights, not to mention all the old boys in the crypt underneath the altar. They must be spinning in their coffins, he thought. But she was good. She sang some hymns with the people, talked to them about the evening and even told a joke or two. Enda, an experienced public performer himself, had to admit that she was very professional and smooth in everything she did. As it came to the time for the ceremony to begin, she quietened the congregation down and began to pray gently with them. When McSorley come on, she had them ready. All in all, it was a stylish and effective performance.

Enda noticed that McSorley, in front of the microphone, and dressed in full priestly regalia – a long, flowing alb and large, beautifully embroidered stole – looked a much more impressive person than he had done in the monastery. He took the microphone in his hand and began walking back and forth across the sanctuary as he addressed the crowd. He spoke with a distinct American accent. He was convincing and fluent, and expressed a familiarity with God and the ways of God. Enda thoroughly disapproved of this because he considered it spurious, but he acknowledged to himself that it sounded impressive. McSorley came across as a man with no doubts about what he was doing and saying. He spoke about how Jesus had gone around healing people in Palestine, and that he was still doing the same, but that now he was using special people as his instruments. Then he went on to tell his own story, how he had been converted and chosen as an instrument of healing. The story contained, Enda noted, all the usual elements of the traditional conversion. He had been living a bad life. McSorley did not go into any detail, but inevitably implied that his badness had been in the sexual area. Then he had had a moment of revelation, and after that his life was changed. Enda always doubted stories like this. In his experience, things didn't happen quite like that. He believed that change came much more slowly and painfully. A person had to work long and hard at developing a new way of life or new attitudes. The contrast in McSorley's story between what he was before and what he suddenly became after the conversion did not ring true. But McSorley wasn't allowing any element of doubt to enter into his narrative. He concluded his personal statement by proclaiming that now he was devoting his life completely to the service of the Lord.

'I am here in the name of Jesus. I am here for one purpose, and one purpose only: to bring the healing power of Jesus to each one of you.'

'You are indeed,' said Enda to himself, 'at five thousand pounds a night!'

Now McSorley changed his tone and posture. He took on a new sense of urgency, and you could see that he was really swinging into action. He began to point to different parts of the church.

'There is somebody down here, in this corner of the church, and the Lord tells me they have a serious heart problem. Are you there? Are you listening to the voice of the Lord? Stand up and let the Lord speak to you.' Eventually an old man clambered to his feet, blushing to the roots of his being.

'The Lord has a message for you tonight. You will be healed of your infirmity. Praise the Lord!'

The woman in the pulpit responded with great energy: 'Praise the Lord! Amen!' And then she repeated it, urging the crowd to join in. They shouted it out with enthusiasm.

Now Enda could sense the atmosphere pick up in the church, and the people beginning to move to the edge of their seats in expectation.

'On this side of the church the Lord is telling me there is a person with chronic back pain. Who is it? Let the Lord see you.'

A woman jumped to her feet. She was clearly excited, and, unlike the old man, had no reluctance about displaying herself.

'Here I am,' she shouted.

'The Lord has shown his favour to you. You too will be healed. Praise the Lord!'

And this time the whole crowd, without needing any encouragement from the pulpit, shouted back, 'Praise the Lord. Alleluia!'

By now the place was electric. McSorley walked to the front seat, where there was a woman sitting in a wheelchair.

'You are welcome, my good woman. The Lord loves you. What is your name?'

The woman's voice came timidly through the microphone.

'Nonie, Reverend Father.'

'And what is the matter with you, Nonie? What is the illness that the Lord, in his own good plan, has asked you to bear?

'Arthritis, Father. I'm crippled with it, and I can't walk.'

'And do you have pain, dear child?'

'Yes, Father. Very bad pain, Father.'

Then McSorley turned to the people.

'The Lord, for his own purposes, has chosen Nonie to suffer. Like Jesus hanging on the cross, she has known pain and affliction. But her suffering has not been in vain. It has brought great blessing. People who are lost in sin, who are in the grip of evil, will be saved because of the suffering of this good woman. But now the Lord in his kindness has looked down on his handmaiden. He is telling me that her time of suffering is ended. He has asked me to release Nonie from her misery.'

He walked over to Nonie. On cue, one of the heavies arrived at his side and took the microphone from him, and held it, so that McSorley could have both his hands free. He raised them over Nonie, and prayed loudly, 'Loving Father, all things are in Your hands. You have created us all, and keep us in being each day. No sickness can resist Your word. In Your name I now lay my hands on Nonie, your handmaiden. Set her free from her illness, just as You cured the mother-in-law of Simon Peter. Make her well again.'

The last sentence was spoken slowly, and with great dramatic effect. There was total attention in the church. McSorley slowly reached out his hands, took the woman's hands in his, and said with strength and power, 'Nonie, beloved child of God, get up. Walk.'

Nonie rose from the wheelchair, at first apparently with some effort, and then more easily, until in a few moments she was walking back and forth across the sanctuary with McSorley holding her hand. The crowd burst into a massive and sustained round of applause.

By the time the excitement had died down McSorley had

slipped quietly into the sacristy and the woman in the business suit had begun to speak from the pulpit once again.

'The Lord is with us here tonight. You can see that for yourselves. Just as surely as he walked the roads of Palestine. He has already poured out his generous love on Nonie. He will do the same for all of us. Every person here tonight will get the opportunity of being blessed individually by Father McSorley, His servant and special instrument. But first we must be willing to give to the Lord. If we are to receive, then we must also give. If our hearts are generous, then the Lord will be even more generous to us. Baskets will be passed around. We ask every person to be as generous as they can. If you give not just from your surplus, but so that it hurts, the Lord will reward you all the more.'

She started to sing a hymn. Enda watched very closely from the organ gallery. This was the part of the night that held most interest for him, because he believed that it was what the whole thing was ultimately about. He saw the three assistants, or the heavies, becoming very active. They armed a team of collectors with plastic buckets – not the baskets that were usually used in the church – and sent them to work among the crowd. From Enda's vantage point he could see the buckets rapidly filling up with notes of all denominations, and in some cases the collectors had to be given a replacement bucket when the one they were using began to overflow. The heavies moved around, making sure that every last person in the crowd, inside and outside the church, had a bucket put in front of them. There was no sense of rush about it. The woman sang and prayed, occasionally interjecting phrases to urge the people to be generous.

'If we are generous to the Lord, he will be generous to us.'

'Indeed he will,' said Enda, in his most sarcastic voice, and it was only when he said it that he realised there were some people in the gallery, which was normally reserved for the organist and members of the community. They had made their way up in search of a seat. He saw some of them looking strangely at him, so he knew they had heard him. He smiled sheepishly. But deep down, he was angry. He knew that when it came to collections in church, the people did not differentiate, and that they would all presume that the monastery was making a big killing from this night. For now he had seen and heard enough, and his lack of sleep the previous night was catching up on him. Before the individual blessings began, he quietly slipped out the back of the church, through the crowd in the car park and into the monastery. He intended to go upstairs and lie on the bed for a while, and come down later for the end of the ceremony.

The door into the living quarters, the private area of the monastery, was wide open. This was most unusual, and made Enda angry. They had had a number of break-ins in the past year, and they always tried to keep this door locked. This night of all nights, with people all over the place, it should have been kept locked. He went through, closed the door securely behind him and made for the stairs leading up to his room. When he came to where the corridor branched off to the refectory, he spotted a man, cloaked in a large anorak, with a hood over his head, disappear out the back door into the garden. He raced down the corridor as quickly as his stiff knees would allow him, and looked out. It was hopeless. There were so many trees in the garden, it would be easy to hide in the dark, and if he had slipped around to the front he would now be mingling with the people gathered outside the church. The glimpse he got of the figure reminded him of what he had seen on the night of Kevin's death, and just as he closed the back door, he thought he heard a strange laugh, like a cackle, but he wasn't sure if he had imagined it. He did one last quick tour around the house, to make sure that everything was secure, and then went up to his room. He was surprised to meet Timothy on the stairs carrying his tool kit. He was going to ask him about the figure he had seen on the bottom corridor, but something about Timothy made him keep his mouth shut. 'I wonder why he isn't out in the church. What could he possibly be up to?' he said to himself.

He lay down on his bed, but sleep didn't come easily to him. His mind was full of questions. Who was this strange individual lurking around the house, and what was he doing? Was he in some way associated with Timothy? Gradually his mind drifted back to the healing ceremony. There were questions about that too. Not least, had Nonie had been paid to get up off the wheelchair? She was certainly someone he had never seen around the place before. Life surely was complicated in this monastery, and he knew that most of the people crammed into the church below were of the impression that everything was simple and easy for the men who lived in St Carthage's. He gradually drifted into sleep.

CHAPTER SEVEN

The healing ceremony ended eventually around ten o'clock, and at least some members of the community returned to the monastery with a sense of elation. They regarded it as a great success. So many people had gone home feeling uplifted, and a number were claiming that they had been cured. Even Brother Bartholomew, cranky and crippled, seemed to be shuffling along with a little more pep in his step than usual, though when Michael asked him had he been cured, he just growled, 'Easy for you to laugh. Wait till your turn comes and you are old like me. Then the laugh will be on the other side of your face.'

'Well, whatever about your body, he didn't do anything for your humour,' Michael said lightly to him. He wasn't going to take Bartholomew too seriously. He had a tendency to complain and give out, but Michael would be the first to concede that, though he had a sharp edge to him, he often spoke the uncomfortable truth. But Michael had his own thoughts on what he had witnessed tonight, and he was uneasy. He could see that the people loved it, and all his training had taught him the importance of listening to the people, but still, the whole event made him decidedly uncomfortable.

The community naturally moved towards the refectory, in need of some refreshment after the long ceremony. It was also the place where people gathered at night to have a chat before going off to their own bedrooms. For a brief while, they had almost forgotten the events of the day, they were in such good form. But that quickly changed when they walked into the refectory. The Superior, Matthew, was seated at a table with a man and woman in their fifties, who were introduced as Paddy Dunne and Catherine Coleman, the brother and sister of Kevin. Matthew was quicker on his feet than normal, and as each member of the community came in and was introduced to the newcomers, he said: 'Catherine and Paddy are shocked to learn of the sudden death of their brother.'

It was enough to let everyone know that the truth had not been told to them as yet. They had been to the hospital, but were not able to see the body, because the post-mortem would not take place till the following morning.

'Where is Father Brown?' Matthew asked. 'I hope he has the bedrooms fixed up for our two guests.'

Father Timothy Brown had the task of looking after the management of the house, and made sure that guests were welcomed and cared for. He may not have seemed the most suitable person to make people feel welcome, but he was a hard worker, and his skill with his hands made it possible to keep the monastery functioning without a caretaker. The fact that he worked so closely with Brendan strengthened the impression that Brendan was the one who was really in charge. But Matthew was willing to accept that in order to have the responsibility lifted from his own shoulders. Though he loved being the Superior, he found it stressful and difficult. At a time like this, knowing Brendan was there to depend on was a great relief. Brendan was bound to know where Timothy was; he had almost certainly sent him there himself.

'Father Brown's dropped up to have a quick look in at Mr Savage, to make sure he's all right for the night,' Brendan said.

'He'll be back in a few minutes.'

'Oh, of course,' said Matthew. 'I should have remembered. He takes great care of Mr Savage.'

'Yes,' said Br Bartholomew, 'It's a pity he wouldn't take such good care of some of the older members of his own community.'

Jack stayed only a few minutes – enough time to show his face to the rest of the community and to give the crowd from the church time to disperse. He had a quick exchange of views with Michael about what they had witnessed, and he was interested to see that the younger man had not been impressed. Neither had he, but right now his mind was on other things. So, as soon as he could decently leave, he slipped out the back, sat into one of the monastery's cars, and drove over to the other side of the town to see Olivia. In the few months since he had got to know her, this little journey had become very familiar to him. And he associated it with the sense of excitement that he now felt building up inside him as he approached his destination.

Olivia Lenihan was alone, waiting for him in her comfortable new house. There was a bright fire in the grate, with two armchairs lined up, one on each side. In between was a coffee table, with a freshly opened bottle of red wine, and two glasses. Her glass was already full, and she was sipping from it. The room was lit by the soft glow of a lamp standing in the corner, and by the pale light of the moon that shone through the back window of the sitting room and spilled across the floor. Olivia had drawn the curtains in the window at the front, but the night was so beautiful, with the full moon low in the sky, that she had left the curtains in the back window open so as not to shut it out. She appreciated the companionship that she had often got from the moon since she started to live alone.

Olivia was in a thoughtful mood. She was contemplating her life, and wondering what she was getting into now. The last thing she had expected to happen was that she would end up having a friendship – or maybe even a relationship – with a priest. She thought she had rejected all that. Religion was part of the life that she had put behind her when she left home and went to university to study law. She had always been a bit of a rebel, but the years in university had made her much more radical in her thinking. She certainly would not be like her mother, living at home on the farm and rearing eight kids. She had never had any life of her own, and was suffering the consequences now. The family was reared, and without any outlet for her emotions, she had become possessive and dependent on them. Olivia was one of the lucky ones who had escaped from home. But she was under pressure to come back every weekend, and when she didn't – and nowadays she didn't go any more than about once a month – her mother would sometimes be in a sulk for the first hour or two. Deep down, she felt sorry for her mother. She didn't know if her parents had ever really loved each other, but it was obvious that now they had very little in common. Their lives were on two parallel lines that never seemed to come together. Her father spent his time on the farm, and went to matches at the weekend. Her mother stayed at home and looked forward to the children coming to visit. They still slept in the same bed, but her mother had confided to Olivia, in a rare moment of personal revelation, that the physical side of their marriage had ceased many years before, after the last child had been born.

'To be honest with you,' she had said to Olivia one Saturday night not long before, when the two of them were sitting at home, and her father was out for a drink, 'I had no regrets when that side of our marriage ended. I was never much for it. It was a duty for me always, nothing more. I often wondered why God didn't think of a nicer way of bringing children into the world.'

Olivia felt it was better not to comment, in case her mother would start asking her about her own life. She certainly wasn't going to discuss her problems in that area with her mother – or the shadow that had lain across her life since her student days. It would be too close to the bone, and too painful. Let her mother believe that everything had changed for her generation, that they could have sex whenever they wished, and enjoy it, without worrying about the consequences. If only it was like that.

But she could remember another occasion, in her final year in secondary school, when she had tackled her mother about the Church's attitude to women. There had been a flaming row. She smiled as she recalled it. It was ironic in view of the fact that she was now sitting waiting for a visit from a priest. She had been doing a project on the 1937 constitution, and in an old newspaper she had come across a photograph of Éamon de Valera kneeling and kissing the ring of the Archbishop of Dublin, John Charles McQuaid. It was they, she learned, who had put together all that stuff about a woman's place being in the home. One evening as she was working on the project at home, she became aware that her mother was looking over her shoulder. She began reading what Olivia had written, and asked her about it. Olivia explained what she was doing. 'It's terrible the way the Church interfered in women's lives. They never listened to our views on anything, but still they told us how we should live.'

She could see the shock on her mother's face. 'What do you mean, Olivia?' she asked.

'For centuries the Church has controlled women, by controlling their sexuality. I'm glad to be growing up in a time when they have lost their power over us. Now we can live as we choose.' She knew she was saying things that her mother would consider terrible, but she felt good. She would grow up to be a radical.

'Don't ever speak like that again,' was her mother's response to her. 'You will draw down the wrath of God on yourself if you speak in that way about His Church.'

And that ended the conversation, but somehow, Olivia felt, it had driven a wedge between herself and her mother that had never quite disappeared. She remembered making two resolutions around that time in order to ensure that she would not grow up to be like her mother. Firstly, she would have a profession of her own. Now she was rapidly beginning to get her feet under her as a solicitor, and loved the work. Secondly, she would not allow religion to dominate her. As soon as she could get away with it she had stopped going to Mass, and now considered herself an unbeliever: maybe not so much in God – that was still an open question – but certainly in organised religion. So what was she doing with a priest? And where was all this going to lead? She heard his car pulling into the yard and his step approaching the door.

'Hello, Jack,' she said.

She stood to greet him when he had let himself in through the back door, and she gave him a hug and an affectionate, friendly kiss on the cheek. She filled his glass, and returned to her chair at the other side of the fire.

Jack noted that Olivia had changed out of her working

clothes and was dressed in an old pair of jeans and a white shirt, which looked really well on her. By any standards, she was an attractive woman. He removed his collar, opened the neck of his clerical shirt and sat back, allowing the peace of the house, and her soothing presence, to relax him.

Even though it was less than twenty-four hours since they had been together, they had a lot to talk about. In spite of the fact that their relationship was still young, they had settled into that easy way of telling each other about their respective days. Jack had the series of events surrounding Kevin's suicide to tell, and he launched into it almost immediately. It wasn't all news to Olivia.

'Everyone was talking about it around the office today. People suspected that something strange had happened, but they weren't quite sure what. The rumours got wilder as the day went on. By evening, most of the office believed that he had been murdered.'

Jack didn't have any qualms about telling Olivia the whole story. He trusted her completely, and gave her all the intimate details about life in the monastery and the various characters who lived there. He smiled to himself as he thought how some of them would be very annoyed if they knew the things he told Olivia about them. Brendan especially, who made a big issue of the monastery being a family, and thought that they should be loyal to each other and keep the details of their life secret from outsiders. But even after only six months, Olivia was now closer to Jack than any member of the community, so he told her in blow-by-blow detail the circumstances of Kevin's death and the gruesome discovery he had made the previous night. As they sat talking and drinking the bottle of wine, he began to think how lucky he was to have met Olivia. The domesticity of this house was in stark contrast to the barrenness of the monastery. What a difference to be sitting here, in the comfort of this warm fire, and in such pleasant and easy company; how different to night-time in the monastery. That was the time he found hardest of all. Normally the refectory was the only place where you could meet anyone for a chat. There was a nice sitting room upstairs, but it was only used on special occasions, when they were having a drink to celebrate something. The refectory was a big, cold. bleak room, particularly in winter. He recalled one widely travelled young visitor comparing it to a Russian restaurant. There was a large table, which wasn't properly cleaned once the women employees left after lunch. It was usually covered with dirty butter dishes, empty milk jugs, bits of marmalade stuck to everything, and lots of breadcrumbs. Every now and then, Brother Bartholomew would give it a sweep with a brush that was left for that purpose on the windowsill. But the brush was dirtier than the table, and served only to turn the blobs of marmalade into streaks, going from one end of the table to the other. And then it was pot luck who might be present. He found himself becoming increasingly intolerant of the people he lived with. The arrogance of Brendan, the pathetic spinelessness of Matthew and the constant complaining of Bartholomew were not conducive to raising morale, or to sending a person to bed in good form. How could any of that compare to sitting here with Olivia?

'So, how do you feel about last night?' Olivia asked suddenly, interrupting his tale of the day's events. She had blurted it out. It was as if something had taken her over, something that was out of her control, and the words were out before she knew it. She could not unsay them, so she felt she must go on. She looked at him directly and intently. 'Listen, Jack. You and me. We spend a lot of time together. I love the times I spend with you. I feel alive and excited; I almost feel reckless, like I couldn't care about anything else, anyone else . . . ' Her voice trailed off.

Jack looked into his glass of wine. This sudden switch into deeply personal conversation had wrong-footed him; it was something that monastic life had not prepared him for.

Before he could think of anything to reply, Olivia said simply, 'I love you.'

Jack had no idea what to make of it all, or how to respond. It was the first time a woman had ever told him that she loved him. Was it just her way of expressing affection and friendliness, or was she saying more? And if she was, what then? His face registered the confusion that her words had thrown him into, and Olivia leaned over, caressed him gently on the cheek and stood up.

'It's all right, darling. I'll make the tea,' she said, and went into the kitchen.

Jack tried to get his thoughts under control. The time he had spent with her the evening before had been wonderful, but also disturbing. It was the first time they had touched each other in a way that was more than just casual affection. He had enjoyed it very much, but even though they had not gone beyond holding each other closely, and kissing, he was full of guilt about it. Would he be able to match Olivia's directness and talk to her about his feelings? He felt that he should, but he wasn't sure if he was able to, or how to go about it.

She returned with the tray, and poured the tea. Then she knelt in front of the fire and began putting on some more coal. He was very conscious of her closeness, and the beautiful curve of her hips as she leant in over the fire. In getting to her feet she reached out for support to the arm of his chair. It seemed such a simple, ordinary thing to do, yet for him the effect was electric. He caught hold of her hand. She paused, half-way between kneeling and standing, and looked at him. He could feel the colour mounting in his face. She smiled and gently moved to sit on the arm of his chair. They sat like this in silence for a time. Then he gradually moved his free hand to encircle her waist, and hugged her closely to him. She slid down so that she was sitting on his lap with her arms round his neck, leant forward and kissed him. They had kissed before: fleeting, affectionate kisses. But this was different. This was definitely more than affection. He broke away from her for a moment.

'Should we be doing this?' he asked, without in any way loosening his tight hold on her body.

'Shhh,' she replied. 'Don't talk. Not now.'

Olivia could feel her body relaxing as she pressed close to him. His kisses were so tentative, almost apologetic. It was lovely. Jack was so gentle that she found her guard collapsing; she felt so safe. He touched her gently, caressing her shoulder. She found herself responding to him, moving her body to the rhythm of his caresses. He gained courage from her response and began to explore, though cautiously. Briefly his hand touched her right breast, but so lightly that she wondered had he done it by accident or design, and then moved up to her face. He pulled back, and gazed at her lovingly. 'You are so beautiful.'

She closed her eyes and began to kiss him again. His hand moved down to her breast once more, this time more assuredly, and he cupped his fingers around it and squeezed it gently. She responded by kissing him more passionately still. But she felt the change come over him almost immediately.

'No! We mustn't!' He pushed her off his knee, jumped up and walked over to the window.

'This isn't right. We must stop.'

She went towards him, reaching out to embrace him, but he stopped her with a gesture. She paused, but still held out her hand to him.

'Don't be upset,' she said. 'It was lovely. Sit down and let's have some tea.'

They sat in their separate chairs, both of them with their eyes cast down, and the silence was deep between them. There was a new closeness, but also a great distance that neither of them seemed to know how to cross. After a while, Olivia took the now stone-cold tea into the kitchen and returned with another bottle of wine. She went over to where Jack was hunched in his chair, bent down and kissed him lightly on the cheek.

'Don't worry about it, love. Let's give ourselves time to work all this out.' She filled his glass with wine. 'Maybe it's something stronger than tea we need just now.'

Gradually they began to relax once more, and though they remained in their separate chairs, with the help of the wine they chatted away happily for the rest of the evening.

About the same time that Jack and Olivia were struggling with passionate feelings, Enda Staunton woke suddenly from sleep. He looked at his watch, and was disgusted to find he had slept through the rest of the healing ceremony. He had wanted to be present to see how it would end, and to keep an eye on what was done with the money. He didn't trust the three heavies. He felt it wouldn't be beyond them to pocket some of the contents of the buckets before it ever got to the bank. But now it was probably too late. Everything must be over for the night. He jumped off the bed, ran down the stairs and went into the refectory. It was almost deserted. Matthew was about to go upstairs to his office. He had just shown Kevin's brother and sister to their bedrooms, and everyone else had retired for the night already. He stayed on for a moment to discuss the latest events with Enda. The Chief Superintendent had been on to him. They had come up with nothing to suggest that Kevin's death had been anything other than a straightforward case of suicide, but they still wanted to clear a few things up. He promised that the gardai would keep a low profile, particularly during the funeral, and not do anything that could provoke speculation or gossip.

On his way back up to his room, Enda met Timothy Brown on the stairs. Timothy was bustling about on his rounds to make sure that everything was locked up for the night. 'Does that man ever sit down, ever relax?' Enda asked himself. 'Or does he spend the whole night wandering around the house like a restless spirit?' Even though Timothy was by no means the brightest person in the community, and had joined the priesthood late in life, still he had a way of controlling things. In his role as house manager, he had the key to everything, so that all life in the monastery tended to revolve around him. Enda got on reasonably well with him, on the whole. He had learned over the years that it made life much easier to be on friendly terms with Timothy. He had a way of making things unpleasant for you otherwise. But Enda wondered about him now. If there was any skulduggery surrounding Kevin Dunne's death – and all the evidence seemed to be pointing in that direction – it was likely that Timothy knew about it, at the very least. Enda wondered if he should discuss it with him, but for the second time that evening he decided against it. There was always something a bit underhand, a bit shady about Timothy. He decided he would sleep on the whole thing, and see how it looked in the bright light of day.

Sleep, which normally came quickly and easily, was eluding Jack. For the second successive night it had been late when he got home. He and Olivia had shared the second bottle of wine while the conversation had flowed freely between them. As he was leaving, they had hugged each other closely, and kissed. Now, lying in his single bed in his room in the monastery, his thoughts were all of her. After spending half an hour or so tossing and turning, he looked over at the telephone on his desk. He got up and dialled the familiar number.

'Darling, did I wake you?'

'No, I was awake. I'm so glad you rang.'

'I wanted to thank you for a lovely night.'

'It was lovely for me, too.'

'Are you all right about what happened between us?'

'Of course I am, love. Are you?' Olivia was speaking in the gentlest of whispers.

'I am now. I love you, Olivia.'

'And I love you.'

'Are you in bed?'

'Yes.'

Jack pictured Olivia in the double bed he had noticed once in her house.

'I'd love to be there with you.'

'That's bold talk for a priest,' she said playfully. 'And I'm certainly not dressed to meet one. In fact, I'm not dressed at all.' She was deliberately playing on Jack's imagination. 'Now, be a good boy and go to sleep, and let me do the same. I have a hard day's work ahead of me tomorrow.'

'Good night, my love.'

'Good night, darling.'

CHAPTER EIGHT

As he had done for more than fifty years, George woke at five thirty in the morning, and immediately got out of bed. He had trained himself at an early age not to lie on after waking, even for a short period of time. In his younger days, that had involved a fair degree of discipline, but now it was second nature to him. He had been told as a young novice that lying on in bed in the morning after waking was a dangerous thing to do. At that time of the morning, when resistance was often at its weakest, unwanted thoughts could come into your mind – temptations against the great virtue of purity – that could lead to committing serious sin. George had heard many confessions of priests in the course of his lifetime, and he had often heard them talk about their struggles against sexual temptation. They had told him their difficulties with bad thoughts and bad actions. He had tried to be as sympathetic as he could, but had found it hard not to be critical of them. He didn't experience any difficulty in this area himself. He thought about this as he began to shave, glad of the hot water that now flowed from the tap into the washbasin in his room, which he found such a comfort compared to all the years when he shaved with a jug of cold water and an enamel basin. Even George had to admit that some of the changes were for the better! He could hardly remember committing a sin against the Sixth or Ninth Commandments in his life. They were the two Commandments which contained the greatest pitfalls and dangers to the eternal salvation of the soul. In case he gave way to pride, he quickly reminded himself that he should give thanks to God for this. But he also knew that he had always been a very disciplined man. He had been rigid in practising modesty of the eyes, as it was called, never allowing himself to look for any length of time on any woman, even his own sisters. This discipline applied even more to his reading, and in more recent years to the very occasional television programme he watched, though he seldom watched anything other than the main evening news. And, careful as he had been with modesty of the eyes, he had been more careful still with his thoughts. This, he felt, was where the real discipline came in. To be able to control your thoughts at all times needed a lot of vigilance. And vigilance was something he was good at. Anything that might remotely resemble a sexual thought was dismissed straightaway, and the three Hail Marys were said immediately, followed by that lovely prayer: 'O Mary, conceived without sin, pray for us who have recourse to thee.' He was a great believer in saying the three Hail Marys, and always in his sermon on purity he would emphasise and encourage the practice. The invocation of Our Lady, the purest of virgins and the model for all women, in time of temptation was the greatest possible protection for the virtue of chastity. His own life was proof of this. She had always been a mother to him, and he loved her more than any human person. He knew that a lot of the difficulties people experienced now were due to the fact that they no longer had devotion to Our Lady and to the three Hail Marys. As he carefully dressed himself this morning, making sure not to touch the intimate areas of his body unnecessarily, he thanked God for the good life he had lived, and asked for His protection throughout the coming day.

The chapel, when he got to it, was empty. For the next hour, as he did his meditation and prepared for Mass, he would have it to himself, unless Brother Bartholomew was unable to sleep and rose early. He hoped that wouldn't happen, because he found Bartholomew an uncomfortable companion in the chapel, even though they both took up their positions at opposite ends and did not speak a word to each other. There was something about the way Bartholomew looked at him with that baleful glare that made him feel he was in some way being judged. Whatever about having God judge you – and he was reasonably confident he would come through that one with the help of God's mercy – he would not like to have to stand up to the assessment of Bartholomew. That one would almost inevitably have a negative outcome. But he comforted himself with the thought that Bartholomew took a negative view of all aspects of life, and that this said more about him than it did about other people.

George let his mind drift back to how, before the changes had begun to happen, the whole community would get up together at five thirty in the morning, and the chapel would be full at this hour for morning meditation. For years he had been the one to lead it, choosing the points for reflection. These were read from some spiritual book at the beginning and also halfway through the time of prayer. He remembered how, when things began to change, but while the younger members of the community were still getting up for morning prayer, they had tried to introduce some modern spiritual writers with names like Michel Quoist and Mark Link, but he had resisted all that. Imagine replacing the spiritual wisdom of the ages with the pop psychology of these American upstarts! They had tried to tell him that unless he compromised, the younger members would stop coming, and that is exactly what had happened, until he now had the chapel mostly to himself. But he had no regrets. There were things in life you could not compromise about, George believed. In fact, he regarded compromise generally as a sign of weakness. In all his years, he had never been appointed Superior of this, or any other, monastery, even for a short period. But if he had been, he thought to himself, he would quickly have straightened out these young fellows with their modern ideas. They would have toed the line, or else have been told where to go. You cannot mess around with something as important as salvation. And self-indulgence was the big enemy. That was what gave the Devil his opportunity. George regarded a lot of what passed as modern as nothing more than self-indulgence. Maybe they had been right not to put him in charge.

This morning his prayer was distracted by these sorts of thoughts, as it so often had been in recent times. And it was time now for him to get ready to say his Mass. In the past, after the time for meditation was over, the priests used to disperse to different side chapels in the main church to say Mass, with one of the lay brothers accompanying each priest in order to serve. That was the time in which you couldn't say Mass without a server. Everything had got so shoddy in recent years, even the celebration of the great Sacrifice of Calvary. He wondered if the young men said Mass at all, a lot of the time. For him it was by far the most important thing he would do each day. To take that little wafer, and speak those words over it, and change it into the Body and Blood of Christ: what could be more important than that? How could they lie on in bed till all hours, and not find time for their Mass? No wonder awful things were happening in the monastery. No good could come of this laziness. Whatever else was said about the old ways – and he was tired of hearing the young crowd criticise them – they didn't promote laziness. Getting up early and spending time at prayer before your breakfast was a good way to begin each day, George believed. There was no substitute for long periods spent in prayer. How else could a person stay on 'the narrow road that leads to life'. That was the phrase from the Gospels that had always meant most to him. The narrow road. And the only way to ensure that you stayed on the narrow road was by discipline, self-control, and regular prayer.

But since he was the only one who was up at this hour of the morning, he said Mass by himself in the community oratory. He knew that some of the younger ones were probably not long in bed. Apart from them not saying their daily Mass, were they saying any prayers at all any more? It was being left up to each one to spend his own time in prayer. From what George knew of human nature, that would not work. Unless you had a rigidly enforced law to give shape and discipline to your life, you would fall into temptation, and ultimately 'the wide road that leads to perdition'.

George was right in at least one of his assumptions. He had finished his prayers, taken his breakfast, had a short walk around the garden and was back in his room settled into reading a life of St Theresa of Avila by the time Jack awoke. If he had known the content of Jack's dreams, it would also have confirmed for him the need for prayer and discipline. Not only did he dream about Olivia, but she also occupied his first waking thoughts. For the second morning in a row, he felt the need to go and talk to Joan. Or maybe it was that he felt the need to talk about Olivia, and he knew that Joan would give him a ready ear.

After a quick bite of breakfast, Jack went up to visit her. As always, she was glad to see him, and before long he had launched into the topic that was closest to his heart. He told her a somewhat sanitised version of the night before, not mentioning the phone call. That seemed to be too intimate even for her.

'I think I am in love with her,' he said. 'And at the rate things are going, I'm afraid your wish will come true and we'll end up in bed together. It was close enough to it last night. What am I going to do?'

'Do you believe in celibacy, Jack? Do you see a value in it?'

'I'm not so sure what I believe any more,' Jack replied, shaking his head slowly.

'But surely you must have given a lot of thought to all of this in the seminary, before you made your decision to become a priest.'

'I suppose I did. It's not easy, looking back now, to be sure what I thought about it at any particular stage. But I do remember being very convinced of its value in the early years. I was involved in a debate in the seminary once, arguing that celibacy was an essential condition of priesthood, that a priest could not have either the personal or emotional freedom necessary for the ministry unless he was celibate.'

'It must seem strange to look back on that now, from your current position.'

'Yes, but I think that said more about my upbringing than my real convictions. You see, I had a very sheltered upbringing. I know that things were different twenty or thirty years ago to how they are now, but even by the standards of those times I was very naive. I wasn't introduced to the realities of life until much later than my contemporaries. It had to do with being marked off at an early stage as a candidate for priesthood. It was only later, in the seminary, when I had my first taste of a crush on a girl, that I began to grasp clearly the choice I was making.'

'Why didn't you leave at that stage?'

'I don't know. I suppose, in a way, I had gone too far. It was just that I had become so much part of the system that it seemed too difficult to turn back.'

'Institutional living is dangerous. It should have a health warning attached to it,' Joan remarked.

'I remember going to the man in charge of us at one stage, and trying to talk to him about my doubts. But he wasn't listening very much. He quoted from the Gospels about how Jesus said that the man who put his hand to the plough and turned back would never be fit for the Kingdom of God. Then he said that I should treat my doubts as temptations, and put them out of my mind. Prayer was the remedy for all such problems, he said.'

'That was good old institutional brainwashing at work,' Joan said, laughing. 'And still, there must be something about the life that appeals to you. Yesterday you were all enthusiastic, telling me about your work up north. You enjoyed that, and seemed to believe that you were doing something worthwhile.'

'Yes, there is a lot about the life that appeals to me. Ever since I was a kid, I've wanted to help people. In school we were told so often that self-sacrifice was a good thing that I became enthusiastic about it. Helping people involved self-sacrifice. And celibacy was part of that. It all seemed to fit in very nicely.'

'But that was before you discovered the pleasure of kissing

Olivia!' Joan was teasing him. Jack began to go red. But Joan continued on a more serious note. 'I don't know, Jack. There was a time when I thought it would be a tragedy if someone like you, who is good and has a lot to offer, left the priesthood. Now I am not so sure. I suppose I've become disillusioned with the Church as I have grown older; this clerical thing, as we call it nowadays, and the arrogance that goes with it. It isn't just the scandals; it's the clinging to power and control. Maybe a lot of what we have known has to fall apart before we can rid ourselves of this oppressive system.' She smiled. 'I really have changed. To hear myself talking like this amazes me. When I was young I was very religious. I suppose I still am, in some ways. God means more to me now than ever, and I try to pray, in my own way. I have plenty of time for that, these days. It's the Church I have problems with. And maybe people like you, who are good priests, are only helping to support a system that must collapse.'

'That certainly is radical talk, coming from a person of your age.'

'I suppose it is, but you know, more and more of my women friends are beginning to think like that. There is a big change happening.' She looked at him candidly. 'There is one other aspect to all of this, Jack.'

'And what is that?'

'Olivia. She needs to be considered too. And you must be fair to her. The danger with you is that you will get so wrapped up in your own issues about the priesthood that you will forget to take her feelings and needs into account. Priests can do that, you know. I think it's because you were trained to believe that the priesthood is a more important vocation that anything else. That's a very dangerous philosophy of life; it can lead to self-centredness. So talk to her. She is just as important in all this as you are.'

While Joan was lecturing Jack about the need to be fair to Olivia, she herself was heading off for lunch with Colette Carey, another young solicitor from the office, and one of her closest friends. The morning had been busy, and Olivia was glad of the work. It took her mind off the events of the night before. She was looking forward to a relaxed lunch with her friend, but Colette immediately came up with the one topic she didn't want to discuss.

'Don't you know all about that crowd up there in the monastery, where the priest is supposed to have committed suicide?' Colette asked. 'You always seem to know what's going on there. What really happened?'

Colette was a good friend to Olivia, yet she hadn't mentioned anything to her about Jack. She hadn't said anything to anyone about Jack. It was all too complicated. Her friends joked with her about her love life, and wondered when she would show up with a man. Now they suspected she was seeing someone, but that she was keeping quiet about it, which made them all the more determined to find out. Clearly Colette had some idea of what was happening.

'I know some of them, but not very well. I didn't know him. I'm not exactly into religion, you know.' Olivia spoke without looking up from the menu, hoping that her offhand tone would convince Colette to drop the subject.

'But you might be into some religious people, might you not?' Colette was enjoying herself. And Olivia felt the need to talk to someone about the situation. She was tempted to open up to Colette. Perhaps she could make sense of what had happened to her in the previous six months.

She had fancied Jack from the first moment she set eyes on him. If anything, the fact that he was a priest made him more interesting. It would be fascinating to find out what he was like behind the collar; to see if there was a real human being there, in spite of all the brainwashing that she believed went on in the Church. She hadn't known much about priests, and she had made a lot of assumptions about them. Looking back now, she could see that she had been deeply prejudiced. She had expected him to be frightened by a woman, to run a mile as soon as she showed any interest. She had also presumed that he would have hardline, traditional attitudes to sex, that he would preach a sermon at her about her own life and the largely inadequate and unsatisfactory relationships she had had. None of her general assumptions had proved to be true in this case.

In many ways she had been very successful in her life. She had managed to get into a profession that she liked, and things were going well for her in work. She was on the way up, and the future looked bright. She loved work, and was always at her best when dealing with clients. It was a different story in her personal life. She had never had much success with men. Despite her polished, self-confident appearance, she was very uneasy with any sort of intimacy, particularly of the physical kind, so she tended to have brief relationships that ended abruptly when things began to get too close. Usually, it was she who ended them. There had been one or two occasions when it was the last thing she wanted to do, but she had been frightened and didn't know how to handle the situation, so the easiest thing to do was to finish it. In this area of her life, she was a coward, and she knew it. She also had a good idea of the reason for all this, but she had never talked about it, not to anyone, and even to think about it was too painful most of the time.

But here was somebody who was different to any of the other men she had known. She was amazed to discover that he was a real human being behind the clerical garb – that he was interesting, and could be great fun to be with. That first evening, at the wedding, they had had a great chat. He was so open: not in any way 'churchy'. He had not been like every other priest she had ever met; they had all seemed to want to preach or condemn others all the time. In fact, he seemed to have at least as many questions about life as she herself had, though he approached them from a different angle. But most of all, what surprised her that evening was what easy company he was, how comfortable and relaxed she felt in his presence. She would not have believed it possible that she could feel that way with a priest. And then, as the weeks went by and they got to know each other a little better, she almost stopped seeing him as a priest at all. He had become a good friend.

But still, he *was* a priest, and that made it a complicated friendship. It had to be kept quiet, or people would start talking about them, and while she believed that she didn't mind that so much, she knew that Jack was very nervous of what people would think. This was where the priest bit came out. He seemed to feel burdened by the notion of giving a good example. But they had grown closer, and in the last few days, since he had returned from working in the north, the relationship had taken a new turn. The first time he'd kissed her, she had been astonished. But the night before had been lovely, so natural, and when he had begun to explore her body, she hadn't tensed up as she had with other men. Instead, she could feel her whole body respond in a way that she hadn't felt for a long time. He was so gentle, so tentative, so clearly uncertain about what he was doing and how to go about it, that she didn't feel in any way threatened by him. She felt safe. But then he had pulled away from her abruptly. She was confused about the whole thing. The temptation to discuss it with Colette was too great to resist.

'I'm not into "religious people", but I am involved with one of them,' she admitted, in answer to Colette's perceptive question. 'Imagine me, of all people, falling in love with a priest.'

'Which of them is it? Not old George that I remember from the time I used to go to Mass there, I presume?'

'No. His name is Jack. He's just a few years older than me.'

'I don't know him. He must have come since I gave up going to Mass. Are you really in love with him?' It was only when she heard Colette's question and realised what she had said herself that she realised how close to Jack she had become, and she suddenly felt frightened.

'Maybe. I might be. I don't know. But he's certainly begun to mean a lot to me.'

'Have you slept with him?' Colette was never one to beat around the bush.

'Oh God, no. Not at all. We've barely kissed. But I'm afraid of where it might end up.'

'I would be too, if I were in your situation.' Even though Colette came from a very religious family – her mother was a daily Mass-goer and a great fan of St Carthage's – she too had given up on religion in her early twenties. 'My advice to you is to run a mile, and do it as quickly as you can, before it's too late.' As she spoke, she suspected by the look on Olivia's face that it might already be too late. 'I know what he'll do. He'll string you along for a while, get you into bed and have a good time with you, and then when he begins to lose interest in you he'll suddenly start feeling guilty. Then he'll go and talk to his bishop, or go on a retreat or something. And one day he'll tell you that the relationship is not appropriate for him as a priest, that he has gone to Confession and repented of his sins, and that he can never see you again. You'll be left high and dry. And when you try to remind him of all the times he said he loved you, he'll pretend it never happened. I know these guys. Deep down, they all hate women. That's why they became priests in the first place. They are taught that women are the source of all the evil in the world – the temptresses. So, when it comes to a choice between you and the Church – and believe me, it will – you haven't got a chance.'

Olivia was sorry she had said anything. Jack mightn't have preached any sermons at her, but Colette certainly had. And at the same time, she knew that what Colette was saying was exactly what she would have said before she met Jack. The problem was, it just might be true. She wasn't so totally in love that she couldn't remember that love can be blind. She had seen too many of her friends over the years believe that their man would love them faithfully and forever, only to be dumped overnight. And that was without the complications involved in trying to love a priest. Still, she knew Jack wasn't like that.

'You don't know him. He's a wonderful, gentle, caring man, and I'm sure I can trust him,' she protested. Colette had been so dogmatic that Olivia wasn't going to admit any more of her doubts to her.

'I'm amazed to hear you talk like that,' said Colette. 'Love's an extraordinary thing, isn't it. You were always an even bigger critic of the Church than me, and here you are now, gone all soft and foolish. You're heading for a fall. And don't say you haven't been warned, or come to me looking for sympathy when it happens.'

'All right!' Olivia, wanting to get off the whole topic, adopted a flippant tone, saying: 'But if it works out, will you come to the wedding?'

'You bet! Anything for a day out!'

Jack was back at the monastery just before lunch. He collected his post. There were a few letters and one small brown packet. He went to his room and opened the packet first. It contained a tape, and nothing else. He thought this was strange, but it wasn't too unusual to be sent a tape; he often got tapes of talks, hymns or relevant songs through the post from various people. He just presumed that whoever had sent this had forgotten to put a note with it. He put it into his tape deck and pressed the 'play' button while he opened the rest of his post. But he was brought up short when he heard his own voice coming from the machine.

'Darling, did I wake you?'

And Olivia answering, in a voice full of affection, 'No, I was awake. I'm so glad you rang.'

As he listened in horror, the tape continued through the telephone conversation of last night. He felt his whole body going red with embarrassment at the point where Olivia said: 'And I'm certainly not dressed to meet one. In fact, I'm not dressed at all.'

Imagine someone else listening in to that. Who could possibly have recorded it? He listened through to the end, to the final 'Good night, darling' from Olivia. Then his blood ran cold as he heard that laugh that sounded like a cackle, the same laugh he had heard the night of Kevin's death. He switched off the machine. Suddenly he didn't feel at all like having his lunch.

CHAPTER NINE

By mid-afternoon, permission had been given for the funeral of Kevin Dunne to proceed, and arrangements were being made for the removal of the body that evening, followed by the funeral Mass and burial the next day. The official result of the post-mortem would not be out for a few weeks, but Brendan had been informed unofficially by the hospital that nothing unusual had been discovered, and that the conclusion was that Kevin had hanged himself, unassisted. In other words, it confirmed that he had committed suicide, although his motivation was still a mystery. He had been dead for about two hours before Jack found him. As was usual in these situations, the phrase used at the inquest would be 'death by misadventure', but maybe Brendan would be able to do something to change that too, in due course. That was not the immediate problem. By now, Matthew had come to accept that there was a real danger that the relatives would hear the true story from some other source, so he had decided reluctantly that he must inform them of what had actually happened.

Kevin's brother and sister were in his office, trying to come to terms with this new information. They were wondering what they would say to their invalid mother, and whether or not she should come to the funeral when there was a knock on the door, and Enda stuck his head in. Matthew knew him as a fairly unflappable individual who observed the world and all its foibles from a distance with wry humour. He could see immediately that something had happened. Enda had an anxious look on his face. As soon as he saw who else was with Matthew, he excused himself and withdrew. Walking back down the corridor, he came face to face with Jack, who grabbed him by the arm.

'I need to talk to you,' Jack said urgently.

'That makes two of us.' Enda was clearly relieved. 'Come into my room.'

Even with so much on his mind, Jack couldn't help noticing how tidy Enda's room was, with everything in its place and not a speck of dust anywhere. The room contained nothing more than the standard monastic furniture – the bare essentials for everyday existence. Enda was not one for accumulating things. He lived in a simple way. The bed was made so carefully that it looked as if nobody ever slept in it. There were just two chairs in the room. They sat down. Jack took out a packet of cigarettes, shaking one out as he did so.

'All right if I smoke?' It didn't seem like the thing to do in such a clean, pristine environment, but he was in desperate need of a cigarette. He was already lighting up as Enda nodded.

'Well, who's first?' Even in the middle of it all, Enda could see the funny side and smile.

Jack was holding the tape in his hand. He threw it down on the desk in front of him but then quickly changed his mind and picked it up again. It would be too embarrassing to let Enda hear this. He had been in a state of shock ever since he had listened to what it contained, a little more than an hour ago. He had considered ringing Olivia straight away, but decided against it. Better wait at least till she got her day's work over before he burdened her with this. And anyway, he needed time to think, to get a grip on the situation. He knew that he needed to talk to someone about it. He could do with someone a little more detached than himself to make an assessment of what was going on and how to deal with it. There really wasn't anyone within the community that he was very close to as a friend. The only other young person there was Michael Moran, and while he liked Michael, Jack didn't feel that he would understand. Michael was very young, and there was an innocent idealism about him that made Jack suspect he would disapprove of the relationship with Olivia. He considered going back to Joan, but with the precarious state of her health he thought it would be unfair to involve her in something as serious as this. At that point he had run into Enda on the corridor.

Enda was worth talking to about this, Jack felt. He wouldn't get caught up in the morality of the situation, but would, hopefully, be able to give some hard-headed and practical advise. And that was what Jack needed. He wondered what was the connection – if any – between the tape and what had happened on the night of Kevin's death. Maybe Enda could throw some light on it. On the other hand, he would need to hear the tape in order to compare the weird laugh at the end with what they had heard the other night. He could hardly ask him to listen to that without hearing all the rest. Jack made up his mind and handed it to him.

'Play that, and I'll take a turn in the corridor with this cigarette while you're listening to it.' It would be easier not to be there when Enda heard what was on the tape.

He returned in a few minutes, and, as he expected, saw a look of amusement on Enda's face.

'An interesting tape, to put it mildly,' he said, with a barely supressed smile. 'I thought a smart man like you would know not to go cooing at your lover down the phone. When did you make that call?'

'Last night, at about one in the morning.'

'So the question is: whose phone's bugged, yours or hers? And this is by no means the only strange thing that's happening around here at present.'

'I knew by the look on your face when I met you outside that something unusual had happened.

'Yes, so much so that I even went to tell Matthew, and you know how slow I am to bring him into anything. But he was busy telling Kevin's family the real story of his death, so I withdrew immediately. I was up in Kevin's room. Matthew had asked me to tidy it up before he brought the relatives up to view his belongings. Not that Kevin's room ever needed much tidying. He was even more compulsive about cleanliness than I am. But Matthew told me that the guards had been up there yesterday searching around for evidence, and asked would I check on it, just in case. I was amazed to discover the room in a complete mess – certainly not in a state that I would expect Kevin to leave it in, even if he was planning to hang himself. Drawers were hanging open, and were untidy. Books were lying around all over the place. Even his clothes had been taken out of the wardrobe and were thrown across the bed. It is hard to believe the guards would have left it in such a state. It looked as if someone else was there, someone who was doing a thorough search for something in particular, but what that may be, I don't know.'

'What did you do?'

'I did what I had to do. I put it back into some sort of shape, because I knew Matthew would be along with the brother and sister, and I couldn't let them see it like that.'

'Did you find anything at all that might give us a clue as to what's going on?' asked Jack.

'I think I might have. Luckily, the guards – and whoever else might have searched that room – are not well up with some of the techniques that are being practised in the spiritual life today.'

Jack snapped his fingers, realising what Enda was driving at. 'I presume you're talking about journalling. Kevin was big into that. I remember him telling me how he did a course on it about fifteen years ago. He had kept it up ever since.'

About a year previously Kevin had invited an expert in the technique – which involved keeping a kind of diary to chronicle spiritual development – to the monastery to give a day's seminar. George had been very upset, because not only was she a woman, but she had been a nun herself and had left the convent. She was now making a living by teaching religious various methods of spiritual growth. George couldn't understand how someone whom he regarded as a renegade and a turncoat could now be brought back to teach them how to pray, of all things. In his way of looking at it, if she had been praying herself she would not have left in the first place. He refused to attend. The others did, but Kevin was disappointed that none of them adopted the technique.

Enda pulled a large hardback notebook out from under his desk. 'There was a shelf full of these, and this is the current one. I've only had the time to go through some of the latest entries. It is teaching me one lesson.'

'What's that?'

'Not that I was ever likely to, because it really isn't my scene, but any temptation I might have had to get into this journalling is well and truly scuppered now. Writing all your personal thoughts and problems down in a book for people to read after you've gone is not my idea of fun. I'll take my secrets with me to the grave.'

'That's enough of a sermon, Enda. Tell me what's in it.'

'A lot about him being gay. As we guessed, he was going through a big struggle over that. Reading between the lines, I gather he was having a relationship with someone: a man older than himself, it would seem. A lot of it is written in fairly cryptic style. He must have worried about someone else reading it. This is the really interesting bit. Listen to what he has written: "Tonight I was threatened with exposure. I don't know if he's serious, or just trying to frighten me. But he has certainly succeeded in doing that. My poor mother! She doesn't deserve this in her old age. To read about her son in the papers. I can't endure it. God, forgive me!" That's the very last entry. I suppose he wrote that just before he went downstairs to hang himself. Sad, isn't it? But unfortunately he doesn't give us any more information.'

Enda went on to tell Jack about the previous evening. He recounted his strange experience when he returned to the monastery during the healing ceremony – finding the door open, seeing the figure at the other end of the corridor and hearing the strange laugh out in the grounds.

'It's definitely the same person that we heard the first night – the one who's on your tape,' Enda said.

Jack frowned. 'The question now is what are we going to do about all this? Our theory that the fellow who looked through the window on the night Kevin died was just some insomniac wandering around the grounds of the monastery is no longer tenable. Also, it's increasingly obvious that there is more to Kevin's death than meets the eye. Not to mention the fact that there's someone out there with evidence about me that could cause me immense embarrassment.'

'Not to mention the harm it could do to Olivia Lenihan,' added Enda.

'Indeed. That goes without saying. I think we should go to the gardai with all the evidence.'

'Even the tape?' That smirk was there again on Enda's face.

'Yes, even that. I'd be prepared to take my chances on it.'

'*You* would, maybe. But what about Olivia? How do you think she would feel about all the guards in the city knowing that she was having an affair with a priest? And she a solicitor, meeting them every day in her work.'

Jack was annoyed to hear Enda talk like this, partly because he realised that he hadn't been taking her side of things into account. 'Leave that to me. I'll worry about Olivia.' The edge in his voice caused a sudden tension to develop in the room.

'Maybe you should have worried about her before now,' Enda said grimly. 'I'm not happy about giving all this evidence to the guards, not just yet. I don't want to be the one to wash the community's dirty linen in public. Kevin is dead, and this journal is a very private affair. I'd be reluctant to show it to anyone. I'm going to keep this for the moment, and I'd appreciate it if you said nothing about its existence to anyone, either inside or outside the monastery. The hospital said he committed suicide. Nothing will bring him back to life. I'd like to know a bit more about what's going on before we do anything. I suggest we wait till after the funeral.'

'I don't know,' said Jack. 'I liked the cut of Bluett, the young garda. If I thought that he'd keep it to himself, and not involve McCormack, I'd chance talking to him.'

A loud knock interrupted their conversation. The door flew

open to reveal the large figure of Matthew standing there. Jack noticed with relief that Enda had quickly slipped the tape and the journal out of sight.

'What's wrong? When you came to my room you had the look of someone with a problem,' Matthew said to Enda, giving a cursory nod to Jack, to acknowledge his presence. But by now Enda had composed himself and was saying nothing about his discovery.

'Oh, nothing at all. What would be wrong? I was only dropping in to tell you that Kevin's room was ready, if you wanted to bring his relations up.'

A look of relief flooded Matthew's face. Clearly he already had more than enough to deal with. He immediately launched into telling them about his conversation with the relatives, and the breaking of the news about the real cause of Kevin's death. They had decided that it was better, under the circumstances, that their mother should not attend the funeral. And since she was in a nursing home many miles away, and beginning to go senile, there may be no need to tell her about the suicide at all. Matthew talked on, glad to have an audience.

Enda only half listened. He could see that Matthew was under pressure. And yet, at the same time, he was relishing being in charge. Like all weak people, he drew his identity from his position, and he needed to be in charge of the monastery more than the monastery needed him. Enda felt that, whatever way they dealt with the situation, the less they involved Matthew the better. He didn't have the same feeling about Bluett that Jack had. He would be slow to trust him. McCormack wasn't very bright, but he understood the monastery, and was devoted to the place. Bluett was in a different category. The fact that he was dealing with priests and an ancient monastery would be irrelevant to him. He would pursue the issue ruthlessly. He would have little or no sensitivity to the older men. And what would he find? Enda didn't know, but he was worried. His reverie was interrupted by Matthew's voice.

'Who will preach at the funeral Mass?' Matthew was a poor speaker, and was frightened of the prospect of having to say something on this occasion. 'Will I ask Father Brendan to do it?'

Over my dead body, Enda thought sourly. This is typical of Matthew. Turning to Brendan in every situation. Always licking up to him. Of course, Brendan would do a polished perform-ance, but considering the circumstances of the last few weeks of Kevin's life, and his open conflict with Brendan, as well as Enda's suspicions about what might really be going on, he thought it would be wrong if Brendan preached at the funeral. And he was damned if he was going to let that happen. There were some things in life – even in a monastery that had long passed its glory days – that were worth fighting for, and this was one of them. Poor Kevin, mixed up and all as he had been, deserved better. The other good preacher in the community – the one who could rise to an occasion like this – was Jack. Enda looked over at him. Would he be able to put his own problems aside and get down to doing it? Enda hoped he would. He spoke up.

'I think Jack should do that job. Kevin would not have wanted Brendan, after all that has happened.'

Jack jumped up from the chair where he had been sitting with his head in his hands, not taking any part in the conversation, and not even listening closely to what was being said.

'I couldn't,' he declared. 'No way. I couldn't do that. It's out of the question.' He addressed his comments directly to Enda, ignoring the presence of Matthew in the room. He was clearly appealing to him to take the circumstances of his own life into account and have a little pity on him. But when Enda really wanted something he could be tougher than any of them, and he was willing to take the risk of pushing Jack into doing it, in order to stymie Brendan and do justice to Kevin.

'You could. And you will.' He turned to Matthew. 'Jack will preach. Put him down for it. And he'll do it well.'

Matthew looked over at Jack, who slowly and reluctantly nodded, cursing Enda internally the while.

Jack had arranged to meet Olivia in the pub after work. It was a place they used occasionally because it was quiet at that time of the evening, and there were a number of little alcoves where they could have privacy. He hadn't said anything to her over the phone about the tape. Indeed, he hadn't used the phone in his own room at all, in case that was where the bug was. Instead, he used one on the bottom corridor that was available to everyone. And even at that, he had said as little as possible. He wondered if he would ever again feel relaxed on the phone.

When he arrived at the pub, she was waiting for him, settled in a quiet corner with a coffee in front of her. He handed her his Walkman and told her to put the earphones on. 'Be ready for a shock,' he said.

He sat and watched as she listened, the blood slowly draining from her face. Then he proceeded to fill her in on all the details and explain the significance of the strange laugh.

'What the hell is going on here?' were the first words she managed, as she gradually pulled herself together.

'I don't know. But I suspect you're getting caught up in something that has nothing to do with you, and probably not very much to do with me either, for that matter.'

'That's no consolation. What are you going to do about it?' Olivia's voice was tight with tension and the look on her face was very different from the last time Jack had been with her, the evening before.

'I want to go to the guards with all the evidence, but Enda thinks we should wait.'

'Do you mean to say you would give that tape to the guards?' Olivia was incredulous.

'Noel Bluett was doing the investigation yesterday. He seemed a sensible sort of a person. Maybe we could depend on him to be discreet.'

'Not on your life, you won't.' Olivia slipped the tape into her bag. 'I'm keeping this. I have to meet these people in court. How could I ever look Bluett in the face, knowing he had listened to that? I don't know if he would be discreet or not, but I could never be sure. I would always imagine a group of them listening to it, having great fun at my expense. If that tape got into their hands, I would have to leave town. The problem is, who else has it?'

Jack was conscious of something that was close to coldness between them. It was far removed from the tenderness of the night before. They talked around the topic for another while, but Olivia had to go to attend a meeting. Jack was almost relieved. From a number of points of view, he had no idea how to deal with this situation. Life was certainly getting complicated.

After finishing their drinks in near-silence, they separated by mutual consent. Jack slipped out the side door of the pub with his anorak pulled up against the cold and the prying eyes of the conservative people who would not approve of him being in a pub. He set off on foot back to the monastery.

'I see I'm not the only one off duty today.' Jack turned and saw a man coming up behind him. Both the voice and the appearance were familiar, but for the moment he couldn't place where he had seen him before. 'Though I suppose, like myself, you're never completely off duty.'

This was enough of a clue for Jack to recognise Noel Bluett, now dressed in casual clothes. 'Oh, good evening, Garda Bluett,' Jack said.

'Noel will do fine, if I can call you Jack.' Jack nodded, and they fell into step together.

'You're just the man I was thinking about,' said Bluett.

'Were you? And why, might I ask?'

'Because I'm trying to work out what's going on in that monastery of yours.'

'And have you reason to believe that there is something going on?'

Jack was playing for time. He thought it uncanny that Bluett should suddenly appear at his shoulder at this precise time. It was almost like a sign from God. On the other hand, maybe it wasn't an accident at all and, in spite of what he had said, Bluett was very much on duty. But how could he tell him about the events of the last few days without involving Olivia?

'I do think there's something going on,' Bluett said. 'I've done many interviews in my time, and I have a fairly good instinct for when people aren't coming clean.'

'Are you saying that some of us weren't telling the truth?'

'There's a difference between not telling the truth and coming clean,' Bluett said, looking keenly into Jack's face. 'I don't know if any of you actually told me lies – though I suspect some did – but most of you didn't tell me everything you knew. And I'm wondering why.'

'Does that include me?' asked Jack.

'I'll leave you to answer that one, and I'd be very happy if you would. Why are you people covering up? It's my first experience of working with priests, and I didn't expect this.'

'I think that some of us are overly concerned about the good name of the monastery, and not letting outsiders see us as we really are. We're really very reserved people, and we value our privacy greatly. And perhaps there are some who have other motives which I can't even guess at.'

'Will you tell me now what's really going on up there?' Bluett's voice was persuasive, and it didn't take too much persuasion to get Jack talking. He told him about the person looking in the window, and hearing the weird laugh, followed by what Enda had seen and heard on the night of the healing ceremony.

'Did you search Kevin Dunne's room?' he asked Bluett.

'We did – not that we found anything of use. What I remember chiefly is how tidy it was, and the difficulty we had in putting everything back as neatly as we had found it.'

'That means that someone else did a thorough search of it afterwards, and wasn't as careful as you.' He explained about the mess Enda had found when he went to look over the room, but he didn't mention the journal. That was for Enda to decide. 'To cap it all,' he concluded, 'I'm being blackmailed!'

'Blackmailed? In what way?'

'Somebody bugged my phone. They taped a personal conversation I had with somebody, and then left a copy of it in the letter box today, with that strange laugh at the end of the tape.'

'That's good!' said Bluett. 'Sorry, I don't mean it's good

that you're being blackmailed. But at least we have a bit of evidence that we might be able to use. Can you give me that tape?'

'I'm afraid not.'

'What do you mean? This could be crucial in discovering what's going on.'

'There's another person involved in the conversation. And that person has got hold of the tape and refuses to give it back to me, because I suggested giving it to you. The other person was totally against that.'

Jack felt very awkward talking in this way, and he knew he was letting Bluett know that it was a woman. But the garda made no comment, except to say, 'Okay. We'll talk about that again. But you've given me a lot to work on for the moment. I have one or two things to check out, and then I think I'll have another chat with Timothy Brown. But this time I won't have a pious colleague looking over my shoulder. And I'll be talking to you again. Thanks for your help, Jack.' Bluett turned down a side street, and was quickly gone.

Jack hoped he had done the right thing, and feared the reaction of Olivia if she found out. He had almost arrived at the monastery. Since the bugging of his phone, he felt uneasy there, as if every aspect of his privacy had been invaded. He had no inclination to go in. Instead he decided to visit Joan. He promised himself that he would not burden her with his latest troubles. He would give her a chance to talk about herself, and give her some news that would brighten up the evening for her – if, in his present state, he could think of any.

CHAPTER TEN

Olivia's mind wasn't really on the meeting, and she was glad when Colette volunteered to chair it. Even though she was sometimes excessively direct in her way of speaking, and she could overdo her teasing about Jack, Colette was sensitive when she wanted to be, and a good friend. She could see straight away that Olivia was not at her best. When the meeting ended, she came straight over to her.

'I need a drink, and by the look of you, you need one even more,' Colette said. 'Come on!'

They settled themselves in the same quiet corner in the same pub that Olivia had occupied with Jack earlier on in the evening.

'Problems with loverboy, the priest?' Colette leant forward expectantly.

Olivia, sitting at the meeting and watching the professional way Colette was handling the whole thing, had already decided that she would tell her about the fix that she was in. So she was glad of the opportunity to talk.

'Yes, big problems by the sound of it.' Olivia told her about somebody bugging the phone line, and the tape Jack had got. She didn't admit to having possession of the tape, in case Colette wanted to listen to it. There were some things too private even for your closest friend, she said to herself. They discussed whether the bug was in the monastery, or at her end, and who might possibly be responsible for it, but they didn't have a lot to go on.

'The one thing I'm fairly sure about is that nobody has been in my house. They couldn't have got in without some sign of a forced entry, and that hasn't happened. I suspect the problem is at his end. And from what he told me, it could have something to do with the whole business of that man who committed suicide, and whatever is behind all of that. I knew that having a relationship with a priest would be complicated, but I didn't expect this. Maybe a certain amount of intrigue in the sense of having to keep it secret. But not blackmail. It's a creepy feeling to know that someone has tapped your phone call.' Olivia shivered. Despite the dramatic possibilities involved in phone-tapping and blackmail, Colette was more interested in the relationship

'What is it about you, Olivia? Why did you get involved with him in the first place? You aren't short of men, if you wanted them. Even at this evening's meeting, did you notice how young Cooney couldn't take his eyes off you? I know he's no great prize, and if that's the best our legal rivals on the other side of town can come up with, we haven't much to worry about. But he clearly has the hots for you.'

'Him? It's guys like him that are the problem.'

'What do you mean?'

'I went out with him one night about three months ago. Never again!'

'Tell me more.' Colette's curiosity was stirred.

'I know we say that men today have only one thing on their minds, but it was certainly true of him. He nearly tore the clothes off me in the car outside my house. I had a job to get away from him.'

'You have a bit of a thing about sex, though, haven't you?' Colette was gently probing.

'If you call not hopping into bed with every man that comes along "having a thing about sex", then you're right, I have. Some of us have standards about these things, you know.'

Colette had never made a secret of the fact that she was sleeping with her current man, even though she sometimes wondered if Olivia disapproved of her doing so.

'But is it not a bit more than that? Is that some of the attraction of Jack? A relationship with a man, without sex coming into it.'

'Yes, professor,' said Olivia sarcastically. 'When exactly did you qualify in psychoanalysis? How much will I have to pay you for this diagnosis?'

Even though Olivia was mocking her, Colette sensed that she was willing – and maybe even anxious – to say more.

'Seriously, though, you have told me yourself before that when things hot up between you and a man you get frightened. I've often wondered why, because that's not the type of person you are. In fact, in a lot of ways, you're the opposite. I wish I had your sex appeal, and by nature you're a touchy-feely type of person, into hugging and embracing. You said the other evening that you have never gone further than kissing Jack. Is that right?'

'That was right the last time I spoke to you, but we had a fairly heavy session last night.'

'I'm all ears.' Colette settled back in the seat, taking a sip of her drink and smiling.

'That was the strange thing about it. When it did get heavy, it was him who stopped, not me.'

'What's strange about that?' asked Colette. 'I would hope that he stopped. After all, hasn't he taken a vow not to do any of that sort of thing?'

'No, I don't mean him. What was strange was that it was the first time in years that I was relaxed in that type of situation. I didn't want him to stop. He could have gone as far as he'd liked. I wished he had. As you said, up to this I have always got so tense when a man began to get close to me that I put a stop to it. I couldn't cope with it. My body went all rigid. But not this time. It was the loveliest feeling. And then he had to go and jump up, and push me away from him, saying it was all wrong.'

'And so it is. Wrong. He shouldn't be doing it.'

'Ah, will you shut up with your moralising,' Olivia snapped at her. 'You're the one who claims to be an atheist, and you're more of a dogmatic, old-style moralist than any of us.'

Even though they spoke strongly to each other at times like this, still there was an ease between them, and Colette chanced probing a little further.

'Why do you tense up when a man gets close to you? Any idea what might be causing it?'

Olivia suddenly began to cry, and Colette reached out and took hold of her hand. After a minute or two of silence, she said, 'Please, tell me, whatever it is. It will help to let it out.'

Gradually Olivia pulled herself together. 'Sorry,' she said. 'I've never spoken about it to anyone. Some things are better left in the past.'

'Please.' Colette continued to hold her hand, and looked into her eyes reassuringly. 'Don't be afraid.'

There was another long silence. A customer in search of a seat stuck his head around the corner and, seeing two women holding hands, quickly withdrew. Colette wondered what conclusion he was drawing about them. Olivia began to speak.

'It was near the end of my first year in college. Tommy Quinn was his name.' She stopped. Clearly this was not easy for her.

'Yes. What about Tommy Quinn?' Colette had let go Olivia's hand but was still sitting at the edge of her seat, keeping close to Olivia and listening attentively.

'He was a third-year, he played rugby for the college and I was head over heels about him. As well as that, it was a great feather in my cap that, as a mousy first-year law student, I was able to nab him. We'd been going together a few months and everything was rosy in the garden – or so I thought.'

'Were you having sex?'

'No. I didn't think it was right at that stage. I was too young. And anyway I was terrified of getting pregnant and having to face my mother. There was the usual bit of groping above the waist but that was all. I liked what he did and he never tried anything more than that.'

Colette listened.

'There was a weekend when my flatmate had gone home, and I stayed in town because Tommy and myself were going to a party on the Saturday night.' Olivia now spoke quickly, as if she wanted to get it over with. 'When he dropped me to the door at the end of the night I invited him in for coffee. I knew he had a good bit of drink taken, and I was concerned about him driving. I though a coffee would sober him up. Of course, before long we were at it on the couch: the usual. It was lovely. I can remember him taking off my bra and how the touch of his hands felt so good. I was relaxed all over.'

'You had a few drinks too, I suppose.'

'I had. But you know me – I never drink much. Two bottles of beer and I've had enough.'

Olivia paused. She turned the stem of her wine glass. When she spoke again, her voice was breaking. But she ploughed on. 'I suddenly felt him trying to push down my panties. He had never done this before. I said no. I asked him to stop. I can even remember saying, "That's out of bounds." I thought he would stop straight away. But he didn't. I began to plead, "Please, Tommy, I don't want that." He wasn't listening. It was as if he was in a separate world, apart from me. He just kept going. I knew he was fumbling with his trousers. I began to scream and tried to get up. But he was on top of me and he was so strong . . . ' Olivia's voice cracked and the tears flowed.

'Oh my God, that was really tough.' Colette put her arms around Olivia and drew her into a tight embrace. 'You surely had a lousy introduction to sex.'

Olivia steadied herself. 'The most horrible part was when it was over. I could see that he just wanted to get away from me. He muttered something – it could have been an apology – and left. And I was glad too. I wanted to be by myself.'

'Didn't you report it to the guards? You'd been raped!'

'No, I never told anybody. I was all confused. You see, I'd been enjoying the early part. I began to think that I'd led him on, that maybe it was my fault. I'd even asked him into the flat. I just didn't know.'

'Come on. Olivia. That was rape. There's no other word for it.'

'I know that now. But I was young then.'

'What happened after?'

'He tried to talk to me the next day but I couldn't look at him. I felt so ashamed, so dirty. I didn't speak to him again, not once during the rest of my time in college. He'd seemed such a nice guy. I couldn't trust anyone after that.'

Two hours later they were nearly the last people left in the pub, and the barman was gathering up the empty glasses. It had been a long night and both women were worn out, physically and emotionally. For the first time since it had happened, Olivia had spoken about Tommy Quinn raping her and at the end of all the talking she wasn't too sure how she felt. There was a great sense of relief in bringing it out into the open at last, and sharing the burden with another human being. And right now she felt closer to Colette than she had ever felt to anyone, and marvelled at how sensitive and affectionate her friend had proved herself to be. But the other side was the pain. In the past two hours she had revisited all the pain, hurt and confusion of that time, and she felt raw and vulnerable inside.

'So where does that leave you and Jack?' Colette asked, as she began to make moves towards leaving.

'That's the problem; I have no idea. Isn't it just my luck that the only person I can feel relaxed with in this way happens to be a priest. You can see now why I didn't want to stop the other night. I was so happy at being able to respond that I couldn't have cared less who or what he was at that moment.'

'But maybe it's precisely because he's a priest that you can be relaxed with him.'

'Possibly. But I don't think so. Or at least not directly. I think it's because he's so inexperienced, so tentative and unsure of himself. I think we respond to each other's insecurities, and that makes me feel easier. I don't feel threatened or over-whelmed, like I do with other men. Especially the experienced, masterful types. Cooney was like that. He acted as if he was in charge, and that he knew exactly what to do. All I had to do was to submit, and go along with what he wanted. Maybe it's me, but I find all young men a bit like that nowadays. I suppose that type of person brings back the image of Quinn, and makes me feel helpless and – I suppose – threatened with rape all over again. When Cooney came on strong with me in the car, I just got this image of Quinn on top of me, and all I wanted to do was run. I'm sure the poor fellow thought I was mad.'

'So that was the meaning of the looks he was giving you this evening. And me thinking that he was lusting after you.'

'Maybe he was doing that too.' Olivia yawned and looked at her watch. 'It's time for us to pack it in for the night, if we're to be in any shape for work in the morning.'

'Right, we'd better. I suppose the question you have to try and answer for yourself is if you are attracted to Jack for himself, or simply because you feel safe with him. And maybe it's only when you've had a bit of counselling, and worked your way through some of this stuff, that you'll be able to get a clear view of it all.'

Olivia nodded. 'I suspect you're right about that. And in the meantime I hope that my name isn't all over the papers for having an affair with a priest.'

Colette was puzzled for a moment. With all that she had heard during the evening, the tape had gone out of her mind.

'Oh, the tape. I'd forgotten about that. Don't worry about it. If anything comes to light – and I suspect it won't – you can deny everything. Put on a posh accent, and say of course it's not your voice on the tape, and stick to that. And when they hear you're a solicitor they'll be terrified of libel, and they'll run a mile.' In a different tone, she asked, 'Will you be all right tonight?'

'Fine. And thanks for everything. For listening.'

'Thanks for trusting me with all of that. It's safe with me.'

They hugged each other briefly, and went their different ways home.

After the removal of the remains, which went off without any complications that evening, Jack felt that he should go to his room and prepare his talk for the funeral the next morning. But he was restless and agitated, and knew that he wouldn't be able to concentrate. And there was something else on his mind that he was under some pressure to attend to. He had promised Mary Anne Savage that he would visit her uncle. Jack decided that this would be as good a way as any of getting through the evening, and taking his mind off his own problems. He walked up to John Street, an old residential area which had once been the exclusive part of the town. The houses were large three-storey buildings, built to look imposing rather than to be comfortable to live in. The ceilings were high, and the rooms large – expensive to heat. Because of this, most of them had now been converted into flats or apartments. Some of the original inhabitants still lived there, like Mary Anne's uncle. Jack knocked on the door of Jim Savage's house. Mary Anne opened the door.

'Oh, Father Jack! I'm so glad you've come, and at a good time too. Uncle Jim is up, sitting by the fire. He'll be glad to see you.' She lowered her voice to a whisper: 'And you won't forget that little job I want you to do for me, will you?'

'What little job?' asked Jack, bemused.

'The will!'

Jack smiled faintly and said nothing. She showed him into the sitting room, where there was a man in his sixties sitting by the fire with a heavy coat wrapped around him. He looked up when Mary Anne introduced the visitor, and Jack could see how thin and worn he was.

'It's good of you to call, Father Jack. You must all be very upset over Father Kevin's death. He was a good man, and a good friend to me. I will miss him very much. I wish I could attend the funeral, but I don't think that will be possible.'

Jack hadn't known that Kevin had been close to Jim Savage

until Mary Anne had told him, but that wasn't really surprising. He knew very little about Kevin's life or friends. And from all that he had been learning in the last few days, it had clearly been a much more interesting life than he'd ever imagined possible. How little we really know about each other, he thought.

'So you knew Father Dunne well.'

'Extremely well. You might say that we were more than friends.' And he lapsed into silence, with his chin sunk into his chest. Jack wasn't sure, but it sounded as if he was sobbing quietly. He waited for a moment, thinking of what Enda had said to him after reading the journal: his suspicion that Kevin had had a relationship with an older man. Could this be him?

'How are you, Mr Savage?'

'Not good, I'm afraid. Ever since I got that stroke before the summer I haven't been right. And I wonder now if I'll ever get back to myself.'

'So you had a stroke?' Jack knew well how to get old people talking, and that most of them were happy to give a detailed, blow-by-blow account of the state of their health. Jim Savage settled down to telling him all about his stroke, and Jack was content to sit back and listen, or at least appear to listen. He might even get some ideas for tomorrow's talk. While the narrative continued slowly, he heard a loud knock on the door, and Mary Anne's steps as she went from the kitchen to answer it. Since the door into the sitting room was left ajar – presumably so that Mary Anne could overhear what he was saying to her uncle about the will – he could easily hear the conversation at the front door.

'Oh, it's you.'

'Yes, it's me. Surprised?' The voice was gravelly and slow.

'Don't you know you aren't welcome here? Not at any time,

but especially not when I'm here.'

'He's my uncle too. I do more for him than you. You can't keep me away from this house. Get out of my way.'

'Take yourself off now, Joe, like a good man. I don't like the company you're keeping, or the people you're bringing around to this house. They're much too smart for you, and they're making a fool of you.'

'How dare you talk like that about my friends! Get out of the way. I'm coming in to see my uncle.'

Jack could hear the voice getting louder and more aggressive. He decided it was time for him to make his presence known to the person at the door. He walked out of the sitting room into the front hall. The man at the door was tall and heavily built. His puffy red face showed the signs of heavy drinking, and his eyes carried very little expression – they almost seemed to be slightly vacant. When he saw Jack, his face broke into a leer, and he said: 'So now I see the sort of company you're keeping, Mary Anne. And you complain about *me*.'

Then he spoke over her shoulder to Jack. 'Wait till you see this evening's paper. That'll take some of the shine off you crowd.'

Jack felt as if he had been punched in the stomach. Somebody must have given them the tape. What sort of spin had they put on it? And would they name Olivia? He was relieved that the big man at the door, having delivered himself of this unanswerable parting shot, had walked out of the gate and away. Jack excused himself to the old man, who was still in the middle of his account. He was confused and upset not to have his audience any more, but Jack couldn't stay any longer. He nodded to Mary Anne, cutting short her confused apologies for her brother's rudeness, and raced out the door. The nearest paper shop was just down the street, in the direction of the monastery. How was he going to walk in and buy it? By now everybody would know about him. It was the local paper, and as he hurried along the street it struck him as surprising that no one in the office had warned him of what they were going to print. As he got nearer the shop, he could see the poster outside the door proclaiming the headline: WOMAN PAID TO WALK. It meant nothing to him. He felt some small consolation that at least he wasn't exposed in the main headline. Looking through the window, he could see a stack of the papers on the floor of the shop. There, beside the main story, was a photograph of Father Brendan. A massive wave of relief flooded over him when he realised that the story in the paper was not about him at all. Smiling broadly, he walked in and picked up a copy. As he paid for it, the woman behind the counter recognised him.

'That's a disgraceful story about Father Brendan. It's awful what they print nowadays. I think I'll stop selling that rag altogether. It couldn't possibly be true. I've known Father Brendan for many years. He's a saint. That's what he is – a saint.'

'I haven't read it yet,' said Jack, as he walked out of the shop and stood outside, quickly glancing through the story. It alleged that Brendan had set up the dramatic cure of the woman who had got up from her wheelchair on the night of the healing ceremony with Father McSorley. The reporter claimed that he had evidence that the woman had been brought down from Dublin and paid five hundred pounds to pretend that she was confined to a wheelchair. They included a photograph of her walking around outside her house in Dublin. Brendan was asked to comment, and he was quoted as being very angry at the suggestions they were making. 'How dare you accuse me of such a thing,' he was reported as having said. And when they showed him the photograph, he had laughed and said: 'Of course the good woman is walking around now. Didn't she have her strength restored to her by Father McSorley, acting on behalf of the Good Lord.'

Jack tucked the paper under his arm, momentarily forgetting his own troubles in taking a certain pleasure in Brendan's discomfiture. Times are certainly changing, he thought. Up to recently, Brendan had all the local media in his pocket. They wouldn't dream of publishing a story like that. But with the outbreak of scandals in the Church, everything changed. Now the clergy were fair game. Young journalists, just like young guards, had none of the traditional sense of reverence and respect for the Church. Jack felt that was probably a good thing, but was slightly concerned that there could be some unpleasant days ahead for all of them.

Back in the monastery, he ran into Matthew and Brendan standing in a corner of the corridor, heads together, studying the paper. Brendan was speaking with considerable indignation.

'A tissue of lies, that's what it is. Not a word of truth in any of it. How dare they publish something like that about me! And that little slip of a reporter who came up earlier today looking for a comment – a comment, if you don't mind – she was a right brazen little hussy. No respect at all. And then when I rang through to O'Connor, the editor, they kept telling me he wasn't available. And that too was a lie. This is the busiest day of the week for them. He never leaves his office on the day the paper's coming out. I'll teach them manners. I'll be talking to my solicitor in the morning.'

Jack had intended joining in with the conversation, but when he heard the tone of it, and saw the way that Matthew was nodding in agreement with everything Brendan said, he decided that he would carry on up to his room. Tomorrow was the funeral, and there was work to be done.

By the time Olivia had got home and gone to bed, Jack, too, was in bed in the monastery. He had managed to put some sort of a talk together for the funeral. He wasn't very happy with it, but it was the best he could do. What could you say at a funeral like that? In bed, thoughts of his own situation and of the fright he had got that evening flooded back to him. And then he thought of Olivia, and wondered how she was, and if she was coping with the shock of hearing about the tape. He looked over at the phone, and was about to pick it up to call her when he thought of the bugging device. He examined the receiver as closely as he could, but he knew nothing about electronics, and he knew that even if there was a bugging device inserted in it, he had no idea where it was likely to be, and he wouldn't recognise it even if he found it. He lay back in the bed and composed himself for sleep. But for once sleep refused to come. His mind was swirling in all directions, and he found himself twisting and turning, feeling more and more agitated. He longed to know how Olivia was. Since he didn't want to take the risk of ringing her, and he couldn't bear the thought of lying on in bed without any prospect of going to sleep, he decided he would get up and drive out to her house. He would just see if there was a light on. If it was in darkness, he would know that she was asleep, and he could come home knowing she was all right. He got out of bed and dressed himself.

Olivia couldn't sleep either. She was exhausted, but her mind was full of images – mostly frightening – chasing one another around in her head. She remembered Tommy Quinn more clearly than she had done in years; the horror of it all revisited her now as she lay in the bed. And when she tried to steer away from that line of thought, the problem of her relationship with Jack and the dreaded possibility of it becoming public began to haunt her. She felt small and afraid. She longed for protection, for someone to look after her, to put their arms around her and hold her. She sat up in bed and turned on the light, wrapping her dressing gown around her. Was that a car slowing down outside? With all the anxious thoughts already occupying her mind, the sound of the car filled her with fear. She got out of bed and peered out, pulling a corner of the curtain back. It was Jack. Her heart skipped a beat. But what was he doing at this hour? There must be something wrong. She heard a gentle tap at the door, and went to open it.

'Oh, Jack! Is there something wrong?' she asked.

'No, nothing at all,' answered Jack, following her into the sitting room. 'Are you all right? I couldn't sleep, worrying about you. And since I couldn't risk using the phone, I decided to come out and see if you were okay.' Olivia nodded.

There was a moment's silence between them, as they stood in the middle of the sitting room floor. Olivia became conscious that her dressing gown was just wrapped around her, and she drew it tighter. Jack moved towards her, and put his arms around her.

'Oh, Olivia!' The dressing gown fell open in front and Jack pressed her body against him. Suddenly all the vows in the world became irrelevant as he felt her warm and naked against him. When he was young and innocent, and full of the fervour of religion, he loved to conjure up images of heaven. But the bed when they reached it was warmer, more comforting, more exciting and more wonderful than any image of heaven that his youthful mind had ever been able to conceive.

CHAPTER ELEVEN

'Dear friends, this is a sad occasion: indeed, a tragic one. We are very grateful that you have taken the time to be with us today to lend your support to the family of Father Dunne, and to us, the community to which he belonged, as we say a last farewell to our brother, friend and colleague.'

Jack was not at ease. Preaching usually didn't cause him any great difficulty. He liked doing it, and, while he might be a little uptight before going out on to the altar, he would usually relax as soon as he stood at the microphone and looked out at the expectant crowd. But this was different. He had got back to his room in the monastery just as dawn was breaking, and collapsed into a deep sleep, from which he had only woken with enough time to shower, dress and have a quick cup of coffee before the funeral. The moment he woke his mind had been assailed with memories of the previous night, and with deep feelings of uneasiness. How could he face going onto the altar after what he had done? He thought briefly of trying to find one of the other priests to go to Confession, but he dismissed that idea. Instead he made a huge effort to discipline himself, and to focus totally on the task in hand. He needed to do that because this was not an ordinary sermon – far from it. He had been on edge for the past twenty-four hours, ever since Enda had cornered him into taking on the task. What could you say on an occasion like this? He had always hated being at funerals where the preacher delivered a eulogy about the person in the coffin that bore no relation to what that person was really like. Sometimes, after listening to the sermon, he wondered if he had gone to the wrong funeral by mistake. But here he was up in the pulpit, and he was intending to do the same thing. Had he any choice? How much of the truth could he speak about Kevin Dunne? At this stage most people knew – or at least suspected – that Kevin had committed suicide. But would it be right to refer to that in public? And what about the fact that he had been gay, and, at least to some extent, a practising gay at that? Surely that could not be spoken, and yet he suspected that it had been a central part of the struggle of Kevin's life. This pulpit, which he liked because it was well positioned for visibility and communication, began to feel decidedly uncomfortable, like a trap he was snared in. And yet his decision had been that the best thing to do was to stick to generalities – or, to put it more bluntly, to give out a mouthful of clichés.

'On days like today we come face to face with the mystery of life and death. We come to know someone, to appreciate them – yes, even to love them – and suddenly they are taken away from us; they are no more. Somebody who is one day vibrant with life and energy is the next day gone forever, almost as if they had never existed. But because of our faith, because of the fact that we believe that Jesus went through the same experience of death, terrible as it was for Him, we have hope.' The thought of George flashed through his mind, and his belief that for someone who committed suicide there was no hope. 'We know that behind the darkness of death there is meaning, and despite all the sadness and sorrow that is contained therein, there is the promise of a new and eternal life.'

Jack paused. He couldn't go on with this, speaking words that had no conviction behind them. It was poor stuff, and he knew it. He even had a phrase for it: cotton-wool preaching. He had done it on occasions before, waffled on in meaningless, flowery language rather than taking up the real issues. Words came easily to him, and he could play around with them and make them sound plausible even if they bore little or no relation to the reality of life.

There was the occasion when the bishop of a diocese was listening to him, and he was preaching on marriage and human relationships. He had backed away from dealing with anything controversial, anything the bishop might disapprove of. He would normally have acknowledged that the word 'family' had many different meanings in the modern world, not just the traditional idea of husband, wife and children. He would have tried to include single parents, separated and divorced people, maybe even same-sex relationships. But, conscious of the bishop, he'd skipped all that. And he'd also avoided the topic of people in second relationships, and whether they were welcome to the sacraments. He still recalled the feeling he had had when a woman came up to him afterwards to tell him how beautiful his sermon was. He felt so disgusted with himself. He had sold out, through fear. He didn't want to bring the disapproval of the bishop down on himself, or even more on his community. The fact that somebody could think that what he had said was good showed how much of a deceiver he could be.

People might think that he was a hypocrite to be up there at all after what he and Olivia had done the night before, but for him the greatest deception and hypocrisy was to speak words that he didn't mean. And he didn't want to do that. Especially not now, when, in a sense, his whole life was beginning to come before him to be questioned and reviewed. Jack must have paused for a long time, though he wasn't conscious of it, because the people, whose attention had drifted away during the early part of his talk as they presumed they weren't going to hear anything interesting, looked up at him to see why he was not continuing. A strong feeling welled up inside him, almost of recklessness. So much had happened in the past few days – the death of Kevin, the upheaval in his own life. He wasn't sure what it all meant, but he had a sense of being at a turning point. In the silence, he made the decision that for the second time in twenty-four hours he would cast the boat adrift; he would speak the truth, whatever the consequences. He would address reality as it was. His voice was now quieter, sensing that he didn't need any dramatic effect to gain attention.

'Kevin Dunne committed suicide. I myself found him hanging from the rafters in the community room two nights ago.' If the pause had brought the attention of the congregation back to him, hushing the shuffling and the coughing, now the silence was electric. There were startled looks on every face as they turned towards him, waiting with bated breath for his next words. He tried to avoid looking directly at the family, but out of the corner of his eye he could see the shock and consternation on the face of Kevin's sister, Catherine.

'We don't expect priests to commit suicide. In fact, there are a lot of things we don't expect priests to do, because we look on them as people who are not like the rest of humanity, who don't have to face the struggles of the ordinary person – who are not fully human. But they are. We are. And some of us get depressed, lonely, hopeless, even despairing, just like other people. Some of us, tragically, take our own lives. When this happens, we cover it up. Oh yes, we in the Church are excellent at covering things up. We justify the cover-up on the basis that the truth would scandalise people, and do damage to their faith. But it also suits us to cover it up because we have taught for centuries that people who end their lives in this way are condemned to hell.

'What an extraordinarily arrogant thing to say! Taking on the role of God. Deciding who will be saved, and who won't. Thinking we had a say not only over matters of life and death, but even of eternity. We became so dogmatic in our beliefs that we even refused them Christian burial. They had to be put into the ground outside the gates of the cemetery. And now, here, today, it has come to our own door. We deserve it. Kevin, in his act of dying, has shown up the cruelty and hypocrisy of the Church. He has shown how uncaring we can be to each other. Kevin, my brother in Christ, I thank you for your final statement to us, and I think it is right that it should be heard. That is what I believe you would have wished. You were a man who, as you went on in life, tried increasingly to live your truth as you understood it, difficult and all as that proved to be. Maybe, like Christ, it was the very struggle of trying to live according to your convictions that led to your death. I know that the God that you believed in was a far greater God than the one the Church presents. Your God was broad-minded, loving, understanding of the weaknesses and inclinations of people.'

Jack heard a loud cough from Father Matthew behind him, and he sensed his restless fidgeting on the celebrant's chair. He knew the fear that was in him. And he knew too that all the other members of the community were on tenterhooks, dreading what he would say next, as they waited to see if he would refer to Kevin's sexual orientation. But now that he was launched, there was no turning back. He would see this one through to the end.

'Kevin, you were a faithful servant of the Church. Even though it is probably doubtful if you ever had a vocation to this way of life, still you gave of your best to it. But the Church was not a kind or loving mother to you. We condemned you, not just in death, but also in life. We disapproved of the way you were, of the fact that you were gay, even though that was the way God had made you. In doing this, we once again set ourselves up as knowing better than God. We told you that you were unnatural; that people like you were twisted and sinful; that you must turn away from what was an essential part of yourself – a part that was at the core of your nature – and become something different, something you were not, in order to be saved. We demanded that you do violence to yourself so as to win the love of that God who formed you in His own image and likeness. And with our attitudes, we promoted and fed the prejudice and narrow-mindedness – indeed, the homophobia – that eventually brought you to your death in that lonely act of two nights ago. I am ashamed today, as I stand in this pulpit, of the Church of which I too am a minister.'

Jack knew the danger inherent in preaching. He knew that, when the mood was on him, he could grab an audience and play on their emotions by the power of his words. It was a gift that could be misused, and needed to be handled with great responsibility. But he had never in his life got the attention of people the way he had at this moment. He could recognise the faces of some of the most loyal devotees of the monastery looking up at him. He could see their shock and dismay. Many of them were traditional Catholics who could not conceive of a priest in the light that Jack was presenting Kevin. And they had never before heard the Church being attacked from this pulpit. One of the core principles of the congregation that Jack belonged to was to be loyal to the Church; never to say anything in public that might seem like criticism, that would suggest anything might be lacking in the Church. He was now very deliberately turning his back on part of that tradition. He no longer believed in it.

'My friends, Kevin was no saint. Neither are the rest of us. I know that some of you like to think that we are. You like to think that we are in some way removed from what you see as the sordid reality of human life – from pain, from passion, from loneliness, from hopelessness. You try to convince yourselves that we are saints in order to feed your own need to believe in an unreal world. But nobody can escape the harsh reality of life and human weakness, either in a monastery or outside it. Those who try to do so ultimately pay a terrible price. Kevin did not try to escape. He grappled with life in all its raw brutality. He grappled with himself, and tried desperately to reconcile his nature with the demands of the institution to which he belonged. And the sad fact is that he was beaten in the end. The forces against him, both at the institutional and personal level, proved too much. To what depth of despair had he come when he decided to end it like this? How could it be that the rest of us who lived with him did not notice? Are we so blind? Are we so wrapped up in our own lives? I feel so guilty today. Kevin, wherever you are, if it is in your power, please forgive me – forgive all of us for failing you in your hour of need.'

Never, in all his years of preaching, had he spoken like this. Never had he touched on so raw a nerve, and at the same time spoken the truth – as he perceived it – so forcefully. None of it was prepared. It seemed to pour out of him, the words coming without any effort, fluent and clear. And still he was not totally absorbed by it, because part of him was able to stand back and observe what was going on. He marvelled at discovering how much anger and rebellion had been buried inside himself all along. It was one of the strange things about being a priest, that you could so easily fool yourself into believing that you belonged in the system, that you accepted all that you were told, all that was part of the package. It was because your whole life was based on it. You had always been told – and even told yourself – that you had been called by God to this way of life, that it was a special and privileged way to live, with blessings in this world, and more especially in the next. Even when doubts arose in your mind, you tended to put them aside, because the consequences of taking them seriously were too great to comprehend. At the back of your mind, you felt that if any part of what you believed was discredited, the whole house of cards might collapse. And then where would you be? The thought of having to rebuild your life from the beginning was frightening. But now he had faced down that fear. He continued.

'From wherever you are – and I use that phrase carefully, because the mystery of what follows death is deep and impenetrable. Is there a life after this one? We don't know. We desperately want to believe that there is. Because if there is nothing, if it all ends at the grave, can we bear that thought? And maybe it does. Maybe this is all there is. We try to cling on to the promise of Jesus, but sometimes even that can seem empty.'

He saw a movement to his right, on the sanctuary, and glanced over. Brendan was on his feet, and was moving towards the microphone at the other side of the altar. Jack waited, as he became conscious of the eyes of the people turning towards

Brendan. Jack had always been somewhat overawed by him. When he'd started out as a priest, Brendan was in the prime of his life. He was full of style and conviction; he was popular and revered. Initially, Jack was happy to settle under his sphere of influence. He felt he could learn a lot, and that maybe by being associated with him he could share some of the reflected glory. But gradually he began to feel stifled, and became more and more critical of Brendan. There was plenty of style, sure, but not a great deal more. He wondered how much of what Brendan preached with such vehemence he really believed. Loyalty to the Church was his abiding principle, and Jack thought that it was possible that you could sell your soul to the Church – that by setting up loyalty as your abiding principle, you could lose any integrity you might have. He tended to keep that sort of idea to himself, but he gradually moved away from Brendan, and in recent times a certain tension had grown up between them. But Jack had never felt confident enough to take him on. This time, though, it was different, and he waited for Brendan to speak, conscious of the rapid beating of his heart, but outwardly unperturbed.

'My dear brethren, I'm afraid that the shock of Father Dunne's sudden death has affected our colleague Father Jack very badly. This is understandable, as they were good friends. As a result, he has said some things here today that, shall we say, have not been well thought out. Neither do they have any basis in fact. And of course, he will regret saying them when he gets a grip on himself again. Father Kevin Dunne was a good man, a holy and devoted priest, and a model religious. Don't believe anything else you hear about him, because it simply is not true. Not true, my friends. And of course there is a next life. We are sure of that. We all have faith, we all believe in the good Lord, who won our salvation for us, and who will forgive Father Kevin his sins and lead him into heaven. We do not doubt that. God is a just God, but He is also kind and loving, and he will call Father Kevin by his name, and welcome him into the eternal happiness of heaven.'

As Brendan spoke, Jack felt the anger welling up inside him. What hypocrisy, he thought to himself. And at the same time he couldn't help admiring Brendan's style, and his coolness under pressure. But talk about the kind and loving God was too much for Jack to take. He forgot about the people below him, and cut into Brendan's dissertation.

'Let's hope that God is more kind and loving to Kevin than you were. You dropped him quickly enough from your sodality team when you discovered that he was gay. You say God will call him by name. I hope the name God will use won't be the same as what you called him when you learned the truth about him. You, more than anyone else, are responsible for Kevin being in that coffin.'

At this point old George, with a speed surprising for his age, moved to the altar and announced in a loud and command-ing voice, 'Let us stand and pray.'

That was enough for Matthew, who had been stuck to the celebrant's chair like a rabbit blinded by the headlights of a car. He was galvanised into action. He stood, grabbed hold of the book and began to lead the prayers. There was a clearly audible release of breath from around the church. Nothing quite like this had ever been seen before in this ancient building.

The rest of the funeral Mass had a sense of anticlimax about it. At the end, Matthew made a fairly incoherent and inadequate attempt to paper over the cracks by apologising to everyone for the fracas, citing the upset of the community generally at the circumstances surrounding Kevin's death. Enda, who after the initial shock had found the whole thing exhilarating, felt it would have been better if he had remained silent.

The walk to the cemetery was short – not more than a few hundred yards – to a lovely corner of the monastery grounds shaded by large oak and beech trees. But short as it was, it gave Catherine, Kevin's sister, and her brother Paddy a chance to collect their thoughts after the drama and revelations of the funeral. Catherine had gone through a whole range of emotions as she listened to Jack's sermon, and now she was simply glad that she was far away from home, and that most of the people at the funeral were complete strangers. In recent years she had been trying to come to terms with the idea that Kevin was gay. She had often regretted the inadequacy of her reaction when he had told her about it. Her way of dealing with the situation was to try not to dwell on it. Not that it was a complete surprise to her. She used to wonder about it when she was younger. It wasn't so much that he was particularly effeminate, or in any way obviously homosexual. But he never, even in his young days, seemed to have any interest in girls. She had tried to convince herself that the reason Kevin kept away from girls was that he was so committed to his vocation that he would not allow himself to get into any situation that might contain danger.

But now, as she walked slowly behind the hearse, she remembered an incident from long ago that she had not thought about for many a year. She must have been about eleven years old, and Kevin, who was ten years older than her, had paid a surprise visit home from the seminary, bringing with him one of his fellow students. On her way home from school, she met her mother, who was rushing to the shop to buy something for the unexpected guests, and she told her about Kevin's visit. At that stage in her life, Catherine had been very close to Kevin, and, excited by his arrival, she ran the rest of the way home. She burst in the door, dropping her bag on the floor in the hall as she passed through, and went straight into the sitting room. Kevin was sitting on the couch with the other student. They jumped up as she came in, leaping apart. But she had seen enough to know that they were locked in an embrace, and were kissing each other on the mouth. There was a moment of embarrassment, and then Kevin recovered and went to Catherine, hugged her and introduced her to his friend.

Catherine was confused at that age about the whole area of homosexuality. She had heard that this sort of thing happened, but it seemed strange and repulsive to her. So she concluded that, if it really did happen, it must be in foreign places and among very strange people. The thought that Kevin might be doing something like that was too much for her. She gradually convinced herself that she had not really seen it, that it was her imagination playing tricks on her, and in due course she succeeded in blotting it out of her mind. As they neared the cemetery, she whispered to Paddy, 'Did you know that he was gay?'

'I was never fully sure, but it doesn't surprise me.' Paddy was younger than Catherine, so he was still only a child when Kevin joined the order and he had not known him very well. 'He never seemed to be at ease with himself. There was always a lot of tension in him. Don't get me wrong, he was welcome when he came to visit us, but both Julie and I were always glad when he left. He was so restless; you could never relax when he was around. And whenever anything about sex came up for discussion, he was obviously uncomfortable, and he fell back on fairly rigid and dogmatic attitudes that always seemed to me to be some sort of refuge for him, because they were at variance with his general outlook on life. So, especially in the last few years, I have suspected there was something the matter.'

'I wonder was Father Jack right in saying he had no vocation. Do you think his homosexuality was the reason why he became a priest?'

'It could well have been.'

Catherine felt a sudden surge of pity for her dead brother. 'Do you think he was unhappy?'

'Probably. Why else would he have done what he did?'

'Oh God, how sad it all is!'

George walked alone, at a considerable distance behind the funeral procession. He couldn't remember the last time he had cried: probably not since he was a child. Crying was one of the many signs of emotion that he would not allow himself. He regarded it as soft and effeminate. But now the tears rolled down his cheeks, and he only made the most feeble attempts to wipe them away. He was sufficiently conscious of them to be glad that he was on his own, with everyone else well ahead of him. He slowed his pace so that he would not catch up with them until he had time to pull himself together. He realised that there were a number of things he was crying for, and that probably Kevin Dunne's death was the least of them. He did feel sad that Kevin would, as he firmly believed, be denied the vision of God for all eternity. That was, he supposed, something that one should cry about. But really, it wasn't what set the tears coursing down his cheeks.

In a way, he felt that Kevin was getting what he deserved. If you lived your life in such a selfish way, pursuing your own pleasure without discipline or control, then you couldn't complain about the consequences. And he could never say that he didn't know what the consequences would be. He had been old enough, and lived long enough, to have been given the real doctrine when he was young, not like the present day, when the young people weren't being taught anything. No! He would not cry for Kevin. The wheel of God's justice turns inexorably, and each one of us must be careful how we live. He hoped, and firmly believed, that he himself would never be caught in such a situation. What then was he crying for, he asked himself. For the disintegration of the way of life that he had committed himself to, the collapse of so much of what he had believed in and on which he had based his life. It was unutterably sad for him, having lived his life so faithfully all these years, observing the vows and the rule of life to the letter, that he should live to see it all falling apart. And this event had brought home to him how much it had fallen apart. The shame of it. Having the whole town know that a member of the community had committed suicide. And worse still, that he was a homosexual. Yes, that was a reason for tears. In the great struggle between good and evil, George felt that now they were in the grip of the Evil One.

He stopped. In the distance he could hear the prayers beginning over the grave. He looked for a moment at the small crowd gathered in a circle around the hole in the ground, in that little plot where he himself would soon be lying. What they were doing was futile, pointless. They were flying in the face of the Word of God, the God of justice. The great book of eternal life had proclaimed the verdict. There was nothing more to say. He would not join them. Slowly, George turned around, and with head bowed and shoulders hunched against the wind, he made his way back to the monastery.

Chapter Twelve

As soon as the prayers at the graveside were over, Jack tried to make himself scarce. He didn't feel ready to meet people just now, least of all the family and friends of Kevin. He presumed that they would be upset and angry with him. But as he walked rapidly towards the shelter of the monastery, he heard steps quickening behind him.

'I could have cheered in there. I was so glad you gave it straight to that man.'

He slowed his walk a moment, and Mary Anne Savage fell into step beside him.

'You don't like Father Brendan Quinn, I gather. Why, might I ask?' Jack enquired.

'I told you. He comes up to see my uncle a lot, and I don't trust him.'

It seemed to Jack that a lot of people from the monastery were in the habit of visiting Jim Savage. Timothy went up every day, assuming the role of a minder; Kevin had been a regular visitor — in what capacity, Jack didn't know, though the old man had described him as 'more than a friend'. And now there was Brendan too. What could be bringing him up there? He usually had a purpose in what he did.

'In what way do you not trust him?'

'I think he's after my uncle's money.'

Jack could believe a lot of things about Brendan, but thought it was unlikely that he would be foolish enough to go after the money of an old man who had plenty of relations.

'I'm sure you're mistaken. What makes you think that?'

'Oh, he's so cute, and such a smooth operator! He sends Timothy to look after everything for Uncle Jim. He must come up at least twice a day, sometimes more, and he has succeeded in making the old man dependent on him. No matter what my uncle wants done, he always asks Timothy before any of us. He even does his shopping for him, and brings him the paper every morning. Not so long ago he arrived at the door with a new television. Jim's television was gone a bit old, and the picture wasn't great. But it did him fine. His sight isn't the best any more, and he wouldn't know the difference. And it isn't as if he'd be short of the money if he wanted to buy one. But Timothy, without so much as a by-your-leave, arrives at the door with this new one, and sets iy up for him, free, gratis and for nothing. Poor Uncle Jim was completely taken in. He couldn't stop telling us how generous Brendan and Timothy were.

Then Brendan comes once a week to hear his Confession and bring him Communion. And that visit is a big deal. It happens at the same time every Friday afternoon. I'm not sure that Uncle Jim particularly wants to go to Confession that often, but it isn't easy to put Brendan off. I believe he's using Confession as a way of getting control over my uncle. You should see the formality and fuss of his arrival. With Timothy coming in before him, like a bloody John the Baptist preparing the way, and they both taking over the house. I wouldn't often be there at that time of the day, because I'd be at work, but since he got the stroke I try to go up as much as I can. The first time Brendan met me there, he said: "Good evening, pet."

Imagine anyone calling me "pet" at this hour of my life. And then he went on, "And who might you be?" as if it was I that was the intruder in the house, and not him. I felt like saying it back to him: 'And who might you be also?' but I hadn't the courage. He's a fairly intimidating character, that Brendan.'

'And Kevin Dunne used to come and visit your uncle? Quite a crowd coming from the monastery! Was he after the money?'

'Oh no, Kevin was different. He was just a good friend, and I liked him a lot. Not that I met him very much either. I think he mostly came at night-time, and he seemed to have his own key and let himself in. I know that when the other two discovered recently that he was coming to visit Uncle Jim, they were very angry.'

'Were they now?' Jack felt he might be beginning to get some clues as to the strange behaviour of the last few days. 'What makes you so sure they're after your uncle's money?'

'I put my ear to the door yesterday evening, after you'd gone, when he came up to hear Uncle Jim's Confession. I heard enough to leave me in no doubt.'

By now they had reached the monastery, and Jack brought Mary Anne into the reception room. After the fracas of the funeral, this was diverting and opened up the possibility of getting one over on Brendan.

'Tell me what you heard when you put your ear to the door?'

Mary Anne settled into the account with relish.

'He addresses my uncle as "my poor child". Did you ever hear the likes of that? A man at least ten years older than him, on his last legs, and he calls him "my poor child". Who the hell does he think he is, anyway? "My poor child," he would say to him, when my uncle had told him a few harmless sins, "God loves you. He will forgive you for everything you have done wrong. He will not hold your sins against you. Because God is loving and generous. But you too must be generous to him. Don't hoard what you have, what God has blessed you with – but give freely to his service by being generous to the poor and to His Church. In this way you will merit the crown of glory that awaits all those who do His will." That's the sort of talk he goes on with. Always talking about how generous God is, and how we must be generous in response. But he doesn't fool me. I know what he's really after.'

Jack felt under no obligation to defend Brendan after what had happened at the funeral, but he still wondered if Mary Anne's interpretation of what she had heard was correct. 'Maybe you're reading too much into this,' he siad. 'All priests tend to do a bit of pious talk when we are visiting an old person, especially after hearing their Confession. We try to put them at ease, and tell them there is nothing to worry about and that God loves them. There aren't too many original ways of saying that. Inevitably we fall back on pious jargon a lot of the time. Maybe that was all Brendan was doing.'

'But why did he try to get my uncle to make a will?' Mary Anne was clearly outraged at the thought of it.

'Make a will? How do you know?'

'From my vantage point outside the door, of course. Just before he left, I heard him at it.'

'You heard him at what? Tell me.'

'I noticed the change in the tone of his voice, and he said to Uncle Jim: "My good man!" He was no longer "poor child"; he was now "my good man", and he was being given an order. "My good man, it is time for you to make a will. I have a friend, a solicitor, in the town, and I will arrange for him to come and visit you tomorrow, and Father Timothy can be here to make sure that everything is done properly."'

'And what did you do?' Jack was enjoying this account, and picturing the scene as she described it.

'I felt that something had to be done at that stage, or all would be lost. I burst in the door and announced loudly: "Uncle Jim will not be here tomorrow afternoon. I am calling for him, and taking him to visit his mother's grave." I knew I was giving it away that I had been listening at the door, but at that stage I didn't care. I could see the look of astonishment on my uncle's face. I had never in my life taken him to visit his mother's grave. He couldn't understand why now. But it did the trick. Brendan backed away and said that maybe they could look after their little bit of business some other afternoon.'

Mary Anne looked at her watch.

'I must run. I promised Uncle Jim that I would come up straight after the funeral, and tell him all about it. Little did I know how much I would have to tell. You really did create a stir today!'

Enda sighed with relief as he and Michael walked out of the monastery and turned towards the river. At last it was over. Poor unfortunate Kevin was buried, the relatives and friends had joined the community for lunch – a fairly tension-ridden affair – and in due course everyone departed. As soon as the coast was clear, they had both changed into their walking shoes, and were now heading for the path by the river.

'It's good to have that over,' said Michael.

'Our relief at having it over must be nothing compared to Matthew's,' Enda replied with a laugh. 'Talk about treading on hot coals. He was in a terrible state during the meal. He didn't know whether to refer to the sermon or not, and if he did mention it, what to say about it. You were lucky. You didn't end up on the top table.'

'Did anyone say anything about it?' asked Michael.

'Not a word. We talked about the weather, the famine in Africa, the economic situation, anything except the funeral. There were long periods of silence. We'll all be suffering from indigestion after it. Kevin's sister, Catherine, was particularly uneasy. She seems to be a nice woman. I felt she wanted to discuss her brother, but didn't know how to start.'

'What did you think of it?' Michael asked Enda.

'The sermon, you mean? After I got over the initial shock I quite enjoyed it. There's a perverse part of me that enjoys seeing people making fools of themselves in public.'

'So is that what you think? That Jack made a fool of himself?'

Enda was silent for a moment as they walked on. 'It's not as simple as that, I suppose. I agree with what he said. I mean, take each point that he made on its own merits and I wouldn't quarrel with the truth of any of them. But there's a time and a place for saying things, and I believe that a funeral Mass is neither the time nor the place for the type of things he came out with. I certainly wouldn't have said any of it.'

Michael laughed. 'I didn't think you would. That's the difference between you and Jack. In many ways you have views that are at least as radical as his, but you are much more cautious.'

'Or is it that I haven't got his courage? I wouldn't take on the institution of the Church and its teaching on suicide and homosexuality in public. And I certainly wouldn't do it without having a carefully prepared script which I could use as evidence of what I said and did not say. He spoke without any script. That was foolish. You can't win against the institution. It's better to keep your head down – don't get over-emotional and lose control of yourself.'

Michael had a way of drawing people out. He had a natural curiosity about the older members of the community, and what was really going on in their lives. He wondered how they coped with life, and what he could learn from them.

'No danger of you getting over-emotional, Enda. You keep that side of yourself well under control.'

'Indeed I do. You have to remember, that was the way we were trained. Obedience was the big virtue in my early days. We were told that the will of the Superior was the will of God. When I think back now, some of the bastards I lived under had little or no connection with God. But that was the way at the time. And you gradually learned to suppress a lot of your own self, and become a good servant of the Order. It was a system that worked well for a long time. It created a unity and cohesiveness that gave religious life great strength and endurance.'

'I'm sure that was true,' said Michael, 'but not any more. People won't accept that way of life now. I admire Jack. Maybe what he did wasn't politically smart, but he spoke the truth as he saw it, and to hell with the consequences. I don't think I would ever have the courage or the ability to do that. But I was really excited listening to him. I wanted to stand up and cheer. I'd like to think that someone would speak like that about me at my funeral.'

'That's all fine. But what's going to happen to him now? He won't get away with it, that's for sure.'

'Maybe there are more important things in life than getting away with it. Maybe there are times when you have to take a stand.' Michael was speaking slowly, thinking it out as he went along, and clearly saying something that was important for himself. 'Enda, would you not think that you do yourself damage by suppressing so much of your own thoughts and emotions?'

Enda was not used to this sort of interrogation. It was the type of conversation that the older members of the community would never have with each other. They had an unwritten law about giving each other lots of personal space. But the new men coming through were into 'caring and sharing', and Michael often tried to turn the conversation in this direction. Enda was uncomfortable, and unsure how to respond.

'Maybe. But life isn't perfect, you know. Not for anyone. And I've managed fine so far, haven't I?' His tone was sharp, and a bit dismissive. Michael had touched on a raw nerve. Enda was aware that he had always kept a very tight rein on his feelings. He understood himself well enough now to be able to recognise that he had gradually developed a hard, cynical side, and that he had done so as a defence mechanism. He no longer liked this side of himself very much, and maybe Michael was right in suggesting that he had done some emotional damage to himself over the years. But how else could he have managed to survive, and remain celibate. Even now, in his fifties, he knew that there were deep longings inside him and he was frightened of them. Sometimes when he thought about it he imagined himself as permanently standing on the edge of an enormous ravine, and if he let go of the tight grip he had on himself for a moment he would topple over, and fall into the abyss. This was a powerful image in his life, and it affected him at a number of different levels.

Every now and again, often provoked by as simple a thing as passing a lovely woman in the street, he would get an intense longing to lose himself in the arms and the body of a woman. It was a feeling of letting go, of sinking down to an unimaginable depth. This wasn't just the physical act of intercourse – although the thought of that in itself contained its own excitement. It was more the emotional letting go, the giving in, the releasing of something so long held in check. But deeply ingrained in him too was the notion of sex as sinful, indeed as the greatest cause of eternal damnation. In his head he had largely freed himself from the image of the fearful, punishing God, and the terror of the fires of hell. But it was much more difficult to get rid of the emotional response. So for him, at an emotional level, closeness was inextricably linked with the temptations of sex, with the possible consequences of serious sin and hell. That was why the ravine in his imagination was an abyss. If he let go of his emotions, if he allowed himself to fall into the ravine, then the consequences would be an eternity of punishment.

So it was better, he had told himself a long time ago, to keep everything in check. Since this life was only a flicker, compared to the endlessness of eternity, it was better to suffer here, to be stunted and unhappy, than to lose your eternal soul. And anyway, he told himself, he wasn't that unhappy; there was a lot that was good about his life, and he had learned to live with it. Maybe the fear of hell no longer held the same power over him. But somehow it was easier to continue to live a largely unemotional life rather than face the inevitable turmoil of allowing the feelings free reign. It was a bit like alcohol. He had seen how some people after years as non-drinkers started drinking in middle age and quickly became alcoholics. He feared that something equally catastrophic would happen to him if he let go of the tight rein he kept on his emotions.

Obviously Michael had got the message that Enda wasn't willing to carry the conversation along the lines that he wished, and had lapsed into silence. They walked a good distance without saying anything more. Michael eventually broke the silence.

'What do you think the consequences will be for Jack? You said that you think he won't get away with that sermon.'

'I'm not sure. But it won't surprise me if Matthew sends in a request to have him moved. Brendan doesn't easily forgive, and he's under pressure already, what with the newspaper story about the healing. He'll want Jack out. And, as I'm sure you've noticed in your short time with us, Matthew tends to do what Brendan wants.'

'I've noticed,' said Michael. 'Tell me, why was Matthew ever given that job? It's obvious that he's unsuited to it, that he can't cope with the pressure. It's unfair to land responsibility on someone who can't handle it.'

'But he's a safe man; he won't do the sort of thing that Jack did. That's why he was appointed. Along with the fact that he wanted the job – wanted it very much, in fact.'

'Did he? Why?' Michael was partly playing the role of being innocent in order to draw Enda out. This was the most forthcoming he had ever been.

'His mother was still alive at the time. He was very close to her, and he knew that she would be very proud to have her son as Superior of the famous and ancient monastery of St Carthage. And of course for an insecure person like Matthew it gives a great boost to the ego to be given a big job. You can draw security and self-belief from your position, if you can't find it in yourself.'

Their conversation was interrupted by the sound of a loud, aggressive female voice. They were on their way back from the river walk, and were coming down John Street. It was only when he heard the raised voices coming from one of the doors in the street that Enda realised they were almost at Jim Savage's house. Instinctively they paused behind the hedge, and peered through the greenery to see what was going on. Timothy Brown was standing outside the door. A woman, slight but tough-looking, was firmly planted on the threshold. Everything about her portrayed aggression.

'Get out of here!' she shouted at Brown. 'I don't ever want to see you near this house again.'

Enda could not hear Timothy's reply, but obviously he was trying to be conciliatory – although not with any great success. He had an anorak pulled up around his ears, and a cap on his head, and, from Enda's vantage point, he looked old.

'Get out, I said! And don't ever come near my uncle again,' the woman repeated.

As Enda watched, fascinated by the scene being played out on the doorstep, Timothy tried once more to calm the situation. He walked towards the door, hands out in a placatory gesture, speaking too quietly for Enda to hear what he said. But obviously it was to no avail. The woman's voice was rising, and, despite her small stature, she occupied the doorway in a very decisive fashion.

'You aren't fooling me with all this holy talk. You're nothing but a bloody hypocrite. All you're interested in is money. And along with ripping off my uncle, you're making a fool of my brother in the process. Get lost, and don't ever come back!' And with that, she banged the door, leaving Timothy standing helpless outside. But only for a moment. The door burst open again, and Enda and Michael were astounded to see the woman send a television set flying out with extraordinary force, the glass of the screen shattering as it hit the pavement.

'And take that back to wherever you got it. We can well

afford to buy our own television sets in this family.'

Enda and Michael stayed under cover as Timothy walked rapidly out of the gate, slamming it shut behind him, and headed back towards the monastery.

'Street theatre wouldn't hold a candle to that for entertainment,' said Enda, and laughed. And they too headed for home.

Mary Anne had left Jack with a lot to think about. He had heard enough of her story to have the beginnings of an idea about what had occured in the previous days, and what he needed now was time to put it together in his mind, and maybe to ring Garda Bluett. But first he needed to escape from the monastery for a while until the meal was over and the relatives had departed. And he desperately needed to try to get some perspective on last night, and what had happened with Olivia. Joan became his refuge again.

'How are you?' she asked. As usual, her tone revealed that she really wanted to know.

'Not very well, I'm afraid.'

'And what's the matter?' Joan looked concerned. 'Is it the funeral or the girl?'

'Both, I'm afraid, or, more precisely, the way I've responded to both,' he said, as he settled into the chair with a mug of coffee. 'A lot has happened.'

'From what I hear, that's an understatement. I have already had two phone calls about the funeral. Interesting, to say the least. So where do we start? Tell me everything.' Joan was smiling, clearly relishing the prospect of hearing all about it.

'So you already heard about the funeral. News certainly spreads fast in this town.' Jack looked down at his feet. 'I don't know. Maybe I was foolish to say what I said. But I don't regret it, and I will take whatever consequences come. Right now I'm more concerned about Olivia. What happened there is something that I expect you predicted.'

'What did I predict? Nothing bad, I hope.'

Jack suddenly began to feel awkward. Even though he was close to Joan, and trusted her completely, still this was something very intimate, and he wondered if she would be shocked. It was one thing to joke with him about the possibility of it happening, as she had done on a few occasions. The actual reality of it was different.

'We . . . you know . . . did . . . we went all the way.' And the last part of the sentence was spoken softly, with his head down. He didn't want to look at her.

Joan was quiet for a moment, but when she spoke, her voice was gentle and light. 'Jack, what's come over you? Attacking the Church in public and making love to your girl, all in the space of twenty-four hours. Not normal behaviour for a priest, wouldn't you say?'

'I suppose not.' And Jack still wouldn't look at her.

'Come on, Jack, lift that head of yours. Don't be acting as if you were a criminal. There's nothing here to be ashamed of. The most it does is raise questions about your future, and that's all right.'

Jack looked up, and smiled at her. 'Joan, I don't know what I'd do without you. I've always felt I could tell you anything, and now I know it's true.'

'Was it nice?' Joan could always surprise Jack with the blunt directness of her questions. It took him a moment to realise what she was asking. Again he began to feel embarrassed and knew that the colour was mounting in his face.

'It was,' he replied, and nodded his head. It was strange

that after telling Joan about it, he felt the same relief that he used to feel in the past when he went to Confession about something that worried him.

'But how do you feel about it? Where does it leave you now?'

'I don't know. It all seems so fast. And this is the first time I have ever been that close to a woman, the first time I have ever had sex. My head tells me that it's the wrong time to make long-term decisions. And yet, to be able to come home to Olivia every evening, and relax in front of the fire in that lovely sitting room; it surely is a more attractive prospect than the monastery.'

'But marriage isn't all relaxing in front of lovely fires. It has its tough times, too. Do you want to leave the priesthood?'

'Again, I don't know for sure. I feel I'm at such an early stage in all this, and there's so much to be thought through. At one level, walking away from the priesthood and religious life would be a great relief. There would be a sense of leaving behind a big burden, one that is getting heavier by the day as the whole thing collapses.'

'Is there anything about it that you'd miss?'

'Definitely, yes. I have access to people that no other profession would give me. People talk to me about the most intimate areas of their lives, and tell me things that they wouldn't tell their nearest and dearest, all because I'm a priest. That's special. And then there's the Mass. Not always, but sometimes, when I celebrate Mass with people who are really involved, it's a great experience. I'd definitely miss that.'

'That's a lot that you would miss. And a lot that you need to think out for yourself.'

They lapsed into silence for a while. Jack loved that aspect of Joan, that you could sit with her in silence without feeling awkward. They were both deep in thought.

'I don't often give you advice, as you know, Jack. I'm not very good at that sort of thing. I've learned enough in trying to handle myself over the years to know that advice can be very facile a lot of the time. But my instinct on this one is that you and Olivia would do well to stay out of bed for a while. Both of you have a lot of things to sort out, and you'll need a bit of space and a clear head. Sex will come between you and both of those things, so try to take your time.' She smiled at him brightly. 'Now, tell me all about the funeral.'

By the time Jack left Joan's house, it was already dark. The few hours he had spent with her had served to calm him down, and helped him to get a grip on himself. He felt ready to face the world and the community again. He parked the car and slipped in through the back door of the monastery. As he walked along the corridor, he stopped at the noticeboard and saw that Matthew had put up a notice announcing that there would be a '*gaudeamus*' that evening. A *gaudeamus* was supposed to be a joyful gathering of the community. Let us rejoice! It usually consisted of a drink and a chat. It was held in the sitting room upstairs, a room that was confined exclusively to the use of the community. He supposed that Matthew had called one because he felt that the community needed time to relax together, to overcome the trauma and to heal their wounds.

'There isn't much to rejoice about around here at the moment!' The voice was that of Bartholomew, who had come up behind him as he read the notice. 'Some hanging themselves off the rafters, and others fighting in public. Not much of a witness to be giving the people, if you ask me.'

'But I didn't ask you.' Jack was sharp with old Bartholomew, but his real annoyance was with the Superior, Matthew. This notice created a problem for him. When the Superior proclaimed a *gaudeamus* there was a certain obligation on each member of the community to be there. But Jack had other plans for the evening. Olivia's cosy house with the warm fire would be a more hospitable place for him, and they had things to talk about. But still, this gathering could be interesting. And if he didn't go, it would be a sign of weakness. He decided that he had better attend.

CHAPTER THIRTEEN

The community had gathered in the upstairs sitting room, where a large fire was burning in the grate. Matthew sat next to the fire. Opposite him was George, with old Bartholomew beside him, hunched over and, despite the fire, tightly wrapped in his cloak. Brendan had taken the seat beside Matthew, and then there was Michael, with Enda just inside the door. The table in the centre held some cans of beer, a bottle each of whiskey, gin and Martini, a selection of soft drinks and some peanuts and sweets. Timothy, whose job it was to provide all these things, arrived with a supply of cheeses and some cream crackers and biscuits. George didn't drink. He'd been a Pioneer all his life, and he intended to die that way. Apart from him, all of the others had filled their glasses – a fairly potent mixture of gin and Martini being the drink favoured by the older ones, a relic of the days when they were allowed to have only one drink, and they tried to pack as much punch as they could into that one. At the instigation of Brendan, they had solemnly toasted Kevin.

'Let us drink to our dear colleague, Father Kevin. May he rest in peace.' They all, including George with his glass of mineral water, raised their glasses and drank solemnly.

The conversation was a bit desultory. They were all clearly tired and in bad form. Some general comments were made about the funeral, but more by way of trying to be sociable than anything else. No one brought up the topic that was on everyone's mind: the homily that Jack had delivered. Enda was totally silent, sitting in the corner feeling lonely, despite the presence of the others. When he'd came home from his walk and seen the notice about the *gaudeamus* he had been irritated. The last thing he wanted was to gather with the rest of the community, this evening of all evenings. And he presumed that there would be no real conversation, that none of the underlying issues of the last few days would be brought up. All his years in religious life had taught him that. Issues were sidestepped rather than faced. He was glad that Jack hadn't come. He had looked for him after he came back from his walk, to tell him about the scene he had witnessed at Jim Savage's front door, and to discuss what it might mean. But Enda hadn't been able to find him. He wasn't around the house.

His reverie was interrupted by Matthew calling for attention. He wished to say a few words.

'My brothers, thank you for gathering here this evening. At a difficult time like this for the whole community – indeed, a tragic time – we need the support of each other more than ever. And that's what our presence is intended to do here. Just by being together, we are telling each other that we are still brothers in Christ. No matter what has happened, no matter what hurtful things might have been said, nothing can change that. Now is a time to forgive. Forgiveness is such a beautiful virtue, especially close to the heart of Our Lord, who himself forgave his enemies on the Cross. These have been stressful days for all of us. We must put all the hurt behind us, and go back to living in peace and harmony, as Jesus wants us to live. So I pray for you all, my brothers, and I call down God's blessing on you.' He raised his hand, and made a quick sign of the cross. 'Now, let's relax and enjoy ourselves.'

This little speech tended to turn Enda even more into himself. If Matthew thought it was that simple to put all that had happened behind them, he was an even bigger fool than Jack already considered him to be. And anyway, there was clearly much more to it than what appeared on the surface, so the community could be in for one or two unexpected and unwelcome surprises yet. He looked over at Timothy. Timothy normally didn't have much to say, tending to sit quietly and unobtrusively, not drawing attention to himself. But he was more than usually subdued tonight. The reception at Jim Savage's door had obviously left its mark on him. Suddenly Enda's thoughts were interrupted. The door opened, and Jack walked into the room. Everybody looked at him, and there was an immediate, palpable increase in tension in the room. There was a second of silence before anyone greeted him. He nodded in response. The ensuing lack of conversation was awkward. Matthew, as always trying to avoid conflict, attempted to relax the situation, in the spirit of the speech that he had just given, saying, 'Well, Jack, how are you? Glad to have all that over, I'm sure.'

'I'm fine,' Jack said shortly, as he took a can of beer and a glass from the table and settled himself beside Enda, near the door. The silence resumed, and continued for what seemed an age. Nobody knew what to say. They were nervous about mentioning the funeral, especially after Matthew's little speech. But it didn't seem possible to sit and discuss ordinary things after the day that had passed.

There was one person in that room, however, whose nature was not to avoid conflict, but to provoke it, especially when he felt that the good of his beloved congregation was at stake.

George broke the silence, and said to Jack, 'I know our good Father Superior has just asked us to forgive – to put these past days behind us. But for me that is impossible. I need to say to you, Father Jack, that what you did today was a disgrace. Bad enough to blacken Father Dunne's name in public, though I am sure that is a small matter compared to the reception he received in the next life, but worse than that, you let us all down. You brought shame and disgrace on the whole community, on this monastery, with its long tradition of service to this town. What did you mean by it? Have you no sense of loyalty?'

After this opening salvo, and before Jack had time to respond, Brendan joined the attack.

'Yes, I agree. You had no right to say those things. Every man is entitled to his good name, and letting the whole town know that Kevin was a homosexual is not right. After all, he was your brother in Christ. You should have shown him greater love.'

Matthew spoke up, doing his best to calm things. 'Let's not fight, tonight of all nights. We are all tired and distraught after our day, and anything we say now, we will regret later.'

'I'm sorry, Matthew,' said Brendan, who, now that he had started, was going to press home his point, 'but some things need to be said. In all my years in the Congregation I have never been so embarrassed. I have never before been provoked to such an extent that I have had to interrupt a colleague as he spoke from the altar. Jack, I hope you are ashamed of yourself. And I suggest that you take yourself off somewhere and do a long retreat, to see if you can get a grip on yourself, and learn how to behave properly when preaching the Word of God.'

Enda sat up. He had noticed after the funeral that Brendan

was surrounded by some of his usual admirers, and that they were praising him for his intervention during Jack's sermon. He could hear from the tone of Brendan's voice that he had no doubt that he had done the right thing, and that the community would agree with him. He could also see that Jack was somewhat taken aback by the severity of this two-pronged attack, and that he didn't know how to respond. Enda was also irked by the pious tone Brendan had adopted. This evening was certainly turning out to be very different from what he had expected. He decided to come to Jack's defence.

'Brendan, will you listen to yourself, for God's sake. You are some bloody hypocrite. As if you were all lily-white yourself, and your name all over the paper for doing something much worse than what you accuse Jack of.'

'That was all lies. That woman was crippled; she hadn't left her wheelchair for years. And now she is running around like a two-year-old. Typical media! They hate to see any good being done. They want to spoil everything. Always about the work of Satan.'

'Leave your sermons for the pulpit, Brendan. They don't cut any ice with us in here. I watched what went on at that ceremony, and I'm inclined to believe what the paper said.'

'Are you calling me a liar?' Brendan's face had reddened, and the temperature in the room had risen dramatically.

'Please, my brothers. Charity. Charity before everything.' Matthew vainly attempted to throw oil on troubled waters.

Enda ignored him, but decided it was time to change the direction of the attack.

'Well, we all know why you got rid of Kevin from the sodality. He was too timid to take you on himself, but he was deeply hurt by your attitude. Many a night he came to my room after your sermons, telling me how disgusted he was by what you had said. You have your fans around you, who tell you that you are a great preacher, but we don't all think that. And what about the day he overheard you and Timothy laughing and joking about how you couldn't stand queers, and how you had to bolt your doors every night in case he assaulted you in your beds. As if he was that hard up! And you knew he could hear what you were saying. But when you went to him a few days later to inform him that he was no longer a member of the sodality team, you hadn't the guts to tell him the real reason why you were dumping him from the job, even though he knew it, and you knew that he knew it. I believe you have to take a lot of the responsibility for Kevin's death.'

'I certainly will not take any responsibility for what that man did.' Brendan spoke with disdain. 'He was a grown man and could make his own decisions. And I make no apologies for not liking queers, and not wanting them in the monastery. It's no place for them.'

'And I agree with that,' said George, who, like Timothy, usually agreed with what Brendan said. 'I never thought I'd live to see the day that such corruption would be discovered between these four walls. What would all the good Holy Fathers who went before us, whose bodies are resting down the vaults, think of all this. I'm glad they died before it happened.'

'Ah, shut up you, too,' Enda cut in, increasingly angry. 'Another old hypocrite. You believe that Kevin is in hell because he was gay and committed suicide. But what have you done in your time to carry into eternity with you? You were so bloody cautious all your life, keeping the rule, doing what your Superior told you. Maybe you didn't commit any big sin, like you believe Kevin did, but it was because you hadn't the courage. And you might have been a bit more human if you had. You spent your life sitting in judgement on everyone else, but did you ever do any bit of good yourself? Did you ever love anyone?' Enda knew that he might be going too far in attacking George in this way, but the assault on Jack had made him very angry. George wasn't used to this sort of direct talk – the bluntness of it – so he fell silent.

Bartholemew wasn't supposed to drink. He was taking quite a lot of medicine, which tended to accentuate the effects of alcohol. Normally, Matthew would have seen to it that he remained sober. This evening, however, he had too much else to think about, and Bartholomew had filled the glass with gin and Martini before he realised what was happening. Trying to take it off him at that stage would have created a scene. But by now it was beginning to affect him, and the effect was dramatic. He became talkative and friendly. From experience, everyone knew that this was only a short phase, before he lapsed into depression, nausea and heavy sleeping.

'Stop all this fighting,' he said in a loud voice. 'We're here to celebrate. To celebrate the fact that we love each other.' And he took another big mouthful of the mixture in his glass. Matthew signalled unobtrusively to Timothy to push the bottles well away from him, so that he couldn't replenish his glass. Indeed, he felt like locking everything away already, even though the night was still young. He already regretted calling this *gaudeamus*. It was having the opposite effect to what he had hoped. Now that whatever bit of rejoicing there might have been was certainly over, the sooner the night came to an end the better.

So far, Jack had not spoken. Now he turned to Enda. 'You're too hard on George,' he said. And he faced the old man. 'George, I know you're upset about what happened these last days, and about the funeral. I don't expect you to understand what I did. But I do respect you and the life that you have lived. All I ask from you is that you try to respect me equally, and appreciate that I need to live my life in a different way, and preach the Word of God in a way that means something to me.'

Poor George didn't know how to respond. First he had had a direct attack from Enda, and now a personal approach from Jack. He was equally uncomfortable with both. He remained silent.

Jack turned to Brendan, and his voice took on a sharper tone.

'But Brendan, I find it harder to have any respect for you. I resent what you did today. Who gave you the right to interfere with the way that I, or anyone else, preach? I know you act as if you were Superior of this community, and you probably think you are. But you're not. You're so arrogant and dogmatic that you feel you're better than the rest of us.' His voice had now begun to quiver with anger, so he paused for a moment to get himself under control. 'I have just one question for you. Why did you try to get Jim Savage to make a will?'

The sudden change in the line of attack took everyone, especially Brendan, completely by surprise. Jack was conscious of Enda squaring himself in his seat, and he could sense the excitement rising beside him. Enda knew that now they were in for a real scrap, and he was relishing the prospect. But Bartholomew had nearly finished his glass, and was rapidly deteriorating as a consequence. Where normally he would only open his mouth to make an occasional acerbic comment, now he could not be kept quiet.

'Jim Savage? What has Jim Savage got to do with all this?

Jack, what are you on about? I know I'm not very bright, but will you explain this to me?'

'Shut up, Bartholomew!' Enda's voice was sharp and peremptory, as for the second time in a few minutes he told someone to be quiet. He knew it wasn't the way to speak to a man in his eighties, but he saw this moment as being much too crucial to allow it to be spoiled by the drunken meandering of Brother Bartholomew. The old man, who was now entering into the depressive stage of his drinking, lapsed into a sullen silence. In the silence everyone looked at Brendan.

'None of you have the right to question the way I deal with any of my penitents. But, if you must know, I always encourage older people to make a will in good time so that they won't leave chaos behind them when they die. Mr Savage, as it happens, is a man of considerable means, with relations who are descending on him like vultures. But he is a good, pious man, and he will do the right thing.'

Jack had learned over the years that if you can manage to keep your head in a quarrel you have a major advantage. He asked quietly, 'Are you a big enough fool to be trying to get Jim Savage to leave his money to you?'

'How dare you make that suggestion! All I am concerned for is the good of the poor man. I want whatever will help him to die in peace, and secure eternal happiness.'

Enda couldn't help admiring Brendan's sheer neck, and his ability to churn out appropriate, convincing words, even under pressure. But he decided it was time for him to re-enter the fray himself.

'Then why was Timothy sent packing from Savage's house this evening, with the door slammed in his face, and a television set flying out after him?'

Enda paused to observe the effect that sentence had on the assembled gathering. He could see from the way Brendan looked at Timothy that he didn't know about it. Timothy himself slid down in his seat, as if wishing he could slide through a hole in the floor. Matthew's eyes were popping out of his head, trying to take in all that was happening around him. Bartholomew seemed to have fallen asleep. George was aghast. Enda was enjoying this. The adrenalin was flowing like never before.

'Is that true?' Brendan asked Timothy.

'Not really – not as he described it. That's not the way it happened.' Timothy was dreadfully uncomfortable. He never liked to have the spotlight on himself. 'The niece was there and she wouldn't let me in; she said her uncle was asleep.'

'That's not what Michael and I heard from behind the hedge as we came back from our walk. It could equally have been heard by the whole street, the shouting was so loud,' said Enda helpfully. He addressed himself to the room in general. 'Do you want to know what the woman really said?' He made a long, dramatic pause. 'What she really said was: "Get out of here, and don't ever come back. All you're interested in is money. Get lost, we never want to see you again. And tell that to your master, Father Brendan Quinn." That's what we heard, loud and clear, out in the street. Clearly, Brendan, you aren't well thought of among Mr Savage's relations. I wonder why that might be? But I don't give a damn what you're up to. What I resent is the fact that, for the second time in a few days, all our names are being blackened by you.'

Jack saw that Brendan was rattled, and decided it was time to press home his advantage.

'And you're the one that's accusing *me* of giving the monastery a bad name!'

Michael hadn't opened his mouth during the whole argument, but now he spoke, in his soft, earnest voice.

'I trust that Brendan and Timothy are not looking for money from Mr Savage. I'm sure they're not. But maybe we all need to be more careful nowadays, especially in dealing with the elderly. We must keep ourselves above suspicion at all times.'

Unfortunately for him, he had picked the wrong moment to speak, because Brendan needed somebody to vent his anger on, and the attack from Jack and Enda, with its element of surprise, had left him wary. He turned on Michael.

'You little whippersnapper, with your earnest talk! Go and live in the real world for a while, and then you might be able to give advice to someone like me.'

It was a vicious attack on the young man, and past the time for Matthew to intervene. He slowly gathered himself up in his chair, and mustered all the authority he could manage. But before he had launched himself into what he had to say, Jack cut in. He wanted to test a hunch he had about recent events.

'My telephone has been interfered with. I have informed the guards about it, and they'll be carrying out an investigation. You wouldn't know anything about that by any chance, Timothy, would you?'

Timothy slumped even further into his seat, and mumbled: 'Me! What could I possibly know about that?'

'That's more than enough for tonight. We'll talk about these matters tomorrow.' Matthew was surprisingly decisive. 'Brothers, let us go to bed and pray that the Lord will forgive us, and help us to forgive each other, and live together in harmony, as we were called to do. Goodnight!'

The traditional respect for the authority of the Superior was still sufficiently alive among them for it to have the effect of breaking up the gathering. They all scattered, heading for their rooms. Jack and Enda met at the end of the corridor and went to the refectory for a cup of tea and an exchange of information. They knew they had had the advantage in the dispute upstairs, that they had outmanoeuvred Brendan and had come out of the whole situation well, and they felt happy about it. It wasn't often they got a chance to be one up on him. But they had a lot of other things to talk about. Jack told Enda what he had learned from Mary Anne Savage, and Enda gave a detailed description of what he had seen and heard at old Mr Savage's house. They began to try to put all that information together and see where it left them. As they talked, Jack thought about how much he had come to know Enda during the last few days, and his increasing appreciation of the man that he was. He was straight and honest – someone you could trust. And even though he could be blunt, and even hurtful at times in the way he spoke, he had never adopted the professional language used by so many religious, that hindered rather than helped communication. Enda, for his part, had forgotten the disapproval he had felt regarding Jack's sermon, and was caught up in the excitement of it all.

'What did you mean about Timothy and the telephone?' he asked Jack.

'I suspect that in some way he's involved in it,' Jack responded, 'though what his motives are, I'm not sure.'

'That's interesting. I was coming to the same conclusion myself. And watching his reaction when you said it to him, I think we're on the right lines. What could be behind it all?'

Jack thought for a while.

'I think it has something to do with Jim Savage. They didn't want Kevin visiting him. And when Mary Anne came to see me the other day for the first time, I noticed Timothy watching us with a fierce scowl on his face. It was the next day I got the tape. I think the message was for me to stay out of that situation. For whatever reason, they want to keep him to themselves.'

'Are they stupid enough to be after Jim Savage's money? And what do they need it for? After all, in our life there isn't much scope for personal money. The community looks after all our needs. But I always suspected Brendan had things going on that we know nothing about. He keeps coming up with a big new car every two years, while the rest of us have to make do with sharing the community cars. And Matthew is afraid to confront him about it. Haven't we always wondered where he got the money?' Enda took a sip from his cup of tea.

'Everyone says he is a genius with money,' Jack countered. 'Along with looking after the community finances, isn't he also on the board which controls the finances of the whole congregation? Everybody thinks very highly of him in this area. Nobody is going to listen to the likes of us if we say he's up to something.'

'The guards would,' said Enda. 'Now that the pieces are all falling into place for us, isn't it time that we reported to them? We should gather all we have together and bring it down to the garda station, and let them deal with it.'

'Well, I've already done that, to some extent,' answered Jack.

'Oh, have you now? You didn't tell me about it.'

'It was just that I ran into Bluett on the street last evening. He's no fool. He knew well we were covering up. I told him about the fellow with the strange laugh, and the tapping of my phone call.'

'Did you? And did you give him the tape? I'm sure Olivia would love that.'

'No, I didn't. But he is trying to get his hands on it. He says it's important evidence.'

'Indeed it is. But evidence of what, beyond giving some idea of the way religious keep their vows nowadays?' And Enda, seeing Jack's embarrassment, laughed. Jack was relieved that Enda didn't know what had happened the previous night.

'I suppose you'd better update him, then, on the latest developments, but I'm still inclined to keep the journal secret. It has too much personal stuff about Kevin. It was never meant for anyone else's eyes.'

'Fair enough. We'll try to keep it like that for the present. I'll get on to him in the morning.'

'The one bit that doesn't fit into any of our theories is the fellow with the anorak and the strange laugh. Who is he, and why is he involved in it all?' Enda was getting up as he talked. 'But I'm whacked. All this excitement is too much for a man of my age. We'll see what tomorrow will bring. I'll see you in the morning. Goodnight.'

'And goodnight to you,' said Jack.

CHAPTER FOURTEEN

Breakfast the following morning in the monastery was conducted in total silence. Matthew had decreed that it would be a retreat day, and that silence would be observed at all times, with readings from a spiritual book at each of the meals. This was a wise decision, because it gave people a little space and time to come to terms with the events of the previous day, and the unpleasantness of the evening gathering. But it also lent an air of heaviness, even of depression to the place, which lasted throughout the day. The community passed each other on the corridor in silence, and went about their business. And there was a clear sense that they were glad not to be talking to each other. Things were just too complicated. So much had been said the night before, and so many accusations thrown around, that nobody was too sure exactly what was happening. Before lunch, they gathered for a community Mass. Matthew was in a quandary as to what he should say, and in the end decided that the wisest thing was to say nothing at all, so, to the relief of everyone, there was no sermon. In the evening, they gathered again for an hour of silent prayer before the Blessed Sacrament. This was easier, as it made no demands of a social nature. In between times, Jack kept himself busy. The first thing he did after breakfast was to ring Bluett and arrange a meeting. Bluett was up within ten minutes, and Jack filled him in on what Enda and himself had discussed.

'What's your reading of the situation now?' asked Bluett.

'I'm not sure. But I wonder if Jim Savage has something to do with it. Not that there seemed to be anything suspicious about him. He looked to me to be a fairly harmless old man, and deeply saddened by what had happened. But he has money: lots of it, apparently. Mary Anne thinks Brendan is out to get it, using Timothy as his lieutenant, as usual. I find that hard to believe. Why would Brendan want the sort of money that Jim Savage has? That's what I can't figure out. For people like us to get a gift of twenty or fifty quid is welcome. We can stick it in our wallet and say nothing about it. And it provides us with pocket money to have a drink, or take a friend for a meal, that sort of thing. It means we don't have to go begging from the bursar. Not that Brendan would have that problem, since he is the bursar and looks after all the money for the community. But I can't see why any of us would want to get our hands on thousands of pounds, or even the millions they say Jim Savage has. All you could do with it is hand it in. And it's unlikely that someone would get involved in the sort of carry-on that is happening here just to hand money to the Congregation.'

'Unless they were in some sort of trouble.'

'What kind of trouble?'

'I have no idea. But as you say, it's unlikely that someone would go after that amount of money just to give it to the Congregation. Have you any idea if Brendan is involved with money in any other area of his life?'

'Yes. He's on the board that decides what is done with the international funds of the Congregation. Most of that is invested, I'm told. And they say Brendan is a genius with the stock market, better than any financial manager. The talk around the Congregation suggests that, at this stage, he's the one who calls the shots regarding all the money controlled by our central government.'

Bluett was immediately interested.

'Would he be a bit of a gambler?'

'Definitely not,' said Jack. 'Brendan is much too shrewd an operator.'

'But you're telling me that he has access to the money of the Congregation worldwide, aren't you?'

'You don't suspect him of some form of embezzlement, surely?'

'I know little or nothing about him, except that he's arrogant. And it's my experience that arrogant people are capable of doing very foolish things at times.'

'There's another thing,' said Jack. 'We've always been aware that Brendan has access to money that the rest of us don't possess. He gets a new car every couple of years, and it's not bought for him by the community.'

'Interesting. There might be something there to go on. By the way, any chance of giving me that tape of the phone call?' There was a glint in Bluett's eyes as he asked the question.

'Not a hope, I'm afraid,' said Jack.

'There must be some really interesting stuff on that tape.' And with that Bluett excused himself and left.

Olivia had woken feeling edgy that morning after a restless night's sleep. She was surprised that Jack hadn't come to visit her the previous evening, and while one part of her was almost relieved, because she was full of confusion about her feelings towards him, another part felt rejected and hurt. Colette's prediction – that he would drop her after he had got her into bed and had his bit of fun – was ringing in her ears, and didn't help her humour. At a much more mundane level she was wondering how the funeral had gone, and what he had said in the homily. He had phoned to say that he had had to attend a function in the community, and was unable to excuse himself from it. He had sounded worried, but when she tried to get him to talk about what had happened, he reminded her of the danger of speaking over the phone and said that he would see her the following evening. When she arrived at the office there were already people waiting for her, and she went straight into the first meeting of the day. But on her way through she could see that Colette had an extra-broad smile. She whispered to Olivia so that the people in the office couldn't hear.

'Well, your lover-boy certainly stirred it up yesterday.'

'What do you mean?'

'At the funeral. Did you not hear?'

Olivia had to go on into the office, so she muttered: 'I'll see you at lunch,' and closed the door behind her. It was hard at first to concentrate on the meeting. She was a bit peeved by Colette's comments. Considering the intimacy of the conversation they had shared the evening before last, she would have expected a bit more sensitivity in return. And she particularly hated that word, 'lover-boy'. All of this was getting a bit out of hand. The morning passed slowly, but eventually it was lunchtime, and she and Colette slipped next door to the pub for a bowl of soup and a sandwich.

'Do you mean to say you haven't heard about the funeral? I thought you two couldn't live without each other for more than an hour at a time.' Colette was clearly enjoying herself, and was going to make the most of this.

'Come on, be serious. Tell me what happened. How do you know about it, anyway? Since when did you become interested in the Church all of a sudden?'

'My mother, of course. She never misses anything that happens at St Carthage's. And she's a great fan of Father Brendan, so your man didn't come well out of her telling of the story at all.'

'What did she tell you?' Olivia had a knot in her stomach, and the sandwich lay untouched on her plate. Why hadn't Jack let her know about all this, so that she wouldn't be hearing it this way?

'Apparently, your boy was preaching at the funeral. And he really cut loose. My mother was scandalised. He said that that guy – what was his name – Kevin Dunne, had, if you'll excuse the pun, done himself in. He had hanged himself off the rafters, that was the way he put it. But even worse than that, he also told the whole church full of people that the man was gay. Imagine that! My mother said she didn't know where to look. It was so embarrassing. For once in my life, I'm sorry I wasn't there. Then he went on to do a big attack on the Church, and its attitude to gays and people who commit suicide. My mother thought it was terrible, but it sounded great to me. She said Father Brendan had to get up and interrupt, and that it was a good job he did. Otherwise, God only knows what would have been said.' Colette was a compulsive talker. She got so wrapped up in what she was saying that she didn't notice how Olivia sat in silence, not touching her food. She continued.

'Whatever else you say about this man of yours, and I've already warned you about him, he has courage, I'll have to grant him that. Maybe more courage than sense. When you see him, you can tell him one thing from me. He'd better start looking for another day job. Because the one he has won't last long if he carries on like that, that's for sure. From anything I know about holy Mother Church, she doesn't take too kindly to that type of rebellious talk from among her own ranks.'

Olivia didn't respond immediately, and a moment of silence settled between them. When she spoke, it was in a soft voice, almost a whisper.

'Maybe that doesn't matter any more.'

'What? What doesn't matter? What are you saying?'

'Well, there's been a bit of a development. Things happened since I was talking to you last.' Suddenly, Olivia found that she couldn't hold it in anymore. She needed to talk to someone. She was so confused. But Colette's mind was still on the funeral, and what Olivia had said didn't fully register.

'What did you say? What happened?'

'Well, he came out to the house late, the night before last, the night I was talking to you. You know the state I was in that night. And . . . well . . . as I said, something happened.'

Colette's eyes opened wide. 'What? Am I right in assuming you're trying to tell me you had sex with Jack?' Her voice was rising.

'Keep your voice down, for God's sake. I don't want the whole pub to know about it.'

'But you will tell me all about it, won't you? What time did he come round, and how did you end up in bed with him?'

'It must have been well after midnight. It was nearly that when we broke up here. He used the excuse that he couldn't ring because of the bug on the phone line.' She sighed. 'That's unfair. Maybe it wasn't an excuse. Maybe it was genuine. I was in bed, but I couldn't sleep, and the next thing, I heard a car pulling up. You know what that's like when you're living on your own. I went to the window and peeped out. I was so glad to see it was him.'

She paused, and Colette, realising the sensitivity of the situation, let the silence last for a while.

'Was it nice? Were you able to do it?'

'I was, and it was.' Again the silence. 'It was wonderful. Lovelier than I could have imagined.'

'So you got over your block.'

'I'm afraid I did. With a vengeance. I can't wait to do it again, but my head is screaming at me to take it easy.'

'That's a wise little head of yours. The question is, are you capable of listening to it?'

'You think I'm walking into trouble?'

'Don't get me wrong, Olivia. I'm delighted it happened for you. And if you needed somebody like him, someone with a collar round his neck, in order to free you from your inhibitions, then so be it. But that's done now. It's time for you to move on.'

'You're tough, aren't you? That would be a rough way to treat him – using him to overcome my fear of sex and then dumping him. I couldn't do that.'

'But that's exactly the sort of thing that men have been doing to us since the beginning of time: using us, I mean. No harm to give them some of their own medicine.'

'I don't know if I could be that cold and calculating. But I am afraid. This is just too complicated. I don't know if it's him I love, or just the fact that he sets me free sexually. Isn't it funny to be saying something like that about a priest?'

'Funny or tragic, I'm not sure which. Can you at least slow the thing down? Take a break for a while?'

'Maybe I should.'

'By the way,' Colette said casually, as they got up to return to the office, 'I hope you're not pregnant. Since you weren't exactly sexually active, I presume you weren't on the pill. In the rush to get into bed with you, did he pause long enough to use anything?'

'Oh God, I never thought about that. I was so excited at doing it that any thought of the consequences never entered my head.'

'Let's hope you're all right. It's poor fools like you, doing it for the first time, that get caught.'

Old George was at a very different stage of life and had radically different views on how it should be lived, but otherwise he shared the same confusion and sense of crisis that Olivia felt. He thought the retreat day would be a blessing, giving him a chance to pray a little more than normal, and hopefully to get his life back into something of its usual disciplined routine. But the opposite was the case. The silence gave him lots of time to think, and his thoughts were out of control. Though he had a tough exterior, he was actually quite insecure in himself, and riddled with self-doubt. The attack Enda had made on him the previous night at the *gaudeamus* had rattled him to the core of his being. After all his years of careful discipline and self-control, to be told that he was a person without any love or humanity in him was not easy to cope with. And to suggest that he would have been better off if he had been more of a sinner seemed scandalous to him. He had always believed that sin was the greatest of all evils. It had caused Our Saviour to shed drops of blood in his agony in the Garden, and to die like a thief on the Cross. What could Enda have meant?

By an unhappy coincidence, the Gospel passage at his Mass that morning, with his mind still full of thoughts of what Enda had said to him, was the one about the two men, the Pharisee and the tax collector, going up to the temple to pray. Jesus had clearly taken the side of the one who was the greater sinner against a man who appeared to be living a good life. What was to be made of all that? Was he like the Pharisee? Enda had accused him of being judgmental in his attitudes towards others all his life. Could that be true, and was it true that he had lived a fruitless, unloving life? George was experiencing something of an identity crisis, though he wouldn't have known such a phrase existed to describe his situation, and if he had known, he wouldn't have used it. Everything he believed in and lived his life by was suddenly becoming shaky. Introspection and self-analysis had never been his favourite pastimes, but now he found that he couldn't avoid them. His mind was full of the most horrible questions. Having lived all his life according to a set pattern, following very definite principles, he suddenly found himself thrown into confusion. Even his faith was shaken. He couldn't pray these last few days like he had been used to. Even though he was up as early as ever, and had the chapel to himself for the hour before he said his Mass, he was upset and disoriented. He no longer felt God close to him, and got no satisfaction from fitting in the hour of prayer, or even from saying his daily breviary. Was it possible that, despite all his efforts, God would still be displeased with him? And was that why He had distanced Himself from him now?

A new sentence from the Bible began to come into his mind and to plague him: 'If I have not love, I am nothing.' During the last years, ever since the changes in the Church began, he had despised all this pervasive talk about love. The task of salvation was a hard, unsentimental battle against the forces of evil. You needed to be tough. Was it possible that he had got it wrong? Never before in his life had he had to face these questions and uncertainties, and he didn't know how to deal with them. He had read in the spiritual books about the saints going through periods of doubt, about St Thérèse, the Little Flower, having doubts on her deathbed about the existence of God. But he never really believed that. He took it as the rambling imagination of the biographers. How could a saint possibly have doubts about the existence of God? And yet the sentence she was supposed to have spoken before she died, that the only thing that mattered was love, had an uncomfortable ring to it. Surely discipline mattered, and self-control. He could never remember having any doubts himself in the past. And it wasn't that he had them now, either. Not real doubts about God. It was doubt about himself that he was having – doubt that he had lived his life as God would want him to live. And trying to deal with that in old age, when he had believed that the hard battles were over, was too difficult for him. He had read about people having crises in their lives. It was something that happened to others – to people with less of a grip on things than he had. It couldn't possibly happen to him. But it was happening, and he was shaken to the core. After two sleepless nights, with a grey, haggard look on his face and rings around his eyes, he went to speak to Matthew.

'Father Superior, I am not feeling well. I need some help.'

Matthew had always found George intimidating, and this opening sentence from the old man was something he could have done without. The haggard, worn face, with its deep lines, which had up to now proclaimed certainty and confidence, but which, in some mysterious way, were softened into indecisiveness and fear, looked across the desk at him. Matthew observed him for a moment. This was an old man in pain, a fragile human being who was suddenly and devastatingly lost. This was not the George he had always known, the strong one. He knew he should respond to him with sympathy and support. But he couldn't do it. The last few days had been too much for him too, and he felt he had no more to give. The sight of George frightened him. Life should not fall apart for someone like George. If it fell apart for him, a man who had been so disciplined, so certain, what chance had the rest of them? What chance had he?

'Don't worry yourself, Father George. You are only upset over the death of Father Kevin, and all the other things that have happened. We're all upset! It's been a terrible time, but it will pass. God is good, and he will take care of us.' He felt a hollow emptiness inside himself as he spoke. 'I know Enda said unfair and unjust things to you. He shouldn't have said them. But they were said in the heat of the moment, and were not meant to be taken seriously. Still, I will speak to him about it.'

'But I think it's more than that, Father Superior. I am all confused. I never felt like this before. I don't know what I believe any more.'

Matthew felt that this could not be happening. People like George did not lose faith.

'Stop worrying and upsetting yourself, Father George. As I said, it will pass. Go back to your room now, and lie down and take a rest. Tomorrow morning take a sleep for yourself, and you will feel a lot better.'

'But Father, I cannot sleep.' And slowly George's face began to crumple, like a building that was disintegrating from the inside, collapsing in on itself. His eyes filled with tears. Matthew was close to panic.

'I'll ring the doctor, and get some tablets for you. You'll be right as rain in a few days. I must go. I have a very busy day today.'

He couldn't handle any more of this. George losing faith, and – in some ways even worse – bursting into tears. How could he possibly support all these sad and unhappy people? He had enough problems of his own. He steered George out the door and back to his room, and left him lying on the bed. Then he rang for the doctor.

There was a knock on Enda's door.

'Come in,' he called.

Matthew opened the door and walked tentatively into the room. Enda could see immediately that he was on edge, so he guessed there was some form of reprimand coming, because when Matthew had to face conflict and confrontation of any sort, he was very uncomfortable.

'Poor Father George is very upset over what you said to him the other night.'

Enda was not in good form. The buzz he had got during the row at the *gaudeamus* had passed, to be replaced by a sullen silence around the house. He and Brendan had spent the day avoiding each other as much as possible. They made sure not to be at the same table for meals, to meet on the corridor only when it could not be avoided, and on these occasions they gave each other the most cursory of nods. So his answer to Matthew was sharp.

'Poor Father George? What's poor about him? He's spent the whole of his life controlling this house, with everyone afraid to cross him in any way. I don't feel any sympathy for him.'

But Matthew was, as usual, trying to be conciliatory. 'Members of religious communities should not fight with each other. It would give terrible scandal to the people outside. And they're bound to notice it. They watch the monastery so closely, they notice everything!' He was doing his best to sound reasonable. 'Behind the tough exterior, George is really quite fragile. And what you said has completely thrown him. He's now worried that his whole life was lived in the wrong way, that all his discipline and self-control were for nothing.'

'If he's come to that conclusion, then maybe I achieved more than I thought possible,' Enda barked.

Enda was so cautious in his own personal life that he reacted more strongly to the way George lived. He saw too much of himself – the part of himself he didn't like – in George.

'But he hasn't slept for the past two nights. Would you please go to him and tell him you're sorry; tell him that you didn't really mean what you said.'

'But I did mean it, every word of it.'

'But go to him, all the same. We can't leave him so upset. Something might happen to him. Assure him that he's a good man, and that he has lived a good life. Remember, at his age he's almost like a baby. He needs lots of reassurance.'

'Oh, all right! Anything for peace.' Enda didn't share Matthew's peace-at-all-costs philosophy, but he was willing to go along with it on this occasion. Deep down, he did feel a bit sorry over the bluntness of his attack on such an old man. But just at that moment, there was commotion in the corridor outside, and Matthew stuck his head out the door. Timothy was coming at a run.

'Father George has just had some kind of attack. Michael is with him, giving him the last rites. The doctor is on his way.'

Matthew and Enda rushed to George's room, and found him lying on the bed with Michael bending over him, anointing him with the oil of the sick. He had his eyes closed, and was breathing slowly, with difficulty. He seemed to be unconscious.

He made no response when they tried to talk to him. Michael finished the anointing and sat on the edge of the bed, holding George's hand. Enda stood by the door, watching in silence. Now he had a real pang of regret for what he had said. George, he thought to himself, was a product of his time, and not the worst of them. Maybe the way he lived was the only way that he could cope with life. He smiled as he saw Michael holding his hand. It was probably the first time that anyone had held George's hand since he was a child. How much of his potential had died in him over the years through the rigidity of his attitudes and lifestyle? What might he have become if he had lived a less lonely and isolated life, in a different time? Who could say?

The doctor's examination of George was somewhat reassuring. Not being skilled in theological issues, he dealt with him at the purely physical level. He pronounced that there was no sign of a heart attack, but that he was showing all the signs of suffering from acute stress, from high levels of anxiety and exhaustion. Matthew explained all this to the doctor as probably the result of the sudden death in the community. He told him that George had been close to Kevin, and had been deeply disturbed by his death. The good name of the community, Enda noted, justified a blatant lie. The doctor prescribed rest and medication, and said that he hoped the the old priest would pull through this and make a good recovery. When he had settled into a deep, drug-assisted sleep, they all quietly tiptoed out of the room.

CHAPTER FIFTEEN

While the drama of George's collapse was working itself out, Jack was sitting in his room, reading a letter. It had arrived in the afternoon post, which was still occasionally delivered to the monastery by a helpful employee of the post office. When he looked at the envelope and realised where it was from, his heart skipped a beat. He sat down in his armchair and opened the letter with trepidation. Looking at the end of it, he confirmed that it was from Kevin's sister, Catherine Coleman. She must have written it immediately on returning home from the funeral. He expected it to be fairly hard-hitting. But he would have to read it anyway. He had not asked her for permission to say what he had said, so she, too, was entitled to have her say about what he had done at her brother's funeral.

Dear Jack

I hope you don't object to me addressing you in such an informal way. Even though we have barely spoken, what has passed between us has made formalities seem strange and, I hope, unnecessary. I am only now beginning to recover from the initial shock of Kevin's death, and all that happened afterwards – not least the funeral. I did not speak to you after the funeral Mass because I was confused – and maybe even a little angry – and I could not trust myself to behave in a civilised fashion. But the journey home gave me time to think, and the purpose of this letter is to thank you for what you said about my brother. I expect that will surprise you. But you see, I have come to the conclusion that you spoke the truth about him. And truth was the one thing that Kevin's life was short on.

I suppose I have known for a long time that he was gay, but I never admitted it to myself until very recently, when he attempted to talk to me about it. But even then, my response was inadequate. I was totally unable to cope and I knew I had let him down. But I had the same rearing he did and I wasn't able to do any better. Within the family we never mentioned the subject. The first time I spoke to my brother Paddy about it was as we were walking to the cemetery, earlier today. All those years – to have that subject hanging in the air between us and not to be able to mention it. How strange! And it took your sermon to get us to talk about it. You see, within our family very few things were ever discussed. Our father was a difficult man: something like a Victorian father. He laid down the law for his children in a cold, righteous way. I suppose you could say he was a moral policeman. He lived a good life himself, according to his own lights, but he seemed to have very little feeling for us. (It is strange to be putting all this down on paper – expressing it for the first time. See what effect your sermon had!) None of us ever stepped out of line. We were model children. Whenever one of the parents in the neighbourhood wanted to reprimand their children they used to say to them: 'Why can't you be like the Dunnes?' You can imagine what that was like for us, to be the model children in the village! It didn't exactly make us the flavour of the month with the other kids. And we suffered for that. But the worst thing was that we were afraid. All our good behaviour was brought about by fear.

Your talk at the funeral has released something in me. I am now able for the first time to look at my father as he really was, and to put words on my feelings about him. It's an awful thing to say, but I can say it now: I not only feared him, I detested him. And that's the worst part. Even though I looked after him in his old age, and right until he died, I never loved him. I couldn't. Love wasn't a word that entered into my relationship with him. I don't think he was capable of love. He was too rigid and repressed. And you can't imagine how good it feels for me to say all these things, to put them into words for another human being to read. It's as if, after all these years, I am at last getting the monkey off my shoulder. But what must it have been like for Kevin in those years of late adolescence, as he gradually began to realise his sexual orientation? How could he possibly face his father with something like that? It must have been such a lonely, even despairing time for him. And surely that is why he chose the priesthood. It was his attempt to get away from it all, and, at the same time, to please his father. And pleasing his father was always a big thing in Kevin's life.

In fact, looking back now, I believe that his whole life was a pathetic attempt to measure up to the impossible standards his father set for him. And yes, his father was pleased that day of his ordination. I can clearly see him parading up the church on the morning of the first Mass, oozing pride and fulfilment. I always wondered in a vague sort of way why I wasn't happy that morning. Now I know. Because somewhere deep inside me I realised that this was not Kevin's happy day, even though he acted out the part well, and probably even believed he was happy. No! It was my father's big day, his crowning glory. He had reared a son who became a priest. I have no doubt now that Kevin never had a vocation, whatever that word means anymore. We will never know the guilt and feelings of self-rejection he carried with him down the years, until a few days ago, when he couldn't carry it any longer and put an end to it all.

It was fitting that words of truth should have been spoken at his funeral – the words of truth that I should have spoken to him the day he revealed his sexual orientation to me. I suppose, in a sense, his last act, committing suicide, was the most honest statement of his whole life. Though in another sense, it was also the ultimate cop-out, the final act of a lifetime of running away, of escaping.

Don't get me wrong, I am not condemning Kevin. Which of us would have done any better in his situation? But I'm glad that you said those words. I'm pleased that some testament was given to the real Kevin, some insight into the monumental struggle that must have been his life. You were a brave man to do it. Thank you. I know now that when Brendan stood up and contradicted you, and spoke about how he had been a good priest and a faithful religious, he was telling a lie. He was doing what the Church so often does, covering up painful and sordid reality with pious talk. Oh how much I have come to hate pious talk! Whatever about Kevin being a good religious, and I am in no position to make a judgement on that, religious life was not good to him. It never helped him to be himself, never helped him to come face-to-face with reality. Instead, it forced him to continue to hide his real nature in a furtive, secretive manner. That is not the way to live.

Jack, do you believe in an afterlife? I always presumed that I did. But now I don't know. There are so many things I don't know any more. Is it possible that Kevin could be happy? Is it possible that all the enormous contradictions with which he tried to live have been resolved by death and that he has found peace? Wouldn't it be wonderful if that could be the case? But is it? I don't know. All I do know is how awfully, unspeakably sad the whole thing has been. In the words of the prayer, may he rest in peace. Rest and peace. How much all of us need these things!

Catherine Coleman

Jack put aside the letter, and became aware that the tears were streaming down his face. It had been so completely unexpected, and at the same time so wonderful. He felt like getting into a car and driving the hundred or so miles to where she lived, just so he could put his arms around her, so that they could cry together for the tragedy of her brother's life. And, as they cried, maybe they would be crying also for the sadness of so many lives, for all the lost opportunities, all the fear that holds people back, all the posturing that was forced on so many by society and Church, all the falseness, all the shame. And for the failure of so many people, including themselves, to respond to the cries for help and understanding that Kevin had made. They could cry for so many people he knew in religious life who seemed to live lives hedged in by high walls, isolated by fear of the consequences of breaking out, and all the time proclaiming their dedication to the One who had come that they might have life, life in all its fullness. They would cry for the irony of all of that. And they would cry for the courage and the bravery of people who still carried on, despite all the impossible obstacles, who still found a reason to live and to hope. They would cry, maybe most of all, for themselves, because so much of the emotion and the pain of Catherine's letter tapped into some deep well of feeling inside himself that he did not understand, that he feared, because if he delved into it maybe there would be no end, and yet he knew that it was where his real self was to be found.

His reverie was interrupted by the shrill ringing of the phone on his desk. Matthew was summoning him to his office. This was not normal. Usually Matthew came to those he wished to speak with, rather than bringing them to his office. But Jack had noticed a new determination about him since the previous night – a set to his jaw which seemed to indicate a decisiveness that had not been there previously. Or maybe it was a case of a weak person being cornered, and striking out on all sides. When he got to the office, he could see this was probably the more accurate interpretation. Everything about Matthew proclaimed him to be under pressure. The fact that he greeted Jack by coming out from behind his desk and giving him a handshake – weak and all as it was – was a real indication that there was something up – that Jack had better be on his guard.

'How are you, Jack?'

Though the question was put in a caring, sincere way, Matthew was so tense that Jack could see he wasn't really looking for an answer. Any possibility of relaxing was quickly dispelled by the way Matthew sat on the edge of his chair, like someone who was ready to make a quick escape by bringing the meeting to a rapid conclusion. Jack had a sense of foreboding. The handshake, and now this apparently caring question. What was coming?

'I'm fine. How are you?'

'Oh, you know. It's been difficult.' He was on the point of launching into a speech about how hard the last few days had been for him, but he realised that it would not be very tactful under the circumstances, so he pulled himself up short with some difficulty. 'People were upset by what you said at the funeral.'

Jack knew that he was now getting down to the real business of the meeting, and he decided that he wouldn't make it easy for him.

'Upset! Were they? Who was upset?'

'His family were upset. Especially his sister, Catherine.'

'Was she now? Did she tell you that she was?' Jack was going to draw out this little victory for as long as possible, because he feared that by the end of the meeting he might have won the battle but in all probability lost the war. Despite the erosion of recent years, authority in religious life could still throw its weight around.

'Well, no, she didn't. But I could see that she was. Isn't it only natural that she would be, considering what you said about her brother?'

'So she didn't tell you that she was upset.'

'She didn't, but everybody was upset by that sermon. It was most inappropriate.'

'Hmm! That's strange! When we can't cope with our own feelings, we often project them onto others, and in this case, maybe onto hordes of faceless others.' Jack was getting angry; his voice had the sharp edge of sarcasm. 'This very afternoon I got a letter from Catherine, thanking me for what I said. She told me that she was grateful I had spoken the truth over her brother's coffin – that it was the first time in his life the real truth had been faced. I can show you the letter if you wish.'

Matthew was immensely taken aback. This was his main line of attack, and it had turned into a rout for him. He tried another approach. 'Is that so? I'm glad to hear it. But what about the other people who were at the funeral?'

'Other people!' Jack said, eyes wide with assumed innocence. 'What other people? Who, precisely? And what about them?'

'I got complaints. I cannot give you the names.'

Everyone in the community knew that complaints from some of the regular church attenders at St Carthage's were part and parcel of life. Any time something new was attempted, you could always assume that there would be complaints. A small group of traditionalists led by the doctor's wife, Eileen, were always on the lookout for any effort at change, and saw it as their role to stymie it. If Matthew was falling back on complaints from this little group, he must be desperate.

'You mean Eileen and her crew didn't like what I said. Since when did that group of fanatics start calling the shots around here?' Jack was now definitely angry, and he showed it. The colour rising in Matthew's cheeks told him that he had hit a bull's-eye. For a second time, Matthew had to change approach.

'It is very bad for the name of the monastery to have two of its best-known preachers disputing in public, especially at a funeral Mass. It has been a source of great scandal around the town. I don't think it will be possible for both of you to continue working here. I intend asking Father General to transfer you to another community.'

So this was it. He was being shafted. Jack had not expected Matthew to go this far, and to do it so quickly, and it took him a moment to absorb the situation.

'I hope you will accept this in the spirit in which it is being done, as something that is best for you and for the Order. I hope you will be able to see it as the will of God for you.'

Jack was aghast at the brazenness of Matthew, coming out with this line of pious sentiment, though he realised it was probably just his way of covering up the embarrassing silence that had come between them. But he did know that the motivation behind having him moved had nothing to do with what was best for him, or with the will of God either. It was Matthew dealing with an awkward situation. Enda had warned him. If you take on the institution, he'd said, don't expect to win. The Church can be ruthless with people if it feels that its position is being threatened. They don't burn people at the stake any more, but otherwise the mentality hasn't changed very much, Enda had said.

'If you remember rightly, it was not me who created the

public confrontation. It was Brendan who challenged what I was saying.' Jack had regained control of himself, and his voice was calm as he spoke. 'Why not ask for him to be transferred?'

He knew the hopelessness of what he was saying. When it came to a toss-up between him and Brendan, in the eyes of Matthew there was no contest.

'Brendan cannot be transferred. He is too important to this house. It couldn't manage without him.'

'The report in the paper about the healing service took some of the shine off him, I would have thought.'

'That was a scandalous lie. We have already been speaking to the editor about it. We have unfortunately come to expect that sort of scurrility from tabloid newspapers, but not from the local press. I have asked that the reporter who wrote the story be severely reprimanded. The only consolation is that I know that nobody will believe it. The people around here know Father Brendan well enough to know that he would not do something like that.'

'Do they now? I wonder. I, for one, am not at all sure that it isn't true.'

'That's a disgraceful thing to say about a fellow member of your community.' Matthew spoke in an outraged tone. 'And it confirms my belief that it is better that you move to another community. Brendan will be staying on here.'

'I see.' Jack couldn't resist a smart comment. 'So if Brendan decided to top himself, like Kevin did, this place would collapse.'

'I'm sorry you're taking it like this,' said Matthew, falling back on the pious tone, and at the same time bringing the interview to an end. 'You have always been such a good religious. I, and all the community, will . . . '

'Don't give me that.' Jack cut in sharply. He got up and

walked out. He went straight to his room, and closed the door behind him. He was shaking with anger and tension. The phone on his desk began to ring, but he left it for a few moments while he composed himself. 'Hello, Father Jack? This is Mary Anne Savage. It's my Uncle Jim. He's not well. I'm afraid he's dying. Can you come quickly?'

Jack grabbed the holy oils and rushed up to John's Street. Mary Anne was waiting for him at the door. She quickly led the way into the sitting room, where Jim was lying on the sofa, apparently unconscious.

'I came up this evening – as I usually do – to see how he was and whether he needed a meal cooked, or any shopping done. I found him lying on the ground in this state. I managed to get him up on the sofa, and rang for the doctor and for yourself.'

'Has he said anything?'

'Nothing at all. Not a word.'

Jack took out the holy oils, said some prayers over the old man and gave him the sacrament of the sick. Then, together, they tried to make him more comfortable on the sofa.

'Oh, I hope he doesn't die,' Mary Anne wailed. 'We don't know if he's made a will or anything.'

Jack smiled sadly to himself. At least she wasn't trying to hide what her real concerns were. Poor Jim Savage might have been a successful businessman, but, whether through his own fault or theirs, his money had become the one thing of interest to his relatives. And the consequence was that he had no one to mourn him, no one of his own to hold his hand into eternity.

'I suspect that he has got to the stage where that's no longer possible,' Jack said. 'So whatever is done is done now. This has all the signs of imminent death to me.'

With that, Jim Savage stirred and began to groan. Mary Anne came with a glass of water and held it to his lips.

'Oh, I wish the doctor would hurry up,' she said, looking down at her uncle's drawn face. She gripped Jack's arm. 'Look!'

They realised that he was trying to say something. They could see his lips moving. Jack bent down and put his ear close to his mouth. He could just hear a faint whisper.

'I want to . . . ' The voice faded out.

'What do you want, Uncle Jim?' Mary Anne was pushing in, edging Jack aside. 'If he has any last wish, I want to hear it; maybe it will be good news for us.'

If the old man heard her, he gave no sign. The struggle continued in his face, and his lips began to move again. Jack bent down once more, with Mary Anne pressing in close beside him.

'Father Jack . . . ' his voice came as only the faintest whisper, 'I want you to see that . . . ' but once again the effort was too great, and he lay back, gasping for breath.

Mary Anne was in a state of desperation. She pushed Jack aside, and knelt down at the side of the sofa. She took her uncle's hand.

'Oh please, Uncle Jim, don't die now. Don't you know me? This is Mary Anne, your niece. You used to love me when I was a little girl. Don't you remember how you used to take me on your knee and tell me stories? And you always said I was your special little girl, your favourite. Don't die without leaving me something. Oh please!' And she burst into tears.

Jack took her by the shoulders and led her over to a chair. Then he returned to the sofa and took the old man's hand. He could see that whatever he had wanted to say would not now be said. His breathing became more laboured, and the gap between each breath lengthened. Jack saw the tension gradually seep out of his face, and the muscles around the mouth begin to relax; he knew that Jim was going. He went over to Mary Anne, took her by the hand and led her back to the sofa.

'Your uncle is leaving us. Just for this moment, forget about the money. Say goodbye to him, and wish him well on his journey.'

Mary Anne looked down at the dying man, with stark horror on her face.

'He can't be dying. He can't go just like that. There's so much still to be decided. Uncle Jim, don't die. I love you. I have always loved you. Please, Uncle Jim, not now. Don't go.' She continued along the same lines, crooning to the dying old man, as she put her arms around his shoulders and drew him to her. Jack watched, seeing the struggle going on in both of them: the old man drawing his last breath, leaving the world, Mary Anne struggling between the genuine love she had for her uncle and her intense desire to get her hands on his money. As he watched this scene being played out in front of him, it took him a few moments to realise that Jim had stopped breathing. He had died quietly, to the sound of his niece's pleadings. Jack leaned forward and gently closed the man's eyes.

'Oh my God,' said Mary Anne. 'Is he dead? He can't be dead.'

Then she tightened her grip on him, and, lifting him up, hugged him closely to her.

'Forgive me, Uncle Jim. Forgive me for being so selfish. Oh, may God forgive me.' And just as the doctor walked into the room, she let go of her uncle and rushed out to the kitchen.

The doctor quickly confirmed that Jim had died a few moments before, but he and Jack stayed standing beside the body for a little while, talking about the dead man. Even in the course of a busy day the passing on of a human being deserved a little time. They reminisced about his life, about the business he had run so successfully, and the doctor talked about the type of person he had been. They were both conscious that Mary Anne had left the room, and that, too, caused them to pause a little longer than they might have done. But eventually the doctor shook hands with Jack, spoke briefly to Mary Anne in the kitchen and departed. Jack then went into the kitchen where he found that Mary Anne had been busy. She had emptied all the cupboards and drawers onto the floor.

'I'm sure you think this is terrible of me, to be searching for his will when he's only just gone. But you don't understand. A chance like this only comes once in a lifetime. I have lived, ever since I was a child, in the hope that one day I would inherit Uncle Jim's money, and have a bit of comfort for myself. If he's given it to those two sleazy companions of yours from the monastery, I'll have nothing left to live for.'

'Whatever's done is done, I'm afraid,' said Jack. 'If he has made a will, the official copy will be with the solicitor. And there's nothing you can do about that. Leave it be for now, Mary Anne. The poor man is dead.'

'I know. And I did love him, I really did. I don't want to be this way. But I have waited for this money for so long.'

Jack felt sorry for Mary Anne, but he was relieved when he heard the doorbell ring. It gave him an excuse to make his exit. Mary Anne didn't move towards it, so he opened the door himself. He couldn't resist a smile when he saw the shocked look on Timothy Brown's face at having the door of Jim Savage's house opened to him by Jack.

'What the hell are you doing here?' Timothy growled, trying

to keep his voice down so that no one would hear the two priests arguing. 'You have no business coming here.' Clearly he was remembering the altercation at the *gaudeamus* the previous night, and suspected that Jack was trying to interfere.

'I was called here to attend to a dying man,' Jack answered, 'and I strongly suspect that you are the one who has no business here now.'

'Dying man! What do you mean?' said Timothy, as he tried to push past Jack.

'Dead man at this stage, I'm afraid,' said Jack. 'Jim Savage passed away about half an hour ago. And if you take my advice, you won't go in there. I don't think you would be a welcome visitor, and that's putting it mildly.'

'Don't tell me where I'm welcome and not welcome,' Timothy said angrily.

'All right, suit yourself.' Jack walked out, leaving the door open behind him for Brown to go through. He had seen enough of this whole sad, sordid business, and was glad to walk away. As he closed the gate, he could hear shouting in the house, and a few minutes later he saw Timothy rushing past him on the other side of the street, on his way home to the monastery. Presumably he was in a rush to acquaint Brendan with this unexpected and probably very unwelcome development.

And indeed, when Jack got to the monastery and heard voices down the corridor, he could see that Brendan wasn't at all pleased.

'I'm a priest. I was that man's spiritual director. Nobody has the right to keep me from him now. I'm going up there at once.'

Timothy Brown always treated Brendan with great deference, so Jack was surprised to hear the firmness with which he spoke.

'I wouldn't advise it. If you go up there now, the door will be slammed in your face, just as it was in mine. That niece of his is a mad woman. And anyway, the man is dead. There's nothing more that can be done.'

Jack slipped quietly around the other way, and went up to his room.

CHAPTER SIXTEEN

The sodality was meeting that evening, and Brendan was searching for Timothy. Eventually the receptionist told him that Timothy was engaged in the parlour with a caller. Brendan was perplexed. Usually Timothy kept him informed about who he was seeing and where he was going.

This, however, had been an unexpected and unwelcome visitor. He'd been surprised when the receptionist told him there was 'a gentleman' to see him. Timothy lived a very quiet life, and didn't have many friends, so a caller for him at the monastery was unusual. Entering the parlour, he was taken aback to find Garda Bluett wearing casual clothes, standing by the window.

'Good evening, Father Brown. I'd like to have a word with you.'

Timothy remained standing. 'What about?' He certainly wasn't going to go out of his way to be nice to this upstart. Bluett could see that the conversation wasn't going to be easy, but then he hadn't expected it to be. He was intrigued by this collection of men who lived in the monastery. They were so different to what he had expected, and he couldn't figure them out. But he had reached the conclusion that Brendan and Timothy were up to something, and that, of the two, Timothy was more likely to break down and give him some information. He decided to try a direct approach.

'Who is this person with the strange laugh who has been hanging around here for the past few days?' He watched closely to see what Timothy's reaction was, but the priest had his head down and it wasn't easy to see his face.

'What person? Strange laugh? What are you talking about?' Timothy's voice was a sullen mutter.

'I have reason to believe you know more about all that has been happening here than you are saying. Who put the bug in Father Jack Daly's phone?'

'What?' Timothy, assuming that Jack was behind this visit, decided to go on the offensive. 'So he told you to come and interrogate me.'

'No one told me to come here. I'm here on my own account, investigating the death of Father Dunne and trying to explain some of the strange things that happened around that event. I understand you're technically skilled. Did you place that bug, and tape Father Jack's phone call?'

'I did not. He has some cheek to go telling you about that, considering what he's up to. For someone who goes around the country preaching sermons, that's strange behaviour to be involved in.'

'I think you've just given the game away, my friend. You seem to know what's on that tape, even though you couldn't possibly have heard it unless you had been involved in recording it.' Although Bluett didn't know exactly what was on the tape, it wasn't hard for him to guess what it might be about. Timothy realised he had made a mistake.

'What tape? What's all this about? Who gave you the right to come in here and question me like this?'

'Could you tell me about your involvement with Mr Jim Savage, who, I understand, died earlier this evening?'

Timothy was beginning to feel trapped. How could he face Brendan if he gave anything away to this young garda?

'That's no business of yours. I have no more to say.' He turned and walked out of the room. Bluett had seen enough to tell him that he was on the right track. But the problem was where to go next. These people were clearly hiding something, but was there anything illegal going on, and had there been any foul play involved in Kevin Dunne's death? If they were ordinary people, he could begin to put a bit of pressure on them. But with the sensitivities of the superintendent, and Jimmy McCormack watching his every move like a hawk, he felt more than usually shackled by procedure in this investigation.

The crowd that gathered for the sodality meeting that evening was a bigger one than the church had seen for a number of years. The sodality of St Clementius had been one of the largest and most famous in the country, but the preceding years had seen an inexorable decline in attendance, as at all religious events. There was a time when the church was full: two evenings each week with women, and one evening with men. Brendan remembered the time when he could stand in the pulpit and address a thousand men. The rot had started about fifteen years ago, when the general government of the Order had commanded that segregation of the sexes could no longer be tolerated at regular religious events. It would be permitted on special occasions, where appropriate, but not as a general rule. Brendan fought tooth and nail against it. He knew what would inevitably happen. And now, sadly, it had. The sodality had become an almost exclusively female affair. There were only two meetings each week, with a little over half the church filled on these evenings. A sprinkling of men, mostly older, could be seen among the women. But the phalanx of young men who used to come when they had an evening to themselves had quickly dispersed. Brendan couldn't understand how stupid his superiors could be, especially when they pedalled politically correct ideas. Political correctness was a recipe for empty churches. Did they know nothing about men? Men, he believed, weren't by nature expressive in their religious practice. Indeed, real men weren't expressive in any aspect of their lives. And when you put them together with women, they were quickly swamped by the religious fervour and emotionalism of the women. The men felt uncomfortable, and as a consequence stayed away. Brendan had always considered himself to be a man's man. He could speak to them in their own language, and they responded to him. He had had very successful years as director of the sodality. But one big mistake that he had made was to take on Kevin Dunne as a member of his team. The last thing that was needed, at a time when men were already uncomfortable in the presence of so many women, was a priest in the pulpit who was in any way effeminate. It took the manliness out of it. After the first few weeks, he knew that he would have to get rid of him, and do it quickly. Matthew had tried to talk him out of it, but when it came to the test he could always steamroll Matthew's objections, which was what he did on that occasion.

Tonight, Brendan was angry. He had tried everything possible for the last few years to hold on to the members that he had, to bring back the ones that had strayed and to entice some young people in as new members. Despite all his efforts, the attendance still continued to decline. He was on the point of giving it up. He did not want to be part of a sinking ship, so he had all but made up his mind to move on to something else. And now, tonight, he saw in front of him what he had worked so hard to achieve: a church filled with people, bursting at the seams and spilling out the doors. He knew they had come out of curiosity to see what he would say, hoping that there might possibly be another public dispute between the priests. He resolved to give them an earful.

'My dear brethren, you all know the old saying that curiosity killed the cat. Lot's wife ended up as a pillar of salt because of her curiosity. But I know that curiosity is the motive that brought many of you here tonight. You know of our troubles in the monastery, and you are hoping that you might witness something unseemly. Shame on you. Shame on you for having so little concern over the tragic death of Father Kevin, who served you so well in this sodality, even if only for a short time. He was a good man, a good priest, and he loved you, his people. It would be more in your line to be on your knees, praying for the repose of his soul, and for the mercy of God on yourselves, so that you will not experience the harsh breath of His anger. Whatever way Father Kevin was – and I thoroughly disapprove of the fact that certain assertions were made about him at his funeral – it is not for us to be passing judgement; it is not for us to victimise him, or to gossip and laugh about him. He was a child of God, just as you and I are. It was my privilege to have him as part of my team, and I will miss him greatly.'

He was getting carried away, and exaggerating somewhat. But he spotted the slight figure of Michael standing amid the crush of people at the back of the church, and it threw him into confusion. He didn't know what it was about Michael Moran, but Brendan, who wasn't easily thrown, found him difficult, even slightly intimidating. It was something about the quiet way he looked at you, as if he was sizing you up. And he was so earnest. Brendan still felt uncomfortable over the way he had turned on him the previous night. He knew that Michael wasn't his real target, and he had only become one because he was disconcerted by the attack of Enda and Jack, and didn't know how to respond. But ever since then he had been conscious of Michael's eyes burning into him. He tried to dismiss him from his mind and get on with the business of the evening. He felt he should pray for Jim Savage, who had been a member of the sodality in his younger life.

'I regret to have to announce the death of the well-known businessman, Mr Jim Savage, who was for many years a good and faithful member of this sodality. I also had the privilege of counting him among my friends. May he rest in peace.'

It was no surprise to him, when the sodality was over and he had returned to the sacristy, to see Michael coming in to talk to him. His voice, when he spoke, was if anything softer than normal.

'Some performance out there tonight, Father Brendan,' he said.

Brendan wasn't sure what line Michael was taking. It was still possible, considering the softness of his voice, that he was actually delivering a compliment. But since the events of the last few days, everything about the monastery was changing, and people were beginning to show themselves in a new light. Brendan had begun to feel threatened in a way he had never done before. Between the newspaper's report on the healing ceremony and the attacks he had endured within the monastery, he felt an insecurity that was totally new to him. He decided to take what Michael was saying at face value, and hope that his positive interpretation was the correct one.

'Thank you, Michael,' he replied, smiling at the young priest.

'I didn't mean it as a compliment, I'm afraid,' and this time

Michael's voice had lost its softness. 'How could you stand up there and say such things about Kevin after the way you treated him?'

'Hold on now,' said Brendan. 'I didn't treat him badly. I took him on the team at a time when no one else wanted him. He wasn't exactly in demand, was he? I can hardly be blamed if his presence on the team was emptying the church from one week to the next. If I hadn't done something, we would have had to close the whole thing down. But there's no point in letting the people know any of that, and that's where Jack made his big mistake. Differences between us must be kept inside the four walls. The people must always be led to believe that we get on well together, and that there's peace and harmony within the monastery. It was the only way I could speak tonight.'

Michael looked at Brendan in silence for a while, almost as if he was waiting for something more. But Brendan wanted to bring this conversation to an end, and he didn't have any more to say. Michael turned to leave, then turned back for his parting shot.

'Do you care for anyone? Is there anyone you wouldn't use for your own ends?' And he walked out. Brendan was glad to see him going, but it left him with an uncomfortable feeling. To be criticised in this way by someone who spoke so softly and gently made it harder to respond and to dismiss from his own mind. This young generation! Maybe it was just as well that not too many of them were joining! How could you live with them?

But he had other urgent things on his mind that evening, and it took him a moment to realise that Mary Anne Savage was standing in front of him. She had a wild look in her eyes.

'My dear, I am so sorry for your trouble.' Brendan spoke in his most caring voice.

'You can keep your bloody sorrow, you hypocrite.' She was almost shouting.

'Hold on a moment, my good woman. I know you're upset over your poor uncle's death . . . '

'It's people like you that upset me. Pretending to be all good and holy, and having all the people licking up to you, and thinking you're great. But I know what you're about. You're only in it for the money. That's all you ever wanted from Uncle Jim.'

'Calm down, now, my dear.' Brendan was at his most patronising. 'Would it not be true to say that it was you who wanted to get your hands on the money? I cared for your uncle. I looked after his spiritual welfare, and because of me, he was ready for death when it came. He had made his Confession and received the sacraments. That was my only interest.'

Mary Anne was unable to cope with the calm way that Brendan spoke to her, with all the talk about sacraments and being ready for death. For her, the only way to conduct a row was two people face to face, shouting at the top of their voices. She didn't know how to respond to apparent calmness. And fighting with a priest went against her basic instincts, against the way she had been brought up. She retreated in confusion, firing a last remark over her shoulder.

'I hope you don't get one penny, and that if you do, it brings you bad luck till the day you die.' And she was gone. Brendan took a deep breath. Two attacks, one after the other, was a lot for even him to take. The next person in was Timothy. One look told him that there was something the matter here, too.

'What's wrong with you, Timothy? Have you seen a ghost or something?'

'No, worse! I had that young garda up asking questions.'

'Bluett? What sort of questions?'

'About Jim Savage, and what used to bring me up there. If I knew anything about Jack's phone, and the tape. And who the fellow with the strange laugh is. He seems to know everything that's going on. Jack must be talking to him.'

'That doesn't surprise me. As we've seen, that fellow has no loyalty. But you should have taken my advice. Bugging phones is not a good idea, especially if you aren't a professional. I hope you've removed it, before they come searching. And call off that fool of a sidekick you have. He's about as subtle as a bull in a china shop. We don't want any more trouble. I hope you told Bluett nothing.'

'Not a word. I don't like that fellow.'

'Good man. I just hope for both our sakes that Jim did the right thing.'

Olivia was sitting beside the fire, sipping a glass of wine. She had opened a bottle when Jack called her to say that he would be out shortly. She was trying to figure out how she felt about his coming. She was both excited and nervous, and uncertain about what she should do. She knew it would take very little for them to end up in bed together again, but she was determined not to let it happen. She needed a clear head, now more than ever, and she knew that the emotions surrounding sex would prevent either of them from thinking straight. She needed to try to work out what she really felt about Jack. There was something special about him, of that she was sure. When she told him she loved him, she meant that she had a deep affection for him, and loved having him in her life, although she certainly didn't mean that she wanted to walk up the aisle straightaway or anything like that. He was great company, and so easy to talk to. They could spend hours discussing all aspects of their lives. But it was even more satisfying that they could spend long periods in companionable silence in each other's company, reading their books or watching a video, feeling relaxed and close to each other. Part of the reason for that, she knew, was that sex hadn't been a part of their relationship. With Jack, she could just chat or be silent.

But now that had changed. Things would never be the same for them again. She could see that. It both excited and frightened her. She was excited and thrilled by the feeling of love, the sense of expansiveness that pervaded her whole being, the new energy she had for living, the intensity with which she experienced the ordinary events of her day. Why was she frightened? Jack was a priest. Even though she had left Catholicism behind her in her head, the heart still had its attachments, its beliefs, its fears. Words like 'spoiled priest', 'Jezebel', 'temptress' kept coming into her mind. These thoughts disturbed her, robbing her of her joy. She feared that it was true that she could not have both Jack and peace. So she was uneasy. She wanted the love, the excitement, the high, but she didn't want the questions. And besides that, she wasn't sure if she really loved him as a man. It was so hard, while he had that collar around his neck, to have an ordinary, clear view of him. Colette was probably right. What she needed was a bit of space and time. But how was she going to handle this evening?

She heard the familiar sound of his car pulling into the driveway. She was surprised, as he came in, at how her feelings of affection could so quickly be overwhelmed by the anger she felt over her embarrassment in front of Colette earlier in the day. Her first words were spoken with a touch of sarcasm.

'Apparently you made a show of yourself yesterday in a big way.'

He was taken aback. 'What do you mean?'

'I had to endure a session with one of my colleagues in the office today. She was giving a dramatic, and she thought funny, account of the funeral. Her mother had been at it. I was annoyed to have to hear it that way. Why didn't you tell me about it? Didn't you know something like this was going to happen?'

Olivia didn't like the sound of her own voice, and wished that she was able to be more affectionate to Jack. But she realised vaguely that she was blaming him for all the confusion and uncertainty she felt in her life at the moment. It was such a contrast to the intense feeling of closeness they had shared at their last meeting, after they had made love. Jack was clearly surprised.

'It's all been so hectic. I'm sorry. I have so much to tell you.'

But she was still angry, and until that subsided, she couldn't listen to his story.

'Why didn't you come out last night?'

'Because Matthew called a *gaudeamus*, and I had to attend.'

'Since when did you become so obedient to Matthew's commands? I thought you were one of the new generation who had minds of their own.'

'Please sit down,' said Jack, 'and don't be angry.' He walked over to her and attempted to put his arms around her. She turned away.

'Not now,' she said. 'Please.'

'What's wrong? Weren't you happy with what happened between us? I thought you were.'

The anger went out of Olivia as quickly as it had come. She kissed him, and said: 'Of course I was happy. It was lovely. But I'm all confused. I don't know what to think any more. Where is all this going?'

Jack had been thinking about what Joan had said to him – that they needed to take things more slowly, and not allow their sexual feelings to sweep them off their feet. But that line of thought was much easier when he was away from Olivia. Now, feeling her body against him for that brief kiss was enough to make him want, more than anything, to go to bed with her again. He tried to pull himself together. But even though what he said next was about thinking things out, in fact he was being driven by his emotions.

'I've been thinking a lot over the last two days,' he said. 'Since the tape, with the danger of public exposure, and more especially since what happened between us the other night, I've thought a lot about you, about us. I've been asking myself if I really love you, and if I want to make a life with you.' As he spoke, he knew that what he was saying had more to do with wanting to be in bed with her now than making a life with her.

'Have you?' Olivia's voice was faint, almost a whisper. She could see that this wasn't going to be easy. It was all happening too quickly for her. But she couldn't think of any way of diverting the conversation now, and Jack seemed more than anxious to continue. 'And what conclusion did you come to?' She knew that asking the question was getting her more deeply into a place she didn't want to go, but she found herself unable to stop herself.

'I felt that I probably would. I like the idea of coming home here to you every evening for the rest of my life.' Jack was warming to the subject, the cautious words of Joan having lost their effect. There was an enthusiasm in his voice that frightened Olivia. She could not respond to it. There were so many questions, so much to be considered. It was all so complicated. She felt that Jack was being simplistic. She got up, walked over to the window and stood playing with the curtain. After what appeared to him to be a very long time, during which she remained in total silence, Jack had to find out what she was thinking.

'And have you anything to say, Olivia? What do you think?' He was rushing her, and that drove her to speak more coldly than she felt.

'I suppose what I have to say is that I'm not ready for this sort of conversation yet. I know that after the other night our relationship has moved on to a new plane, but I'm not able to handle it. I need time and space. I'm sorry, Jack.'

'But you did say that you loved me. Please don't tell me now that that was just sexual desire – that I mean no more to you than that.' Jack was aware that there was a touch of petulance in his voice, and he wished it wasn't there. Many times he had given talks to groups of young people or engaged couples and told them that love was a free gift, that it couldn't be demanded from anyone, that the moment you began to demand it you were already destroying it. Now he was beginning to learn the difference between the theory and the practice.

Olivia answered him, speaking slowly and with effort. 'Yes, I do love you, Jack. I love having you in my life. I've never been as close to anyone as I am to you. But there's a lot about me that you don't understand. You think I'm experienced, but I'm not. Our night together was the first time I'd ever made love. It's only because you're inexperienced too that you didn't notice. I was never able to respond physically to any man before I met you. There are reasons for that, but please don't ask me what they are; I don't want to talk about them now. I have a lot to work out. I know that I'm very fond of you, but I'm not in a position to be sure of anything. That's why your talk about the possibility of us making a life together frightens me. That's a big step, a huge step, and I think it's too early for that. Too early, not just for me, but for you too. You aren't even remotely near making a decision about your future in the priesthood. And there are practical considerations to be thought of. What work would you do? How would you make a living? And there's your family, my family, to consider. What would your father say? And after all, we've only known each other for six months.'

Olivia had said more than she had intended, and it had come out differently to how she wanted, lacking in warmth and affection. She felt deflated, depressed, and her voice had a weariness about it. She had been looking forward to Jack's visit, to hearing about the funeral and his sermon, but now the atmosphere had changed. An air of silent conflict, of two people at odds, wanting different things – apart, not close – pervaded her sitting room. The closed curtains shut out the night and trapped the two of them in their separate lives. Talk of the events surrounding the funeral, or indeed of anything else, didn't now seem possible, and an uncomfortable silence dragged on between them. She was afraid, however, to show affection. If she allowed herself to respond to Jack, where would it end?

Jack, too, was upset. He couldn't help feeling disappointed at Olivia's response. He had hoped for something warmer, more positive. He sat hunched up in his chair, feeling sorry for himself. He wasn't sure what he had hoped for in coming out to see her, but it was certainly something different to this.

'Are you sorry we made love?'

'No, Jack, I'm not. But I am afraid that I might use you. And I don't want to do that.'

'Use me! How could you possibly do that?' Jack's image of Olivia, in which she was so romantic and desirable, didn't allow for the possibility that she might be capable of using him.

'To sort out my own problems. You're a very good man, and I'm very fond of you. I don't want to hurt you. As I said, I'm very confused.'

She took his hand and held it in silence for a while. Gradually, a calmness descended on them, and the tension subsided.

'How do you feel about the other night?' she asked.

Now that Jack had overcome his initial disappointment, and his intense desire for her had eased, he was able to speak more clearly. 'A whole mixture of feelings. Love for you. I have never felt anything so intense as the way I feel about you now. And desire. I would happily go straight to bed with you again. But I do know that you are right, that we shouldn't do that. And of course guilt. Lots of guilt. My vows, and all that. Have I the right to say Mass, to preach, after what I have done? There is a strong urge in me to go to Confession, but I haven't done it yet. My head tells me I should wait, and try to work out where I stand on it all first. That's part of what I feel.'

Olivia felt a cold chill going through her. 'All that talk about Confession makes me squirm a little. I can't see how this is anybody else's business but ours. I hate the thought of you going off and telling some old fellow in a dark box about me. And I'm sure he'd give you quite a lecture. Are you afraid you'll go to hell for making love to me?'

'When you put it like that, I'm not. But you aren't the only one around here who's confused.'

'All the more reason why both of us need to take time, and not rush into things.'

'I suppose you're right.' Jack wished there wasn't such a tone of disappointment in his voice.

The rest of the evening was pleasant. They drank the bottle

of wine, and were careful not to engage in any physical contact beyond the occasional light and fleeting touch. Having told her all about the funeral, Jack said: 'Matthew has asked the General to move me to another community. He says that Brendan and I can't remain together in the one monastery after what happened.'

'Didn't he move quickly on it? He doesn't usually act with such decisiveness. How do you feel about it?'

'Angry,' Jack answered. 'I didn't really expect Matthew to take my side against Brendan, but it's still upsetting when it happens. And being away from you; I can't bear to think about it.'

'I know that will be difficult, but maybe it's exactly what both of us need for a while. Will you go?'

'It's either that or get out. And maybe you're right to say that I'm not ready to do that yet. I think, coming here tonight, I half-hoped that you would solve the problem for me by agreeing to marry me.'

'We might create more problems than we'd solve.'

'I know you're right. But I don't want to lose you. Let's have time to work out how we feel, but let's not lose contact with each other, even if I have to move.'

'That's fine with me. It's what I want too.'

Jack went home early. Being with Olivia, and not being able to kiss and hold her, was getting harder as the night went on. So after they had begun to exhaust their topics of conversation, it was easier to go home.

CHAPTER SEVENTEEN

Jim Savage's funeral took place in St Patrick's, one of the other churches in the city. Beyond attending the ceremony, the priests of St Carthage's had no official role to perform. Timothy was there, up on the altar, concelebrating the Mass, but Jack was surprised to see that there was no sign of Brendan. Jack had felt he should attend, considering he was the one who had been called to him at the end, and in deference to Mary Anne, but he tried to be as unobtrusive as possible. Mary Anne and her two brothers were the chief mourners. Jack recognised one of them as the man who had come to the door on the first occasion he had visited Jim Savage, and had had the altercation with Mary Anne. He was tall and heavily built, and while he was in the same pew as his sister, he kept as far away from her as he could. The other brother stood beside her, in a very supportive way. As funerals go, it was uneventful, and Jack was glad when the ceremony was over. He decided he had done enough, and could skip the burial.

When he got back to the monastery, it was about midday, and the first person he met on the corridor was Enda. He could see immediately that there was news.

'We have a visitor in the monastery!' said Enda, with a conspiratorial smile on his face.

That in itself was not unusual, as St Carthage's prided itself on hospitality. But Jack could see from Enda's glee that this was no ordinary visitor.

'Who?' he asked.

'A member of our General Government arrived unexpectedly this morning. Even Matthew seemed to be unaware of his coming.' The General Government was based in Rome. There were six members on the governing council, all from different parts of the world. A visit from any of them was a rare enough occurrence, but for someone to arrive unannounced was unheard of.

'Which of them came?' Jack didn't know a lot about the General Government, but he could remember the names of most of them.

'The American. Bob Quinnell is his name. A small fellow, wiry, and they say he's as tough as they come. He's reputed to be the one who's always sent when a hatchet job needs to be done.'

'A hatchet job? Is that what brought him here? Could it be true that my little homily at the funeral has brought such an instantaneous reaction from the heart of Christendom?'

'That's assuming that it's you who's going to feel the edge of the hatchet, and my impression is that it's someone else they're after,' said Enda. 'He and Matthew were closeted together all morning, until a few minutes ago. And judging by the grey, haggard look on Matthew's face when I met him just now, I'd guess it has to do with something more serious than your little misdemeanours. Having Rome's assistance in dealing with you wouldn't put the look I saw on Matthew's face. Was Brendan at the funeral?'

'No, he wasn't, which surprised me. I was sure he'd be there.'

'That figures,' said Enda thoughtfully. 'Whatever it is that brought the head honcho from Rome, Brendan is in it somehow.'

'Do you know something I don't?' asked Jack. But just at that moment their conversation was interrupted by Jack being called to the phone.

'Could I speak to Father Jack Daly, please?' The voice on the phone was soft, but well-spoken.

'Speaking!'

'My name is Martin Ryan, and I'm a solicitor. I'm dealing with the affairs of Mr Jim Savage. I understand you attended him when he was dying.'

'That is correct.'

'The reading of his last will and testament takes place this afternoon in my office. I fear it may not be the easiest of occasions. I would appreciate it if you could attend. In fact, one of his relatives, a Miss Mary Anne Savage, has specifically asked that you be there.'

'But I have no business there. I couldn't say that I knew the man, having only met him once before being called to attend him as he was dying.'

'Will you come, please? I have a prior appointment myself, so I won't be able to be present. One of my younger assistants, a Miss Olivia Lenihan, will be in charge. In case things get a little rowdy, it would be good to have someone else there.'

God! Jack said to himself. Olivia! But he tried to keep his voice normal.

'Have you reason to believe that it may get rowdy?'

'You never know with situations like this. A quick glance over his will this morning makes me believe that it may not be to the liking of some of the people present.'

Jack noted the irony of the situation. What a strange twist that he should end up being requested to give moral support to

Olivia at the reading of Jim Savage's will. Curiosity alone would make it hard for him to refuse this one. He agreed to go.

Lunch in the monastery that day was full of a sense of foreboding. Everybody was wondering what the Roman visitor was doing in the house, and a notice on the board told them that there would be a community meeting at four o'clock. Neither Matthew nor the visitor were at lunch. They were seen leaving the monastery a little after noon, and Brendan was with them. People were reluctant even to speculate, because they feared that something really serious was afoot.

Mary Anne Savage stood up to welcome Jack when he entered the waiting room of the solicitor's office. She looked tired and worn. Her two brothers were with her. As in the church, the younger, more lightly built one was sitting beside her. The other one, whose name, Jack recalled, was Joe, sat on the other side of the small room and said nothing. But Jack could see that he wasn't happy with this latest arrival. He decided to ignore it, took a seat and waited. It was his first chance to get a close look at Joe. He was a fairly rough-looking character, with a badly fitting suit and unkempt hair. He had clearly shaved for the occasion, but being the sort who only handled a razor about once a week, he was less than expert, and his face proclaimed as much. There was something familiar about him, but Jack couldn't work out exactly what it was. After a short time spent sitting in total silence, they were ushered by the secretary into the office. Jack had had no idea if Olivia knew that he was coming, but the look on her face was one of surprise, followed quickly by a wry smile. He thought she looked beautiful in her suit, perfectly cut to accentuate the slim curves of her body. He felt a pang at the thought that he could be moving away, and his relationship with her coming to an end. She quickly got down to business. Having welcomed everybody, she began to read.

'This is the last will and testament of Jim Savage . . . ' He was surprised at how different her voice sounded, speaking the strange and antiquated language of the legal profession. The first part didn't contain anything of interest: instructions about covering the expenses of the funeral, and some minor items about his business affairs. A small amount of money was left for Masses for the repose of his soul, to be said at St Carthage's. But then Jack heard a sound that made his blood run cold. It was a laugh, strange yet familiar. It had come from Joe on hearing that the paltry sum of one hundred pounds was being left to Mary Anne as a reward for her care for her uncle during his last months. He caught Olivia's eye, and could see that she too had heard and recognised the sound as the one that was on the tape. Her voice faltered, but she continued.

'All the rest, residue and remainder of my estate of which I die possessed of or entitled to I leave to Father Kevin Dunne, of the monastery of St Carthage. But in the event of him not being able to freely accept both property and money, and dispose of them as he chooses, I leave everything instead to the Society for the Promotion of Minority Rights. Signed, published and declared by the above-named . . . '

Jack didn't hear any more. He was observing the looks of total consternation around the room, while at the same time wondering what the will could possibly mean. He had heard of the Society for the Promotion of Minority Rights. It had sprung from the gay movement, and while it officially espoused the causes of all minority groups, its real interest was to protect the rights of lesbians and homosexuals, and to fight all forms of discrimination and violence against them.

'What's she saying?' The brother who was sitting beside Mary Anne seemed to be slow at catching up.

'She's saying that your uncle left us nothing. That's what she's saying.' Mary Anne was almost choking. 'But this can't be. Father Jack, this is unfair. Can nothing be done about it? I had it wrong all the time. I thought it was Brendan who was going to get all the money. But it's all the same. None of it's coming to us. A hundred pounds. He broke his heart.'

'What? What? What are you saying, Mary Anne? Are we not getting the money?' Her brother still hadn't worked out what was happening. Mary Anne ignored him.

'We'll contest this will. Yes, that's what we'll do!' And she burst into tears. 'He couldn't have done that to me, after all I did for him.'

'You may contest the will, Miss Savage, if you choose.' Olivia was even more businesslike than before. 'But let me warn you that this will is perfectly legal and that you stand no chance of overturning it. Everything was done properly.'

'Nothing was done properly. This was all a fix.' Joe spoke up for the first time. Mary Anne immediately turned on him, with a vicious look in her eyes.

'You're the cause of all the problems. You're a stupid fool, the way you let that pair make a stooge of you, thinking you would get something from them. If you'd stayed with me, and not been taken in by them, we would all have come better out of this.'

Jack could see that Olivia was on the point of bringing this exchange to an end and declaring the reading of the will completed, but he made a sign to her to stay quiet and let it continue.

'I was no stooge. Those two men promised me they would look after me if it all worked out right. They are good men, and I believed them.' And Jack was amazed to see tears begin to course down the big man's cheeks.

'That was always your problem,' answered Mary Anne. 'You were always too quick to believe that people would look after you when they were only using you. What promise did they make to you?'

Joe seemed to have softened towards Mary Anne, and he even edged over in the seat closer to her. 'They said they would see that I was well rewarded. But that's no good now. Timothy will be very angry with me.'

'Were you helping Timothy in all of this? What were you doing for him?' Jack couldn't resist coming in with the question, but he could see immediately that he had made a mistake. A quick change came over Joe, and he turned aggressively towards him.

'I was doing nothing. I didn't go near your phone. And anyway, who are you two to talk, and what you are up to?' Jack was amazed at the strange mixture of naivety and slyness in the man. Now Olivia interrupted decisively.

'That's enough. The will has been read, and the business done. This meeting is now ended. You may leave.' She got up and went to the door, opened it and waited for them to leave. Jack was last to go, and he whispered to her that he would meet her in the pub when she'd finished her day's work.

He still had a little time before the community meeting, so he decided to drop around by the barracks and see if Noel Bluett was on duty.

'I was just about to go in search of you,' Bluett greeted him. 'Some interesting things are happening around here.'

'Not to mention the interesting things I have to tell you,' said Jack, and he launched into a description of the reading of the will, and his discovery of who the person with the strange laugh was. 'He seems to be a bit simple in some ways, but volatile, and with quite a temper. Timothy has some sort of hold on him, though. Clearly, he was involved in tapping the phone and delivering the threat to Kevin on the night he died. All done at the instigation of Timothy, whose motive was to keep both Kevin and me away from Jim Savage. Now the only question is what they wanted the money for.'

'And I may have just come up with the answer to that. Apparently some money belonging to your congregation has gone missing. The Italian police were on to us. Around five million pounds has been misappropriated, and they have traced its path as far as a bank here in the town. But from there it disappeared into a black hole. The name on the account is not anyone of your community. But that means nothing. They've asked us to investigate.'

'And that explains something else,' said Jack, enlightened. 'We've had an unexpected visitor from our General Government in Rome this morning. He was closeted with Matthew all morning, and clearly there's something up. He's addressing the community at four o'clock, so I'd better rush. I wouldn't want to miss this for the world.'

There was a sense of great expectancy in the room where the members of the community were gathered, waiting for Quinnell to join them. Jack immediately noticed that there was one absentee: Brendan. Enda, who had spent all day in the house, watching every move that the American had made, whispered to him that, whatever was going on, it definitely involved

Brendan. Jack was about to tell him what he had learned at the reading of the will and the meeting with Bluett, but before he had a chance, Quinnell entered. Immediately, he walked to the head of the room and addressed the community.

'I must apologise for my unannounced arrival here this morning, and for the secret nature of my business. Unfortunately, circumstances made that approach imperative. Now I am in a position to explain everything to you all. But it saddens me to do so. It is my unpleasant task to inform you that a member of this community has been involved in a number of activities that are totally inappropriate for a religious – indeed for anybody. I refer to Father Brendan Quinn.'

A loud gasp was heard around the room, loudest of all from old George.

'What do you mean?' he quavered. 'Father Brendan has always been an exemplary religious.'

'He may well have been, Father George,' answered Quinnell. Jack could see that, despite the delicacy of the situation, he was very much in control. Clearly he was a man with considerable experience of coming into communities and dealing with difficult situations. 'But I'm sorry to say there is nothing exemplary in what I have to tell you.' He paused, and Jack could have sworn it was a pause for effect: that, like any good communicator, he was finding it hard to resist the temptation to milk the drama of the situation. 'Brendan Quinn took possession of five million pounds of the congregation's money without any authorisation, and it has now gone missing. He is unable to return it.' This time there was no need to work on creating the effect. Even Enda's mouth had fallen open.

'Five million!' he whispered to Jack. 'What in the name of God was he up to?'

Quinnell continued. 'I wish I didn't have to break this news to you. I feel it is better that I say no more about it.'

There was a murmur around the room, and again George spoke up.

'Father Quinnell, since you are making such dreadful accusations against our brother, I feel it is necessary that you tell us more.'

'Father Brendan has, of course, already left this community, and he will not be returning. I consider, for the sake of his good name, it might be better if nothing else was revealed about this whole sorry event. I have discussed with your Superior what might be said to the people. He will convey that to you at another time.'

'But I agree with George,' Jack said, joining in. 'Earlier on this afternoon, one of the local guards was able to tell me a good bit of what you have revealed. The Italian police were talking to them, following the path of the money. It's better that we know the whole story.'

Quinnell looked over at Matthew, who looked helpless and lost but eventually nodded his head.

He turned again to the assembled gathering.

'Maybe you're right. I'll tell you, but I must ask you to treat this as you would information you received in the confessional. As you are aware, Father Quinn was considered to have great skill with money, and had proved himself so adept that he was appointed to the governing body which looks after all our investments. Unfortunately, it was precisely this idea that he was highly skilled that went to his head, and led him into temptation. Pride, as they say, comes before a fall. Your country has been experiencing a great economic boom. Property prices, in particular, have been spiralling. Father Brendan seems to have had a friend who was involved in property development. He persuaded Brendan to put up five million pounds to buy some land on the edge of Dublin. Apparently he had a definite promise from a local politician that it was going to be rezoned for development. I know you've had your scandals about land rezoning and the involvement of politicians. I cannot say whether Brendan or his friend were involved in bribing this particular politican. Anyway, in the last election, as you know, there was a change of government, and the particular man they were depending on to see to the rezoning lost his seat. The new people in power decided that this area would be retained as a green space for public amenities and would be the subject of a compulsory purchase order. Immediately, of course, its value plummeted, and the money Brendan had given for the purchase was gone. That, as I understand it, is what happened. I know it must be a shock to you to hear that one of your own community was involved in this type of underhand dealing.'

Jack turned to look at Enda, and he could see that for once in his life he was reduced to silence. Michael was the one who came up with a question.

'For what purpose was Father Quinn trying to make this money?'

'I questioned him closely on that,' answered Quinnell. 'He's emphatic that he was doing it for the good of the Congregation – that he intended all profits to go into the community coffers.'

'Do you believe him?' Enda had found his voice.

'It is not for me to answer that question. But if he had come to me for advice, I could have told him that whatever bit of expertise he had acquired in dealing with the congregation's money was very inadequate in the cut and thrust of the property market. Smarter people than Brendan Quinn have lost their shirt on this type of speculation.'

He now turned to Matthew. 'Father Superior, I think it's time we brought this meeting to a close.'

Again Jack spoke up. 'I'm afraid the matter can't be left at that. There are further aspects to it of which you aren't aware.' Jack was conscious of Timothy sitting in the corner of the room, as was his custom at meetings. He was bent over, with his head in his hands, saying nothing. But the lack of surprise being registered by him indicated that none of this was new to him.

'What do you mean, Father Jack?' asked Quinnell.

'There have been a lot of strange things happening in this house in the last few days, and only now are they all beginning to fit into place. There's another member of this community you need to speak to. I refer to Father Timothy Brown, who is over there.'

Timothy didn't stir. It was almost as if he didn't hear what was being said. Jack continued, conscious of the eyes of all the community fixed firmly on him.

'Clearly Brendan, in his desperation to return the money before it would be missed, got both himself and Timothy involved in some very unpleasant activity. They tried to persuade a dying man to leave all his money to them. They tried to shut out the man's relatives. They even tried to prevent other members of the community from getting near him, in case their plans were interefered with. They weren't beyond using intimidation in their efforts to get their hands on the old man's money. The most serious thing of all, I think, is that they seem to have been at least partly responsible for the death of Kevin Dunne. He was friendly with the old man, and in trying to frighten him off they threatened to expose his sexual orientation. I think that was what tipped the scales in the end, and made him decide to end it all.'

'Are you sure of what you are saying, Father Jack?' asked Quinnell.

'Yes. And so is Garda Noel Bluett in the local garda station. I suspect he is considering criminal charges at this moment.'

Quinnell was clearly shocked. Even he had never come across something quite like this.

'Have you anything to say in your defence, Father Timothy?'

Timothy stirred himself, and looked, not at Quinnell, but at Jack. He was clearly lost and disorientated by the sudden departure of Brendan, and he had no idea how to handle this situation. But he came out of his corner fighting.

'Who are you to talk, and you spending your time hopping in and out of bed with that Lenihan lady?'

'Hold it now,' interjected Quinnell. 'This dirt-throwing won't resolve anything.'

'He is referring to the fact,' said Jack, enraged, 'that he bugged my phone and taped some of my conversations with my friends. He is drawing some fairly far-fetched conclusions from them.'

'Not too far-fetched, if you ask me, from what I heard.' And Timothy lapsed back into silence.

'Well, it would appear that there is much more to this. I will need to extend my stay, and look into the matter more thoroughly. For the present, we will bring this meeting to a close.' Quinnell was so taken aback that he even forgot the usual practice of ending all community meetings with a prayer.

CHAPTER EIGHTEEN

Not long after the meeting ended, Jack met Matthew in the corridor.

'Jack.' Matthew clearly had something to say, but he was so shattered by the pace and nature of events of the day that it took him a while to work out how to begin. 'I hope you will forget the conversation we had the other day.'

'What conversation?' Jack knew exactly what he was referring to, but he was going to make him spell it out.

'About your leaving the community. I have spoken to Father Quinnell, and we both think that it would be better for all concerned if you stayed.'

'For all concerned? Maybe not for me.'

'Please forget what I said. I want you to stay. This community needs you.'

'Such a change of tune in such a short time. I'll think about it.' And Jack walked away. He looked at his watch and realised that Olivia would have finished work already and be waiting for him in the pub.

Settled in their usual corner of the pub with photographs of Michael Collins and Dan Breen over their heads, Jack and Olivia smiled nervously at each other. Though they had a lot to talk about, they were both conscious of an uneasiness between them – a distance that had not been there before. Jack tried to reach across the divide by chatting about the reading of the will.

'I'm really sorry I didn't know Jim Savage better. Anybody who could make a will like that must have been worth knowing.' He filled her in on all that had happened in the last few hours.

'I'm amazed that Brendan got caught out. I thought he was smarter than that. He usually reads his prey well. But on this occasion he got it all wrong. Good for Jim Savage. He must certainly be having a laugh at them all.'

'That is, if he exists any more,' said Olivia. 'If there is an eternity, it will need to be very big, or he could be in serious trouble when Mary Anne and the two brothers arrive up there. There could be mayhem in heaven.'

'In my Father's house there are many mansions,' Jack quoted from the Bible.

'I hope they have big fences around them,' said Olivia. 'If I ever get to heaven, I have no great wish to spend it with the crawthumpers who seem to presume they'll be the first in the door.' They had gone back to their very first conversation, talking about faith, but now there was more of an edge and less warmth about the way Olivia spoke.

Jack, on the other hand, was longing for closeness between them again. He had been through so much in the preceding days, and he felt so alienated from the monastery and all that it stood for, that he would have loved to put his arms around her. The sight of her at the reading of the will, dressed in her business suit and looking so efficient and competent had brought back all his desire for her.

'Matthew has changed his mind. He wants me to stay.'

'Because Brendan is gone?'

'Yes. I suppose he feels he couldn't cope without one or other of us.'

'What are you going to do?'

'I don't know yet. I need time to think about it. It's impossible to think straight at the moment.'

'I'm sure it is. Do you have a choice? Can you still go if you want to?'

'I suppose so. I have so many questions at the moment, I don't even know where to begin.'

Olivia was silent. Jack was taken aback by the way she seemed to be so detached about the question. She was discussing it as if it had nothing to do with her. He was anxiously trying to scrutinise her reactions, to see if she showed any sign of personal interest. How she felt about him was going to influence the decision he made. He tried to provoke some response.

'What do you think I should do? Or maybe what I really mean is, what do you want me to do?'

'No, Jack, don't do this to me. Don't try to involve me in this decision. It's for you to make, and you must make it alone. After all, it's your life.'

'But I thought we were friends. I thought we were maybe even a little more than that . . . '

'I've done a lot of thinking. There's too much of the Catholic in me, Jack, in spite of all my efforts to shake it off. I don't want to be responsible for taking a man away from the priesthood. I don't want to be the one who takes the collar from round your neck. I'd be afraid that the ghosts of my ancestors would rise up and haunt me. Not to mention that I don't know how I could face my mother.'

'You, the unbeliever! I think you're more traditional than me.'

'Maybe I am. I think that's part of what happens to those of us who give up on the Church and religion after being brought up in it. We retain, in spite of ourselves, the ideas we learned as children, and we never completely succeed in replacing them with anything better. A traditional notion of God is still very much part of our emotional response to life. That's why ex-Catholics, if they ever allow themselves to be religious again, are much more traditional than those who have stayed with the Church and struggled through times of change. Knowing you over the past six months has taught me that. I'm still afraid that if I was responsible for you leaving the priesthood God would wreak some vengeance, some punishment, on me. I know it's laughable, but that's the way I am.'

Jack was amazed. One of the things he had always loved about Olivia was her freedom. And now he saw that it was, to some extent, an illusion. In many ways, she was less free than he was. But maybe this was all just a cover-up, a sign that she wanted to get rid of him. Was it proof of what he had always feared: that she only found him interesting because he was a priest?

'But do you love me?'

'Jack, we went through all that the other evening.' Her voice had an edge of impatience.

'Did we? I didn't think so. I thought that having me in your life made some difference to you.' Jack was beginning to feel trapped, as if he was in a large, bare room, with one door after another slamming shut and being bolted from the outside. Olivia heard the hurt in his voice.

'Come on now, Jack,' and she spoke gently, while at the same time reaching out to touch his arm in as unobtrusive a way as possible, so that the other customers in the bar wouldn't notice. 'Of course having you in my life has been wonderful. Haven't I often told you so? If you leave this town, I'll be very upset, and I'll miss you very much. But it's a small country and we'll still be able to see each other, I hope. What's important now is that you try to make your decision as far as possible without being influenced by me. I have said that I am not ready to discuss marriage, commitment or any of that stuff. If you did decide to leave, maybe we could continue to see each other, and in a year or two we might begin to talk in those terms, depending on how the relationship was going. But not now. It's much too early. And you have too many other things to sort out.'

'But I can't understand you. You've shown me so much affection over the last few months. You've made me believe that I meant the world to you. And now you're saying the opposite. You're saying I must decide for myself, and that you can't help me. Have I been getting the signals wrong?'

'No, you haven't. But this is typical of the difference between men and women. You expect me to be consistent. And when we're dealing with such deep emotions, consistency isn't always possible.'

'Are you dealing with deep emotions? Do I mean that much to you?' Jack was desperate for something to hold on to.

'Yes, Jack, you do. Very much so. But I must try to keep my emotions under control, for both our sakes.'

Their drinks were finished.

'Another one?' he asked, half-heartedly.

'No,' she replied, shaking her head firmly. 'It's time to go.'

They got up, and walked out to her car. In silence, she drove him back up to the monastery and parked outside the gate. He sat in the passenger seat, making no attempt to get out. She reached over and drew him into her arms. For a long time they held each other, oblivious to the danger of being seen by passers-by. Then they kissed, and still without a word, he got out, and stood on the footpath. She rolled down the window.

'Goodbye, Jack.'

'Goodbye, Olivia.'

She drove away while he stood where he was, and in the rear mirror she could see him giving a small half-wave and returning his hand to his pocket. She felt empty and desolate and suddenly, for the first time in her life, she felt old.

Jack stood at the gate of the monastery and watched Olivia's car drive away. He could see the outline of her head until she came to a bend in the road and disappeared from his sight. He had never in his life felt so lonely. Was she gone from his life forever? If she was, how could he live without her? He was also frightened. The future seemed to stretch before him interminably. Would he ever know happiness again? The monastery building was dark and brooding as he walked up to the heavy wooden door. He pushed in the key and opened the lock. It seemed to take all his strength to push the door open and walk into the dark hall. He was glad that he met no one on his way to his room.

There was a message on his answering machine from Noel Bluett, giving his home number and asking that he call whenever he came in. He was glad of the distraction.

'Hello, Noel, Jack here. How are you?'

'Not good, I'm afraid.'

'What's the matter with you? I thought you'd solved the mystery of the monastery.'

'I have. But my hands have been tied. I can't act on it.'

'What do you mean?'

'This evening, just before I went off duty, the Super called me in. He informed me that he was taking me off the case. I objected, telling him what I had discovered. I told him there was plenty of evidence of criminal activity. You won't believe what he said to me.'

'I think I might,' answered Jack. 'I know how these things work.'

'He told me that the authorities in the Order were dealing with the situation and that we could safely leave it to them. Then he just dismissed me from his office, saying that that was the end of the matter.'

'Nothing in that surprises me,' said Jack.

'All I can say,' Bluett concluded, in an angry voice, 'is that I am even more convinced after this experience that I want to have nothing further to do with the Church. And I can't understand why you stay in it.'

Breakfast at St Carthage's the following morning was in many ways similar to how it had been for centuries. Matthew intoned the grace before the meal, gave the blessing and then took his place at the head of the table. George, who had made sufficient recovery to be back in his regular place, read a paragraph from Thomas à Kempis's classic medieval text, *The Imitation of Christ*, and sat down. Matthew smiled at the assembled community and opened the conversation.

'A nice mild morning, thanks be to God.'

'But the porridge is cold. How are we expected to eat that?' Bartholomew was complaining as usual.

'Will you shut up!' Enda was back to his irascible self. 'Take a good mouthful and it might keep you quiet for a while.'

'Today is First Friday,' said Matthew, 'the day that the sick and housebound members of the sodality are visited in their homes and in the hospital. Enda and Michael, would you be willing to do it? I have the list of names here.'

Both of them nodded agreement.

'Thanks be to God you both have the health and the energy for the work.'

'Maybe one of you could visit me while you're at it,' said Bartholomew, giggling creakily to himself.

George spoke in the voice that he used for leading the community in prayer. 'And may the Lord bless us all, so that our troubles will be behind us, and that we may have peace in this community.' It was obvious that he was speaking from the heart. It had all been too much for him.

'And I say Amen to that,' said Matthew.

Jack sat at the bottom of the table. He finished his breakfast quickly, without speaking a word. Then he got up and headed out into the garden. The dawn was just breaking, but a dense fog had settled on the countryside overnight. The trees in the garden looked like giant ghosts, enveloped in a cloak of mist. He stepped out and walked into the fog.